MURDER
HAS A
MEMORY

A ROBERTA LAW MYSTERY

KATHRYN DAWN O'BRIEN

KING PELLEY PUBLISHING

MURDER HAS A MEMORY

Library of Congress Control Number: 2011915856

ISBN 978-0-9839713-0-6

Published by:

King Pelley Publishing
Sherman Oaks, CA 91403-1330
www.robertalawmysteries.com

Book design by Kimberly Martin

First Edition

For Gerry,
without whom this book would not have been possible

ACKNOWLEDGMENTS

The author wishes to offer her sincerest thanks to the following individuals and organizations—Topanga Medical Clinic; the California Highway Patrol; the Los Angeles County Sheriff's Department, Malibu/Lost Hills Station; Captain Chris Casillas, Los Angeles County Fire Department, Fire Station 69, Topanga; Marvin Quarles, Jail Supervisor, Glendale Police Station; Jerrilyn Farmer; Geraldine Farrell, my ever patient and diligent editor; the loving, loyal and supportive staff at King Pelley Publishing, Lucky, Laci and Jimmy; Lillian O'Brien, for always believing in my talent; and Max, the beagle, for inspiring the character Lex.

CHAPTER ONE

I WAS HOME THAT DAY, at work in my office, prepping for the next client. By ten minutes to five it was apparent my four o'clock was a definite no-show. The appointment was a freebie. Part of a promotion I ran the previous month at the 2004 Global Heartbeat Convergence, a New Age expo in Santa Monica. The lucky winner received a free hypnosis session with Roberta Law, Certified Hypnotherapist—that's me.

I gazed at the pale green winning entrant's form nestled inside the manila folder on my desk.

NAME: Ben Cohen
OCCUPATION: Researcher.
WHAT WOULD YOU LIKE TO ACCOMPLISH
THROUGH HYPNOSIS: ???

Maybe it was time to stop plying my wares at alternative trade shows. My booth had been wedged between a dentist who channeled cosmic messages of global importance through his patients' fillings, and a shamanic belly dancer who cleansed and aligned chakras by shakin' her groove thing on your back. Ouch! While I consider myself to be open-minded and liberal, even I have my limits. Hypnosis is a tough sell. Still a little too out on the fringes for mainstream America, and a little too mainstream for fringe America. What's an entrepreneurial gal to do?

Picking up the phone, I decided to give Mr. Cohen one last chance to claim his prize before relegating him to the flake pile in the bottom drawer of my filing cabinet. My dialing was halted by the scream of a child. Dropping the phone, I rushed to the front door and flung it open. An African-American woman in a nurse's uniform was struggling with a feisty little girl on my doorstep.

"It's not going to hurt," the woman said, attempting to grasp the squirming child around the waist.

"Please don't make me talk about it, Mommy," the desperate girl pleaded. "I promise to sleep tonight."

The woman turned to me with a look of embarrassed apology. "She's not usually like this, Mrs. Law. LaVonne hasn't had a good night's sleep in weeks. I'm at my wit's end."

It was my five o'clock appointment—LaVonne Jefferson, a ten-year-old suffering from acute insomnia. Referred by her pediatrician, after he failed to find any identifiable physical or psychological causes behind her condition.

"Please come in," I said, as if there was a remote possibility to get this terrified child to come anywhere near me.

"No! I won't! I won't! I won't! …" the hellish, screeching mantra kicked up a notch.

"We'll just have a little talk," I continued. *Before one of my neighbors reports me to the police.* "Get to know one another."

Her contorted faced relaxed and eased into a toothy smile.

Darn I'm good.

"Can I pet your dog?" LaVonne asked.

Standing behind me, waiting to intervene like a canine Dr. Phil, was my trusty beagle Lex. In all the excitement I had neglected to close the door leading to the living area of my home.

"Sure," I replied. "But let's go inside. I don't want him to run away."

As if Lex would ever contemplate leaving while a single ounce of food remained inside this house. It would take a car made of Krispy Kremes to get him running. When it came to sweets, Lex lost his fine-tuned Zen mind. I attribute this to his living with a pair of dotty octogenarian sisters during those crucial first two formative years of life. One of them thought he was a cat, while the other fed him a steady diet of jelly doughnuts. When I got him from Beagle Rescue four years ago he was a sorry sight—thirty pounds overweight and often mistaken for a pot-bellied pig.

"What's his name?" LaVonne asked, as I shut the door behind her.

"His name is Lex. Would you like to play with him out back while I talk to your mom?"

She looked at her mother, who nodded her approval.

Child and beagle followed me out onto the patio behind my office. I returned to find Mrs. Jefferson seated in the recliner sobbing.

"We can keep an eye on her through the window," I said, offering a box of tissues.

"Forgive me. I haven't had much sleep myself lately," she said, wiping away mascara-streaked tears. "I just don't know what to do anymore. You're my last hope. This has got to work."

"Dr. Maxwell tells me the insomnia was triggered by a series of nightmares."

"Yes. They started over a month ago. It was sporadic at first. She'd come into my room afraid and ask to sleep in my bed. I'd hug her until she drifted off. Then she stopped coming to my room. Instead, she'd wake up in the middle of the night shrieking. When I asked about the dreams, she never remembered them. I spoke with her teachers and friends to see if anything had happened at school. Nothing. Finally, I took her to the school psychologist. She couldn't find anything emotionally wrong and suggested I have my pediatrician take a look at her. That's how we ended up here. Now she refuses to go to sleep at all." She reached for some more tissues.

"In hypnosis I'll be able to get her to recall the nightmares. Then, at least, we can see what's scaring her so much. Once we know that, I can begin to diffuse the situation by reframing the imagery and replacing it with something more benign. Twenty minutes in hypnosis is equivalent to a few hours of REM sleep. That alone will be very beneficial for her at this point. You may want to do a few sessions for relaxation yourself."

She shifted in her seat. "I'll relax once I know my baby's okay."

"Dr. Maxwell forwarded a written referral to me, but I'll still need you to fill out a few forms. Including one for parental consent." I handed her a pen, and a clipboard filled with paperwork. "I'd like to work with her alone today. If that's okay with you? Children are less self-conscious and more willing to open up when not around their parents. I'll tape the session so you can listen to it later."

"That's fine. I wouldn't mind catching a nap in my car."

After Mrs. Jefferson said goodbye to her daughter I went out to the patio. "LaVonne, will you come back into my office now?"

"Why does my mom have to stay in the car?" she asked, petting Lex.

"Because my office is small and I don't have a waiting room."

Studying me, she still seemed unsure of my intentions. "Can Lex come, too?"

"I don't see why not."

"Okay, then," she said, budging from her perch.

We followed Lex into the office. *And a little beagle shall lead them.*

"You can sit in this big comfy chair." I steered her toward the recliner before positioning myself behind my desk.

Lex settled in for a nap on the blue-green oval area rug that lay between us.

I hadn't done a lot of work with children. Don't really know why. I liked kids, having been one myself for many years. For the most part they were pretty straightforward. So it didn't take long to get a handle on the core issues.

"My daddy says you're a witch doctor."

Now I remember why I don't work with kids ... their parents can be a royal pain in the butt. Not all parents, but enough to get my attention. "Well, I'm not a doctor. And do I look like a witch to you?"

She scanned my pale freckled face and frizzy auburn hair.

5

I shouldn't have asked that ... kids aren't big on rhetorical questions.

Looking into my green eyes, I could see her flipping through her catalogue of witch mug shots—searching for a match. "That's silly!" she giggled.

It was so good to see her relaxed enough to laugh. I laughed right along with her. Not much of a laugher himself, Lex let loose a raspy beagle whoop. The more he howled, the louder LaVonne and I hooted. Our silliness helped ease the way for the difficult journey ahead.

After we settled down I opened the top center drawer of my desk. Somewhere under the scattered bank statements, notepads, stamps and envelopes was a green velvet pouch. Inside was a cut crystal pendulum on a 14-carat gold chain, a graduation gift from my brother. I discovered the small bag hidden in the back. It had been a while since I last used it.

"What's that?" LaVonne asked with wide-eyed wonder.

I lifted the glistening orb from its dark pocket. "Do you like to make-believe?"

She sat entranced. Watching the piece as it dangled from my fingers, twirling in the air, catching stray rays of sunlight and transforming them into dancing rainbows on the walls. When dealing with children, a little razzle-dazzle never hurts.

"This is a magical stone," I said. "It helps people tell stories, make wishes and dream dreams without falling asleep. Would you like to see how it works?"

LaVonne tilted her head. "Can I make a wish?"

"Certainly." I rolled my chair closer to her. "What's your wish?"

"To make those bad dreams go away. They aren't nice and they scare me." She reached for the spinning crystal.

"Hold on," I lifted the chain out of her reach, "before the magical stone can grant your wish, you must stare at it. Watch it moving back and forth, from side to side."

She followed the slow, steady pace of the swinging pendulum.

"Don't take your eyes off it. Keep thinking about your wish until it becomes the only thought in your head. As you notice your eyes blinking more and more, they will begin to feel heavier and heavier. That's a sign the magic is starting to work."

Her breathing deepened, eyelids fluttering half-shut.

"When your eyelids get too heavy, it's okay to let them shut and rest awhile."

Her eyes closed right on cue.

"That's better. When I count backwards from five down to zero, you will go even deeper into this restful state. Five—four."

Her breathing continued to deepen.

"Three—two."

Her head drooped forward onto her chest.

"One—zero—deep sleep." I snapped my fingers.

She was in trance.

I covered her with a soft, blue and gold throw decorated with images of the sun, the moon and the stars, before adjusting her chair into the reclining position. It is not atypical for body temperature to drop when in hypnosis. I did not want a sudden case of the chills to pop her out of trance.

"Each and every time I say sleep, you will sleep quickly, soundly and deeply."

After inserting a blank cassette into the tape deck, concealed in the wall unit between my desk and the recliner, I pressed the record button and returned to my seat.

"Now, LaVonne, I want you to imagine that you have discovered a hidden playroom in your house. It is a very special place, but you had forgotten all about it being there until now. Take a good look around this room. What color is it painted?"

"Yellow," she replied in a distant preoccupied voice.

"Are there any toys in this room?"

"Lots."

"There's a big orange TV in the corner of the room. Do you see it?"

"Ah-huh."

"Pick up the remote from next to the TV."

Her little hand reached into the air, picking up the invisible gadget.

"Turn it on."

She pressed her thumb down.

"Do you see the number twenty in the upper right-hand corner of the screen?"

"Yes," she nodded.

"Okay, then. Find the button for channel surfing. Press it. Watch the numbers going backwards from twenty down to zero. One by one, station after station passes by. Each playing a different program. None of these shows interest you right now, because you're looking for the dream channel. You will find it on channel zero. Today it's showing LaVonne's dreams."

She fidgeted in her seat.

"Are you okay?"

"Don't want to watch," she said in the sluggish language of deep trance states.

"Everything's all right," I reassured her. "It's not real, only imaginary. Just a bunch of talking pictures and stories. They can't harm you or anyone else."

Her tiny hands flailed in front of her, as if struggling with invisible monsters. "No! No! No! Hurt lady!" she screamed.

I reached over and gave her head a soothing stroke. "You're safe. I'm right here"

She grasped my arm.

"What are you seeing?"

Her nails dug in to my flesh.

I yelped.

Her iron vise hold on me loosened, the hand fell from my arm. "Dying. Dying. Dead," she said in a weak whisper. She laid there limp and lifeless, like a forgotten rag doll tossed into a corner.

I moved my aching arm out of harm's way. That didn't feel anything like the grip of a small child.

She was now resting quietly.

Feeling it was best to end the session for that day, I rolled my chair back over to the desk and jotted a few quick notes in her file.

"It's all over, LaVonne. Just allow yourself to let go. Relax." Then I decided to give it one more try. "And let yourself drift down even deeper."

She sighed, but showed no signs of the previous distress.

"Can you tell me what you saw?"

She bolted upright in the chair, throwing the blanket to the floor. Both eyes popped open and fixed a zombie-like stare at me. I could have sworn her dark brown eyes had changed to light blue.

"My murder!" she shouted in a strange, grown-up sounding voice. Then she fell back in the recliner and collapsed into silence.

* * *

Mrs. Jefferson returned to find a cheerful daughter out on the patio playing with Lex. Other than the tape I had made, not a trace of incriminating evidence remained from the scene played out earlier.

She handed me the completed paperwork. "How'd my little girl do?"

"LaVonne's a very good subject. She responded quite well to the trance state," I said with caution, still not quite sure how to explain what had gone on.

"Did you find out anything about the nightmares?"

"A little bit. I still don't have a complete picture." *Here goes … let's test the water before diving in.* "She appears to be witnessing a murder."

"A murder! If I find out my ex-husband has been letting her watch those damn scary movies he loves so much …"

"Her father is a horror movie fan?" A sense of relief filled me. *Okay … now that makes sense … she's replaying a scene repressed in*

10

her subconscious … it's trapped in there … and just needs to be pro-cessed.

"He used to drive me crazy watching those things—promised me he wouldn't watch them during LaVonne's visits. If I get him to stop will her nightmares cease?"

"That should help prevent any new episodes. But, I haven't been able to fully root out what's already in there. It may take a couple more sessions. I don't want to push her too hard."

"Is tomorrow too soon? I need to put an end to this right now. My child needs to get a good night's sleep. If this doesn't work, Dr. Maxwell is going to prescribe some mild sleeping pills. I'd like to avoid that if possible."

I opened the large black appointment book on top of my desk and turned to Friday. *Three clients in the morning … late lunch date with Louie … remainder of the afternoon free.* "Does tomorrow at six work?"

"Yes, we can come right after I get off work. Will she be able to sleep tonight?"

"I hope so. As I was bringing her out of trance, I put in a post-hypnotic suggestion for her to be able to fall fast asleep. When you tuck her into bed, give her a gentle kiss on the forehead and say, 'sweet dreams.' This will trigger the suggestion. However, I can't guarantee she'll sleep through the night. We'll have to wait and see on that one."

"Well, at least she'll get some sleep." She extended her right hand. "Thank you so much, Mrs. Law."

"Actually," I said, shaking her hand, "it's Ms., but please call me Roberta, Mrs. Jefferson."

"Only if you call me Sharon." She handed me a check for one hundred dollars.

Sounds of mirth and barking drifted into the room. We walked out onto the patio.

"She certainly has taken to that dog of yours."

"She sure has," I replied, enjoying the first smile to brighten Sharon's haggard face. *Should I let her know about the strange sounding voice I heard? … was it necessary to add any more worries to her plate?* "Oh, I almost forgot. Do you mind if I hold on to the recording I made? I'd like to review it to help prepare for tomorrow's session."

In blissful ignorance, watching her child at play, Sharon Jefferson nodded her consent.

* * *

By six-thirty I had reviewed my clinical notes for the next morning—a soon-to-be nonsmoker, a flying phobia, and a weight loss client. It was comforting to be back on track in the real world—unlike my extraordinary encounter with LaVonne.

A mournful baying broke my concentration.

"What's the problem? The door to the backyard is open and you ate dinner half an hour ago."

Lex looked up at me with those big, plaintive, amber eyes—half understanding, half not caring what I said. Planting himself at the front door to my office, he resumed his yowling.

"Why must you personally inspect every cat, dog, child and crow that passes by this house?" I said, opening the door to prove my point.

A six-foot, one-inch feast of sheer masculinity stood in my doorway.

Wow! ... dark brown hair ... hint of gray at the temples ... steel-blue eyes ... I'd give him mid-to-late forties ... preliminary inspection passed. Even by LA's lofty standards, this guy was drop dead gorgeous. The perfect complement to my five-foot, eight-inch, auburn-haired, green-eyed, forty-two-year old self.

Tail wagging, Lex crossed over the threshold and entertained himself with the personal "scent" history of the stranger who stood before us.

While Lex sniffed the pair of brown leather, Fratelli Rossetti loafers that fate had delivered to our doorstep, I opted for the less efficient human mode of information gathering—talking. "May I help you?"

"Sorry I'm late," mystery man said.

Better late than never.

"Can you squeeze me in?"

Well, big boy ...

"I realize I should have called earlier, but I misplaced your phone number. You'll have to excuse my absent-mindedness, this is the first time I've ever won anything."

Won? "Oh," I said in shocked disappointment. "You must be my missing four o'clock appointment." *Too bad ... professional ethics frown on lusting after one's clients.*

13

"Yes. I'm the profusely apologetic, Ben Cohen. If you can't see me right now, I understand." He turned to go.

"No, wait!" *Why'd I say that? ... I should be giving this guy the brush-off ... it's not my problem if he missed his appointment.* In defiance of my strict "Pay-or-Play" policy, I extended my hand. "I'm Roberta Law. Pleased to meet you."

He stared at my hand with a look of uncertainty. "If you don't mind, I'd prefer not to shake hands right now."

Germaphobe.

I retracted my weapon of mass destruction. "Please, come in and have a seat." *Better not waste time getting started with this one ... it's a wonder he showed up at all.*

"Can't be too careful when it comes to mingling etheric energies," he said, walking into my office. "Let's wait till we get to know each other a little better." His eyes locked onto mine.

There was something unsettling about the way this man's eyes penetrated me. *Note to self ... no more freebies.*

Before locking the door, I placed my "IN SESSION, DO NOT DISTURB" sign outside—half wondering if I should make a "HELP! CALL 9-1-1" sign for the future. I crossed over to my desk, indicating he should use the recliner. "Have a seat, Mr. Cohen."

Lex bounded into his lap.

I jumped up from my chair. "Oh, I'm so sorry." *The impending shower of doggy breath kisses might send the poor guy into shock.* "Let me get him out of here."

"I don't mind," he said in obvious enjoyment of his four-legged admirer.

Peculiar behavior for a germaphobe. "Lex, get down from there! You know better than that."

No, he didn't. Truth be told, I was the permissive parent of an obedience school dropout. Grabbing my brash hound by the collar, I made a futile display of take-charge authoritarianism. That stubborn beagle wouldn't budge.

Smiling, Ben lifted Lex down onto the floor. "Maybe you should take another stab at obedience school?"

"I would if it wasn't so embarrassing," I said, leading Lex out of the room. *How does he know we flunked out?*

"Lucky guess."

"Did you say 'lucky guess'?" *This is getting a little spooky.*

"Yeah, guess I was lucky ..." Ben hesitated, as if searching for the right words. "To win a complimentary hypnosis session with you."

"Right." *Does he have some type of verbal dyslexia?* "Just give me a minute to locate your file." I sat back behind my desk. "There's some preliminary paperwork I need you to fill out. Just some intake information for my files." I handed him the forms.

He touched the other end of the clipboard and a sudden flash of heat raced through my body.

Great ... I must be perimenopausal. Wild erotic thoughts raced through my mind. *How nice ... I get one last run-through of my sexual exploits ... before being put out to pasture.* Except in this version, every boy and man I ever kissed, or made love to in my entire life, had turned into Ben Cohen. I looked up from my desk. *Please God ... tell me I'm not blushing.*

Ben fixed those amazing electric eyes of his onto mine. "You're not blushing," he said in a deliciously sexy dulcet tone. "But I think I am."

Feeling faint, I let go the clipboard and took a huge gulp of water from the glass on my desk. Still half-dazed by the experience, I opened the window behind my desk hoping a little fresh air might bring me back to my senses. That's when it hit me—"Wait a minute! What do you mean, 'not blushing'? How do you know ..."

"There must be some substance in this clipboard that acts as a natural conductor for subtle energies," Ben explained. "If you let me borrow it I can run some tests to find out."

Might not be wise to hypnotize this one ... may need to get a psychiatric referral first ... keep him happy ... remain calm ... avoid any sudden movements.

"Do I really need to fill this out?" Ben asked. "After what just occurred I think, for the time being, you know everything you need to about me."

My head kept telling me—certifiable kook, head for the hills. My body kept telling me—rip your clothes off, jump into his lap. So far this was not my typical session. "Look, I'm not feeling very well. Do you mind if we postpone?" *There, I did it ... hypno interruptus!*

"That's okay. I understand. I didn't really come to be hypnotized anyway."

So why did you come? If I wasn't so afraid of the answer, I might have asked him.

He stood up and opened the door. "This is in case you need to reach me." He dropped his business card into my mailbox. "All my numbers are on it."

I walked to the doorway and watched him head toward a silver Evie parked across the street.

Figures he would have an electric car ... probably charges it by thrusting his finger into the lighter socket.

As he drove away, I fought an overwhelming urge to get in my car and follow him.

Who is this man?

I looked at the card he had left in my mailbox, "California Center for Parapsychology & Paranormal Research, Benjamin R. Cohen, PhD., Founding Director."

What does he want with me?

I turned the card over. On the back was handwritten, "Answer: twin flames. I'll call to discuss."

I wish he'd stop doing that.

CHAPTER TWO

MY YELLOW VW BUG crossed over the hills, which separated The Valley from Tinseltown, by way of Laurel Canyon. Once the enclave of artists and hippies, there was little left of its psychedelic past other than a few faded flowers painted on the side of the Canyon Country Store, and an abandoned school bus emblazoned with the words "MR. MOJO RISIN'," slowly rotting in the front yard of a soon to be razed eyesore property. Driving past the old Houdini estate, thoughts of the previous days events played on my mind. The one person who could put my life back into perspective was Louie Lopez. We were meeting for lunch at his favorite hangout, Sunset Strip Sushi in West Hollywood, where as Louie puts it—"The food is cold and the men are hot!"

Louie and I met while performing in the chorus of a touring production of *Gypsy*. His swarthy Latin lover looks, coupled with his wicked sense of humor, helped put him at the top of every show's popularity list. Our friendship was cemented about midway through the run, the night we discovered we were both being two-timed by the same guy. We went legit in the early nineties. He was now a talent manager and often referred clients to me.

I arrived at the restaurant to find Louie camped out in his favorite corner booth.

"Sorry, honey," he said. "These waters have been overfished. I've been here for fifteen minutes and not a nibble on my line."

I sat across from him. "Maybe you need to get a new line. What about the one over there?" I pointed out the chiseled, blonde Adonis perched on a black leather stool at the end of the sushi bar.

"Under the legal limit. I'd have to throw him back."

I doubted his call. "How can you tell?"

"Threw him back yesterday."

We both laughed.

"Thanks," I said. "I needed that."

"*Trouble in Tahiti*?" Louie asked. He liked to talk in song and show titles. He was a real music buff. If a song were being written today, he'd have a copy of it tomorrow.

"More like 'Ball of Confusion,' " I volleyed back.

"So which one is it? 'Heat Wave,' 'Bewitched, Bothered and Bewildered' or 'She Works Hard for the Money.' "

"You got it."

"A trifecta—weather, love life and work? Sorry, can't help with the weather. Gimme the 4-1-1 on the other horizons."

We ordered lunch and ate while I filled him in on the puzzling events of the last twenty-four hours of my life.

"Sounds like the kid is suffering from some 'Instant Karma,' " he said in between bites of tuna sashimi.

"Translation, please."

"You know. A holdover from a past life or something."

"Don't be ridiculous!" I snapped. "All right, I'll admit it. The thought did cross my mind."

"Do a past life regression. Isn't that what you hypnotists do?"

"She's a child. What would her parents think? Besides, you know I don't go in for all that hocus-pocus stuff."

"Call 'Danny Boy.' See what he thinks."

"My brother?"

My older brother, Danny, had journeyed from boy genius—to Harvard Medical School grad—to groundbreaking psychiatrist—to card-carrying schizophrenic. Our relationship was strained at best. The last time I saw him in person he was a born-again evangelical Christian, preaching about Armageddon on the streets of Atlanta. That was six years ago. To date, he's been an Orthodox Jew, a Mormon, a Bahá'í, a Jehovah's Witness and God knows what else.

In an effort to stay in touch and show he cares, he sends me an endless barrage of greeting cards, religious tracts, prophecies and fortune cookie inserts. That's when he can remember my address. I, in turn, deposit money into his bank account to ease the pain of my sisterly love.

"Louie, I have no idea where he is or who he is right now."

"He's a Buddhist. I visited him last weekend at the Mt. Baldy Zen Center."

"You promised."

"I'm okay. Nothing happened."

21

Did I mention that Louie and my brother knew—as in biblical—each other? "When are you going to get over him?"

"I can't. I think we're twin flames."

Twin flames? ... I haven't told him about my encounter with Ben Cohen ... Louie must be up to his old tricks ... this is all part of one of his elaborate practical jokes.

Like the time he set me up on a blind date with a Hare Krishna. The guy showed up at my door dressed in flowing saffron-colored robes and presented me with a handmade wax lantern. I didn't have the heart to turn him away. At least I got a George Harrison concert out of it. Turned out he was an actor client of Louie's, which I didn't find out for another month. In the meantime, he kept calling and inviting me to the free Love Feast at his temple.

"What exactly is a twin flame?" I asked, taking the bait. "I met someone who brought the subject up recently."

"Do tell," he said in a gossipmongering tone.

"You first. Spill the beans on this twin flames business."

Louie moved in closer. "I heard about it when I went to keep you company at the Global Heartbeat Convergence."

No kidding. I feigned surprise. "Really?"

"I picked up a pamphlet about it at one of the other booths. From what I was able to gather, a twin flame is like a soul mate, but better. Soul mates can be friends, lovers or business partners. They're like members of the same spiritual family who have shared a lot of lives together. You and I are soul mates."

I nodded my head, silently appreciating the elaborateness of his prank. *This one must have taken a lot of planning ... that conference was held over a month ago.*

"Twin flames are more like a part of ourselves in another body," Louie continued. "One soul that splits into two prior to beginning a series of earthly incarnations. They travel parallel paths for many lifetimes. When the time is right, they meet up again and reunite. Because their connection is so intense and powerful, they must be spiritually prepared to receive one another before fully coming back together. That moment will signal the end of this cycle of three-dimensional reality for them."

"It's amazing how much you remembered." *Guess that's because you made the whole thing up.*

"Not really. I'd forgotten all about it, until I found this in my jacket pocket this morning." He pulled out a pamphlet and threw it on the table. "Synchronicity, I guess."

I picked up the pamphlet. It was published by the California Center for Parapsychology & Paranormal Research. "Very funny, you almost had me. So is Benjamin Cohen his real name?"

"Whose real name?"

"The jig's up, buddy. I still haven't figured out how you rigged my contest, but I will. You can take the boy out of the theater, but . . ."

"What are you rambling on about? I feel like I'm having a conversation with your brother."

"Twin flames? California Center for Parapsychology & Paranormal Research? Benjamin Cohen, Founding Director and winner of my draw for a free hypnotherapy session? He was magnificent. An actor, right? There was something very familiar about him. Louie,

I'll kill you if he's not straight and unattached. I'm really attracted to that guy."

"Honestly, I don't have a clue who he is. But if he turns out to be gay, please be a good citizen and recycle."

"Look I can't play this game with you all day." I reached inside my purse. "I still have some errands to run before my last appointment." Taking out my cell phone, I called the number on the pamphlet.

On the third ring, a woman answered, "California Center for Parapsychology & Paranormal Research. How may I help you?"

"Benjamin Cohen, please."

"One moment, please hold," she said.

A chorus of singing whales crooned in my ear. "Female receptionist. Nice touch." I looked Louie straight in the eyes. "Better be his sister."

The woman came back on the line, "May I say who's calling?"

"Sure, sweetheart. Tell him it's his twin flame and her fairy friend."

Louie chuckled. "I can hardly wait to tell this one to the guys at the gym."

"Do either of you have a name I can use?" the receptionist asked dryly.

"Believe me, he'll know," I fired back. The whales returned for an encore.

Louie surveyed the room. "Are we on one of those practical joke shows?"

"You tell me."

The underwater concert came to an abrupt end.

"Hi, Roberta. It's Ben."

An electrical surge raced through my entire body, almost knocking the phone from my hand.

"I didn't know you were interested in fairies," Ben said. "Perhaps we could discuss some of my research in that area over dinner tonight? I'll pick you up at eight."

Please, God … don't let him be bi … my sharing days are over.

"There's someone here who'd like to speak with you." I shoved my cell at Louie.

He shook his head like a temperamental little boy refusing to take his medicine.

"Go on," I insisted. "You started this."

Giving in, he took the phone. "Hi, my name's Louie Lopez. I read your pamphlet, 'Reuniting Twin Flames.' Do you know where I can get some more information?" He listened for a moment, nodding his head. "Thanks, I'll be sure to do that. Bye." Louie handed back my phone. "He said you'd be able to tell me all about it by tomorrow. Should be quite an interesting evening." A note of amusement crept into his voice. "I can hardly wait."

"Fine. Have it your way." I got up from the table to leave. "We'll see who has the last laugh on this one."

* * *

After lunch I made a quick stop at the Bodhi Tree bookstore—having decided it might be a good idea to do a little reading up on the subject of reincarnation—before heading back to The Valley.

I had studied past life regression in hypnotherapy school. Upon client request, I'd performed a couple of them since going into private practice. What they were exactly—imagination or memory—I didn't really know. Let's be real, folks. How many people could possibly have been Cleopatra, Elizabeth I or Marie Antoinette? All I cared about was whether or not it worked therapeutically. If you believed this was the only way to get rid of your fear or phobia, who was I to rain on your parade? On the other hand, suggesting to a child's parents that a past life regression is called for was an entirely different matter. That could lose me a client, as well as future referrals from doctors and psychologists. Her father already thought I was a practitioner of the occult arts.

There must be a way of doing this without alarming the parents … could I be sued?… Danny did quite a bit of research in this area before checking out of the "Sanity Hotel" … should I just give in and go see my brother? "Do you have the book, *Doorways To Yesterday*, by Dr. Daniel Law?" I asked the girl behind the counter.

"Oh, I love that book. Let me check," she replied, punching an endless stream of computer keys. "You know, I was Betsy Ross in a past life."

Here we go. "Really."

"Nowadays I couldn't sew a button on a shirt if my life depended on it."

That's all right … there's not much demand for flag seamstresses these days.

"It's an older title," she continued. "We're out of stock. I can order you a copy if you like."

"How long will that take?"

"Two to three weeks."

"Okay," I said, handing her a business card. "Give me a call when it's in."

She looked at the card. "Are you Dr. Law's sister?"

"Yes. Why do you ask?"

"Well, you both have the same last name, and he asked me to give this to you if you happened to drop by." She handed me a large envelope with my name written on it.

"When was my brother here?"

"Last month. He gave a lecture on the Noble Eightfold Path of Buddhism, and how it relates to Jungian numerology and sacred geometry. Blew my mind!"

"His, too," I said under my breath. "Thank you."

I sat down in a comfy vintage armchair and opened the package. Inside, there was a copy of Danny's book and a flier for his lecture, "Crazy Eights: How to Play Your Hand in the Cosmic Card Game." He had given the talk on the eighth of August at eight p.m. *Of course, when else?*

On the back of the paper he had scrawled one of his cryptic notes, "If you receive this on the eighth, do not contact me. I will contact you. If you receive it on the eighteenth, leave a message for me at the Mount Baldy Zen Center. If you receive this on the twenty-eighth, wait a day and then come visit me at the Center. Love, Danny. P.S. I knew you'd want a copy of this book one day."

It was the twenty-eighth of September. *Do I really need his craziness in my life right now?*

Mount Baldy is about an hour's drive northeast of Los Angeles. The only thing I knew about the place, singer-songwriter-poet and sixties icon, Leonard Cohen was rumored to be living there. Louie had gone up to get him to autograph a 45rpm of 'Suzanne.'

I bet that's how he found my brother ... or did Danny tell him about Leonard Cohen? ... then again ... this whole thing might be part of a convoluted practical joke.

Leonard Cohen, Ben Cohen, LaVonne Jefferson, Danny ... somehow I sensed everything was related. All I needed to do was connect the dots, fit the pieces together. Or was I becoming as paranoid as my brother?

Hoping there would be no need for any of it, I stuffed the flier and book into my bag.

What if it is just because Daddy let her watch some scary movies one night? ... let's see what happens in today's session.

I left the store and walked back to my car.

Wonderful ... my parking meter's expired. I removed the paper from underneath my windshield wiper. It wasn't a ticket. "SACRED SEX SALVATION: CALL 1-800-2 FLAMES" was printed in large red letters on the front.

This is starting to get creepy.

* * *

LaVonne and her mother arrived ten minutes ahead of schedule.

"Sorry, we're early," Sharon said, walking into my office. "Traffic was light and she was all excited about coming here today."

"Lex is waiting for you on the patio, LaVonne," I said.

Smiling and happy, she raced out back. Altogether, a very different little girl from the one I had met yesterday.

"Looks like she got some sleep last night, Sharon."

"We both did. Thanks."

"Did she sleep through the night?"

"Almost. She got in six hours before the nightmares started up again. I called my ex this morning and gave him a piece of my mind."

"Did he tell you which movies he let her watch?"

"No. He's sticking to his story. Maybe you'll be able to find out today."

"Maybe." I wasn't quite sure how to broach the next topic. "I did some research earlier this afternoon. Let's suppose her father is telling the truth. We may need to leave the door open for exploring some other options."

"Other options?"

"Yes. She said something interesting while in trance yesterday." *Do it now, Roberta ... or you'll never do it.* "There's a possibility she may be witnessing her own murder." *Cue mother to grab child ... and run out of crazy lady's office.*

"Past or future?" Sharon calmly asked.

"Future?"

"Well, if you're willing to entertain the possibility of seeing into a past life, why not consider the fact that time travels in both directions."

It was hard to tell if she was serious or putting me on.

"I'm just relieved you were the one to bring the subject up. My ex already thinks I'm a prime candidate for the nuthouse. He practically had me convinced of it, until one morning I woke up and realized he was the one with the problem. His world was too small and narrow for me to function in. Frank thinks anyone who's not a Bible-thumping Christian is on the road to hellfire and damnation. He spends so much time thinking and worrying about the devil, there's no time left for loving Jesus."

"Do you believe in reincarnation?"

"I believe I'm an eternal being created in the image and likeness of God. And since I haven't always been here, I must have been somewhere else before and will probably be somewhere else after. Where that is, I don't really know. But I'm open to finding out.

"I'd like to do a past life regression with LaVonne. Will you give your permission?"

"May I be present?"

"Yes."

"Okay. You have my permission."

"Then let's start."

I ushered LaVonne and Lex back into the office. She climbed into the recliner and he reclaimed his spot on the circular rug. Sharon sat in the straight back wooden chair next to my desk.

I focused my attention on LaVonne. "Your mom's going to stay in here with us today, if that's okay with you?"

"Are you going to get hypnotized, too?" she asked Sharon with gleeful excitement.

"Not today, baby," Sharon replied. "I'm just going to watch."

Thanks to the trust I had established with her the day before, LaVonne went into trance almost immediately.

My stomach fluttered with stage fright. I hadn't done this in a while and never with a child. The audience factor wasn't helping any either.

Snippets of Danny's book floated through my mind. "Let's go back to the dream you watched on your special TV yesterday." *Stay calm and centered, Roberta … you can call "Scene" anytime you want.* "After you find the right channel, I want you to go and take a nap on the sofa in the corner of the playroom. Do you see the sofa?"

"Lex is on it," LaVonne said in a drowsy tone.

"Good. He can watch over you while you sleep. Now pick up the remote and start surfing the channels. I will count backwards from twenty down to zero, while you watch the numbers go by on the screen. The more I count, the sleepier you become. When we get to zero, the dream channel will be playing. You will be too tired to pay any attention to what is on it."

Number after number, she drifted deeper and deeper into trance. By the time I reached zero, her breathing was slow and rhythmic.

Sharon sat and watched, motionless. Her own breathing synchronized with her daughter's.

"In a moment LaVonne, you will join Lex on the sofa. While you take your nap, I will talk to the lady on the dream channel. Nothing she says or does will have any effect on you. You will be fast asleep, dreaming only the sweetest of dreams. Nod your head if you understand me."

Her head bobbed lethargically and fell to her chest.

I snapped my fingers. "You are asleep on the sofa. Lex is snuggled up beside you.

She was in delta state. If I went any deeper she really would be asleep. I gave Sharon a look of reassurance, and proceeded with the past life regression.

"I am no longer speaking to LaVonne. My words and my questions are only for the person on the dream channel. What is your name?"

LaVonne's head rose from her chest. She parted her lips but did not speak. Both eyes opened wide.

Sharon gasped.

I hadn't imagined it yesterday; LaVonne's irises were a glassy blue. Her jaw moved mechanically up and down, and reminded me of one of those movies where a sinister doll comes to life. I had half a mind to end it right there—then she spoke.

"Who are you?" The words were remote. The voice not La-Vonne's. It was not the voice of any child. This was definitely a woman speaking.

"My name is Roberta Law. I am a hypnotherapist."

"Are you here to help me?" She sounded tentative and afraid.

"Yes, if you help me and stop bothering this little girl. She needs her rest."

"She will rest, when I can rest." The woman panted, as if trying to catch her breath.

"When will you rest?"

"The day my murderer is caught." The panting grew louder, more persistent. "I don't have much time left. Please help me," she pleaded.

"Do you know who murdered you?"

"The alley. The alley. There's no way out of the alley." She moaned. "Oh my God, he's stabbing me. Help! Help! Someone please help!" she screamed.

"Who's stabbing you? Tell me what you see," I exhorted, feeling impotent. How could I help someone when I wasn't really there, and they weren't really here? Unable to rescue the victim or see the killer, all I could do was talk and listen.

"Father," she said in a faint whisper.

"Who are you?" I was losing her. "Give me a name."

Her response was staccato. "Lo. Ri. Tay. Lor. Sing. Er." Both eyes snapped shut and she fell back in the chair.

Sharon and I sat there in numbed silence.

I felt like calling the police. *What would I say? ... hi ... I'd like to report a woman named Lori Taylor Singer was stabbed to death ... by her father ... in an alley somewhere ... no, I don't know where or when ... the body? ... it seems to be trapped inside a ten-year-old girl ... no, my meds don't need adjusting.*

"What should we do?" Sharon asked.

"Nothing. Lavonne's all right. She's still resting comfortably on her imaginary sofa."

"What about the woman?"

"LaVonne won't remember any of this."

"But we just witnessed a murder." Sharon sounded as frustrated as I felt. "We've got to do something."

"What? Where would we start? Lori Taylor Singer doesn't sound like an uncommon name. We don't know when she lived, where she lived, or if she ever lived. This entire incident could be the figment of a child's imagination."

"How do you explain those eyes? That voice? It was like La-Vonne was no longer in the room."

Sharon did have a point. Phenomena this striking wasn't easy to explain away. *Didn't I once read people suffering from multiple personality disorder have been known to exhibit similar traits?... if only I could remember where I saw that.*

"I need to sort out my notes and do some more research before deciding on how best to proceed with this." I had no choice but to pay my brother a visit on Sunday. If he was having a lucid spell I could benefit from his clinical knowledge and years of experience. "There's a colleague I would like to consult with over the weekend. Can we do our next session at the same time on Monday?"

Sharon looked apprehensive. "Will she be able to sleep over the weekend?"

"Well, she was able to get some rest during today's session. This will continue to build off of yesterday's work, so she should have a relatively uneventful weekend. Call me if anything unusual happens." *Like this whole thing isn't unusual.* "I'll put in some more post-hypnotic triggers before I bring her out of trance." *With any luck they'll hold her through the weekend ... giving me some time to come up with a plan of action.*

* * *

Ben arrived at eight sharp. He looked stunning in his black Armani suit, with violet shirt and black tie.

My black silk cocktail dress, with violet shawl, was the perfect complement to his attire. "See you got my fashion memo," I said.

He laughed and shook his head. "I'm not surprised something like this happened. Guess we'll have to get used to it."

"Wait. Don't tell me. The twin flames have struck again." *He's certainly a diligent practical joker.* "You can drop the gag now. How do you know Louie? Are you one of his clients?"

"Louie? The friend you put on the phone this afternoon? I'm not sure I know what you're talking about."

"Welcome to the club. Why don't you come in and have a drink? It may refresh your memory."

I escorted my date into the living room and strategically placed him on the loveseat in front of the fireplace. It was too hot for a fire in the old hearth, but I wasn't opposed to starting one up somewhere else.

"Martini, Cosmo or bourbon?" I asked.

"Cosmo."

That was a trick question. Louie and I had devised a liquor litmus test, as a way of sorting men when we went barhopping together. Bourbon equaled straight. Martini hinted at bisexual undertones. And Cosmo was gay all the way. Silly as it may sound, it rarely failed.

Looks like this girl's sailing into another lonely night. Dejected, I went into the kitchen to prepare the drinks.

"Virgin," Ben shouted out.

"No," I called back. "Are you?"

"I want a virgin."

Good luck.

My head was halfway in the fridge, trying to locate the cranberry juice, when I sensed Ben standing behind me. Even with all that cold air swirling round, I was starting to feel uncomfortably hot.

"There you are," I said to the cranberry juice. Clutching the bottle, I held it to my flushed cheek before standing to face him.

"No," Ben said, talking hold of my waist—pulling me into his body. "Here I am." Then he kissed me.

A throbbing ache coursed through my body, making me want to pull away and move in closer at the same time. The intoxicating spell was broken by the thud of plastic bottle crashing onto tile.

Ben abruptly released me from his embrace. A moment of awkward silence passed between us.

"I shouldn't have allowed that to happen," he said.

Why not? ... didn't you feel what I just did?

"Sorry, Roberta."

I won't hold it against you ... I'd rather be holding you against me.

He retrieved the bottle of cranberry juice from the floor. "I'll drink my Virgin Cosmo and promise to be a good boy for the rest of the evening."

Is there such a thing as a closet heterosexual? "Look is there something you want to tell me? Anything you want to get off your chest?"

"Are you married?" He picked Danny's book up off the kitchen counter. "Is Daniel Law your husband?"

Is that why he stopped kissing me? "No. He's my brother." *Now let's get back to smooching.*

"I'm a great admirer of his work. Would you mind setting up an introduction?"

What am I … a gay dating service? "You may want to clear that one through your friend, Louie."

"Why do you keeping calling him my friend? I've never met the guy."

"Can we drop the charade now? It's grown quite tiresome. Let's lay all our cards on the table. What do you want from me?"

"You sound upset. It's because the kiss was too soon."

"What in God's name are you talking about?"

"The reason I'm here—twin flames."

"Not that, again. How much is Louie paying you for this?

"I don't know what you mean?"

"Tell you what," I said pushing him toward the front door. "Why don't you try and figure it out on your way home?"

"What about dinner?"

"I seem to have lost my appetite. Louie might be free tonight. Why don't you give him a call? I'm sure he'll pick up the tab. You can tell him all about me—this evening—the twin flames." I opened the door, waiting for him to exit.

"This is difficult to understand. It baffles even me. We may be rushing things a bit, so I'll leave." He strode down my front walk and stopped halfway. "But don't worry, this doesn't mean I'm giving up. You'll come around. When you're ready, you'll call me."

I shouted out to him just before he reached his car. "Wait!"

He stopped to look back at me.

"Don't forget to let Louie know you're interested in my brother. He can take you up to the Mount Baldy Zen Center the next time he pays Danny a visit."

A devilishly sexy grin adorned Ben's face. "Sounds like a plan; will do." He got in his car and sped off into the night.

I stood there all alone. Wishing I'd never met him, wishing I were with him.

CHAPTER THREE

I HAD NO CLIENTS BOOKED on Saturday, so I hibernated in bed. Looking out from my bedroom window, the day was as gray as my mood. The phone rang a few times; the answering machine took the messages. I was through with men. All men. Gay, straight or bi—sane or insane—living or dead; none of them mattered anymore.

This woman's declaring herself a testosterone free zone ... there are other options open to me ... though the only ones I can think of are lesbian or nun.

Lex bayed from somewhere in the house.

All right ... he'll be the one exception to my new rule ... why can't men be more like dogs? ... is that asking too much? ... dogs are loyal ...dependable ... lovable ... and devoted.

Lex jumped up on the bed and snuggled next to me. After a couple of perfunctory licks, he gave me the look—five o'clock, time for his dinner.

So even dogs have an agenda ... at least it's not hidden. "Okay, boy. Kibble time it is."

I dragged my carcass into the kitchen.

Perhaps I should eat something myself … a woman can't live by chocolate alone … not if she wants to maintain her five-foot-eight figure at one hundred and forty pounds.

For a female with a medium-sized frame, I thought I was doing all right—the weight of a contender by American Medical Association standards. Unfortunately, it's the weight of a has-been by Hollywood agent standards. It's a cruel joke that the acronym for the professional actors' union is SAG, but my show biz life was far behind me now; I was much happier in my new profession.

Turning on the radio, to drown out the annoying beep of my answering machine, I caught the last few notes of an old song.

"That was Lori Taylor singing, 'Blue Tomorrow,' a mellow male voice relayed through the speakers.

How apropos for my mood.

As I scooped kibble into Lex's bowl, the announcer's voice repeated in my head, "Lori Taylor singing."

Lori Taylor singing? … or Lori Taylor Singer? … or Lori Taylor, the singer? … is she dead? … I thought she was one of the fortunate ones who made it out of the sixties alive … coincidence? … another case of believing you were someone famous in a past life? … would a ten-year-old even know who Lori Taylor was?

Lex pawed my leg.

"Sorry, fella." I set his bowl down on the kitchen floor. *What next? … waste valuable time researching this on the Internet?… or get the whole story from Louie in ten seconds flat? … what kind of profes-*

sional would I be if I let being pissed off at Louie get in the way of my work?

I went into the living room and picked up the cordless. The doorbell rang. Lex and I both ignored it. He was busy devouring his dinner, and I was busy trying to avoid being devoured by my anger at Louie for playing stupid practical jokes.

The doorbell rang again and again. I marveled at the annoying persistence of salespeople. Now that telemarketing was next to impossible to do in the state of California, it was back to the personal touch—face-to-face harassment. After a few moments of blessed silence, assured my uninvited guest had hit the road, I punched in the number for Louie's cell.

My living room window, hidden behind closed drapes, made a noisy rattle.

Wind must be picking up.

The old wooden frame creaked and scraped. It was located on the side of the house hidden from street view. Motion detector lights were installed to thwart any would-be robbers. Of course, they don't help much in the light of day.

The curtains fluttered.

A strong breeze might be able to jangle a window … but I've never heard of it opening one.

A body moved behind the drapery.

What kind of nut breaks into a house … in a residential neighborhood … on a Saturday afternoon? … do I want to hang around and find out?

Seizing Lex, I hurried into my office and closed the door behind us. *Damn! ... should have put a lock on this door.*

I was about to call 9-1-1, when I heard Louie calling from the cordless phone still clenched in my hand. "Hello? Hello? Is anyone there?"

"Oh, thank God, you answered. I need your help,"

"Are you okay, Roberta? Where are you?"

I heard a muffled voice in the living room.

"Hurry, I'm in my office. Call the pol ..."

"Don't go anywhere. I'll be right there." Louie hung up.

If he manages to get me out of this one ... I'm going to kiss that guy when I see him.

Lex squirmed in my arms.

Heavy footsteps made their way through the house, as the intruder drew closer to my office.

Can't wait for Louie ... better make a run for it ... and pray no one else is waiting outside.

I reached for the front doorknob. Lex dropped to the floor and made a beeline for the other door. Turning back, I caught hold of his collar.

The office door cracked open.

An ear-piercing scream emanated from the very depths of my being, only to be trumped by the vociferous cry of a petrified male. The door slammed shut again.

What the hell is happening?

"What are you doing in there?" asked the spooked phantom from behind the door.

That voice. I flung the door wide open. "What are you doing?" I shouted. "Why did you break into my house?"

Louie stood there looking shell-shocked. "I happened to be in the neighborhood and saw your car parked out front. You had me worried when you didn't return any of my phone calls. I rang the doorbell, but you didn't answer that either." He wiped the perspiration off his brow. "Something might have happened to you. You could have been lying injured on the floor. I don't know how many meals that dog would be willing to miss before deciding to snack on you."

"Lex? He's a beagle, you idiot, not a pit-bull."

"It could happen. You hear about it all the time."

"Right. Today on *Jerry Springer*—'Beagles Gone Bad.' "

Adrenalin depleted, our self-invented terrors gave way to relieved laughter.

"You can't blame me for wanting to check in on you after last night's date," Louie said.

"So you've come to apologize."

"For what?"

"Didn't old Benny boy fill you in?"

Taking me by the shoulders, Louie looked straight into my eyes. "I swear on Judy Garland's grave, I don't know the guy. Picking up that pamphlet of his was nothing other than a coincidence." Louie was serious; he never joked about Judy Garland. "When I couldn't get a hold of you today, crazy thoughts started running through my head. What if it turned out he really was a nut? That's why I was checking up on you. So how was the date? I want all the dirt."

I slumped down into the recliner.

" 'Man That Got Away?' " he asked.

"More like chased away."

Louie nodded and gave me an empathetic shrug. "Weirdo?"

"You can say that again."

"I was right about him then."

"No, I'm the weirdo. What must Ben think of me? I behaved like a total idiot."

"Call him up and explain. It was an honest misunderstanding."

Humble pie was never my favorite dish, and I'd have to enter a pie-eating contest to get myself out of this predicament.

"I'll think about it," I said. Do you want a drink?"

"Well, it is cocktail hour. Make mine a Cosmo."

"I'm pouring whiskeys."

"Sour?"

"No, straight."

"How Miss Kitty of you," Louie said in a western drawl.

"Not in the mood," I said with a cutting glance.

"Beg your pardon, Marshal Dillon."

I poured a couple of shots.

We sat together in the living room, drinking in silence.

Is it possible to feel any worse than I've felt all day long? I took another swig from my glass; the answer was a resounding yes. I hated whiskey. *What's this bottle doing in my house? ... must have been a gift ... fitting punishment for my pig-headed stupidity.* I got up to pour myself another one.

"You're having more?" Louie asked.

"Yeah. You want some?"

"God, no. This stuff is horrible." He came into the kitchen and threw the remainder of his drink down the sink. "Whisky a Go Go," he said, waving it a fond farewell. "Wonder if that's how they came up with the name for the club? I haven't been in there since Lori Taylor was at the top of the charts."

"Is she dead?"

"Who?"

"Lori Taylor?"

"May as well be. She retired and went into seclusion."

"How long ago?"

"A year or two. She quit the business after reuniting with her long-lost daughter. Why all the interest in the golden oldies?"

"I took your advice yesterday and did a past life regression with my child insomniac, claims she was murdered in a past life. When I asked what her name was she said three words—Lori, Taylor, Singer. So either her name was Lori Taylor Singer or she was Lori Taylor, the singer."

"Maybe Lori Taylor died and no one knows yet because she dropped out of sight."

"She'd have to have died at least ten years ago to be reincarnated as my client."

"I've got it! Lori Taylor killed her."

"Nope. Claims to have been murdered by her father."

"What's his name?"

"I have no idea. She referred to him only as 'father.'"

"What if he was a priest?"

"I never thought about that."

"What if he was a Father who was her father? There's your motive." Louie was getting carried away with the idea of playing Watson to my Holmes. He always loved the challenge and excitement of being cast in a new role.

"Here's a better theory," I said in a conspiratorial tone, drawing him closer to me. "What if the whole thing's just a figment of a child's overactive imagination?"

He came back at me defiantly. "And what if it's not?"

"In that case, I have a murder to solve and not a clue of how to go about it."

"If I help, will you give me first dibs on the movie rights? This could turn into another *Erin Brokovich*. Antonio Banderas can play me. Now who'll we get for your part?"

"Aren't you jumping the gun a bit?"

"Guns? I didn't think about that. We might need them."

"No guns. You're dangerous enough with a cell phone."

"Does that mean we're partners?"

"We'll see. Let me put you on probation first. Since I have no idea where to start on something like this, you can accompany me to the Mt. Baldy Zen Center tomorrow."

"Danny. He'll know what to do. What about Shirley MacLaine?"

"Don't tell me she's up there, too."

"No. She can play you in the movie."

"Thanks," I replied sarcastically. We can pick up some camera gauze on the way."

* * *

Louie came by bright and early Sunday morning. Okay, it was ten a.m.—that qualifies as a rooster call in the theatre world. His SUV was better equipped for twisting mountain roads than my VW Bug, and his presence would make seeing my brother a little less uncomfortable.

About a quarter of the way up Mount Baldy, we passed a faded sign advertising tire chains. People loved to stand by the side of the road and sell things in LA. Flowers for Valentine's Day, Santa hats for Christmas, big stuffed bunnies for Easter, and bags of oranges for what I haven't the faintest idea.

"I called ahead and made arrangements for our visit," Louie said, when we were about halfway there. "Danny already knew we were coming."

"The Bodhi Tree must have told him I received his package."

"No, I don't think so. He said it was one of his 'knowings.'"

"Don't you mean delusions?"

"Well, we are driving up there, aren't we?"

He had me there. My brother's madness both fascinated and terrified me. Was it genetic? Did the same fate await me? Having exhibited not an inkling of my brother's intellectual brilliance, I figured I was safe. Yet the puzzling challenges of the past few days reminded me that, perhaps, even I didn't have the slightest idea of what was real and what wasn't.

Louie pulled into a cramped, gravel parking area just off the side of the road. "This is it."

Except for the presence of a weather-beaten, nondescript, wooden sign identifying the Center, there were no other indications that four-and-a-half acres of Tibet lay hidden behind the deciduous and evergreen trees surrounding the property.

We parked and climbed up a stone staircase that led to a winding dirt road. Set on a hillside, a series of small and unadorned buildings came into view as we made our way along the path.

"I loved it up here as a kid," Louie said.

"You were a Buddhist?"

"No, a Boy Scout. This place used to be a camp. It was heaven to be out in nature surrounded by hundreds of other boys. I had my first summer romance here." Louie launched into an off-the-cuff rendition of the song, 'Black Boys,' from the Broadway musical, *Hair.*

"Shhh ... Keep it down. We're at a religious center."

"It's okay. He's a Pentecostal minister in Orange County now."

Feigning exasperation, I reached for my air mic singing, 'Summer Nights' from *Grease.*

Louie joined me in the duet. Another voice, from behind one of the buildings, turned us into a trio. A singing Danny ran up and wrapped his arms around Louie and me. For an instant, we were transported back to the days when our most pressing concern was which party to attend on a Saturday night.

"Good to see ya haven't lost your touch, sis." My brother seemed like his old self. It was good to have him back.

"Are you back on your meds?" I asked.

"I'm fine," he said.

"You didn't answer my question."

Danny went Zen on me. "Every answered question leads to a questioned answer. Let's not get on the merry-go-round today. Okay?"

My head nodded in agreement, but in the back of my mind I wondered how long this spurt of sanity would last?

"Let me show you two around the place before we get down to business."

Danny escorted us around the grounds, pointing out key buildings along the way. He showed us the zendo, where he sat in daily meditation—the dining room, where he took his meals—and the sutra hall, where he studied the teachings of the compassionate Buddha. We passed by a shower building, sewing hut, office, library, and various cabins used for housing monks, nuns, and visitors.

The place was filled with a peaceful purposefulness, which seemed to have a soothing effect on my brother. His navy blue eyes had lost their torment. The trembling hands had been replaced with an unseen strength. Even his once jet-black hair had relaxed into the rhythm of this new life; the graying curls no longer clenched to his head. They were softer, longer, more willing to let go and just be.

"These are my digs," he said, opening the door of a tiny unadorned hut. "Make yourselves comfortable." Danny sat cross-legged on the floor.

It was evident that comfy wasn't what the designer had in mind. There was a utilitarian bunk with a green sleeping bag on it in one corner. On the back wall, under a solitary window, sat a small table with a straight back bamboo chair. Louie claimed the bunk. I went for the chair.

"I don't mean to rush you but this is a work afternoon up here," Danny explained. "There are still a lot of roofs we need to repair before winter sets in."

The image of my brother doing manual labor did not compute. He was a bookworm, through and through.

"Do you mind if I watch?" I teased. "Gotta get a picture for the family album."

"No photo ops unless you help," Danny said.

"I'll help," Louie offered. "I look fabulous in a tool belt."

"So, Roberta, did you finally read my book?"

"Yes, but I'm still a little skeptical."

"Hard to believe you're the artist in the family, and I'm the scientist," Danny said shaking his head.

"I <u>was</u> an artist, now I'm a hypnotherapist. And I know the difference between fact and fiction."

"No, you don't," Danny countered. "Isn't that why you're here? Why we're all here?"

"I came because we're working on a cold case file," Louie said.

"Have you two opened a detective agency on the side?"

"No. I'm dealing with an insomnia case. The client's a child. She's afraid to sleep due to horrific nightmares. While in trance she displayed some unusual physical phenomena. She may—and I stress <u>may</u>—be spontaneously regressing to a possible past life, where she keeps witnessing her own murder. The woman she keeps seeing vows not to rest until her murder is solved. Her name was Lori Taylor Singer, and her father was the killer."

"He was a priest," Louie blurted.

"Catholic?" Danny asked.

"Don't start jumping to conclusions," I said. "We don't know if he was a priest or not. I'm not even sure if her name is Lori Taylor Singer or if she's claiming to be Lori Taylor, the singer."

"Lori Taylor isn't dead. She was up here a few weeks ago," Danny said.

"Did you get her autograph?" Louie asked.

"Why would I do that?"

"Because she's a reclusive folk-rock legend," Louie answered. "And it would be a real collector's item."

"I have enough of my own baggage to unload; why start accumulating someone else's? We're just fellow sentient beings traveling the road to enlightenment. She was not in the best shape."

"What do you mean?" I asked. "Did she look ill?"

"Hard to say, I didn't get very close to her. She had an entourage following her everywhere. There was this fragile look about her, like she could break at any minute."

"Who was in the entourage?" I was intrigued by the enigma that was Lori Taylor. Though well-known, due to her vast body of work spanning four decades, there was not much I knew about the woman. Always publicity shy, her songs served as the sole testament of her life and times.

"There were two people with her, a woman and a man. The woman was younger and looked a lot like her. The man was about the same age as Lori. I'd seen him somewhere before, but I couldn't put a name to the face."

"Must be the long lost daughter I told you about." Louie seemed proud that his encyclopedic knowledge of music trivia might, at long last, serve a useful purpose.

"So who's the guy?" I asked.

"I bet I'd know him if I saw him. If he looked familiar to Danny, he must be a somebody."

"We're all somebody, Louie." Danny philosophized.

"True enough." Louie switched to an Asian accent. "But some bodies are nobodies, little grasshopper,"

"It doesn't matter who he is or isn't," I said. "That's Lori Taylor's problem. Let's get back to my client. How do I help her through this?"

"Listen." Danny closed his eyes.

Listen to what?

Louie and I sat staring at each other.

At first I heard nothing, then I noticed the quiet hum of chanting in the distance. "People are chanting. What's that supposed to tell me?" I asked Danny.

"Listen some more," he instructed.

I heard the chanting again. After a few more minutes of this exercise in futility, I opened my mouth to speak.

Danny pressed his right index finger to his lips, begging my patience.

I continued listening and noticed a louder, closer, more usual sound than chanting. *Chirping.* "Birds. I hear birds and chanting." Somehow I hadn't noticed them before.

"Better," Danny counseled. "Continue to listen."

This inane game was starting to annoy me. "I don't see how this is going to help me with my client."

"Not yet, but you will," Danny said.

Louie was lying on the bunk with his eyes closed. I had never seen him so quiet for so long. He was either fast asleep or dead.

I closed both eyes, too. My auditory awareness heightened by this one simple gesture. In addition to the birds and the chanting, I heard other sounds I had missed. Layer after layer, I peeled away each sound exposing another hidden underneath. A gentle wind rustled in the trees—feet shuffled through fallen leaves—a broom scratched over dirt and stone—the faint echo of a woman singing—Louie snoring—my own breathing. I opened my eyes.

Danny smiled at me.

I smiled back. "I heard a lot more this time."

"The longer you listen, the more you hear. Anything interesting to report?" Danny asked.

"I was surprised by how I noticed distant sounds before becoming aware of the ones close by."

"Humankind's eternal quest in a nutshell." Danny shrugged. "Lifetimes spent in outer exploration, until we finally turn within and realize what we were seeking had been inside, waiting for us all along. Closer than our hands and feet, nearer than our breath."

Louie sat up in the bunk. "There's no place like home. There's no place like home."

"Welcome back, Dorothy," I replied. "Did you have a nice sleep?"

"I was resting. It helps me listen. I've never heard that Lori Taylor song before."

"You were dreaming, Louie," I reminded him.

"I heard a woman singing," Danny said.

"So did I," I admitted. "But it was way too faint to make out."

"Not to the ear of a true connoisseur of music," Louie said.

"He makes a salient point," Danny agreed. "We hear what we want to hear and see what we want to see; which was the reason for this entire exercise. Roberta, when working with your client it is essential you maintain an open mind. Don't judge, don't analyze. Just listen. Close your eyes if you must. Try to hear everything, not just what you want to or expect to. When you can do this, the puzzle will solve itself. The answer is closer than you realize. Go with your instincts."

A gong reverberated through the cabin.

"I must go now." Danny got up and showed us to the door.

"What you said was helpful, but do you have anything a little more concrete for me to go on?" I asked. "Like, precisely how I'm supposed to do this?"

"Ben Cohen will help you," Danny replied.

I froze in my tracks. "Ben Cohen? How do you know Ben Cohen?"

"He dropped by yesterday and paid me a visit. We had a long discussion about my book and clinical findings in the field of past life research."

Louie threw up his hands. "Don't look at me. I had nothing to do with any of this. Judy Garland swear," he said, crossing his heart.

"Why do you look so surprised?" Danny asked. "He said you told him I was living up here."

With reluctance, I recalled the night I threw Ben Cohen out of my house. "I guess I did. Sorry."

"Don't apologize. He's a fascinating man. I think you've met your match."

"More like a flame," I added.

"He mentioned that, sounds intriguing. I haven't had a chance to go over any of the literature he left me. Why don't you come together next time and we can talk about it?"

With Danny in the lead, we all exited the cabin.

"You'll have to excuse me. I don't want to be late for meditation." Danny strolled off down the path leading to the zendo.

"Now what?" I asked Louie. "Do you want to see if we can find Lori Taylor and get an autograph before we leave?"

"She's not here."

"I thought you heard her singing."

"It was a recording. I could hear the tape being rewound."

"You do have incredible hearing. Let's go then. We can get down the mountain before it gets dark. I hate driving on these zigzagging roads at night."

"Afraid of aliens?"

"No, deer. I don't want you to hit one."

On our way back to the parking lot, I speculated about whether I'd gotten anything of value out of the trip. At least my brother seemed to be doing better. Maybe there would be a miracle and this time it would stick.

I climbed into the SUV and fastened my seatbelt. "How do you know Lori Taylor wasn't the one listening to the tape?" I asked Louie as we pulled onto the road.

"She has a phobia about listening to herself sing."

"I could help her with that."

"Speaking of help, are you going to call Ben?"

A part of me was happy to have an excuse for calling him, while another part feared behaving like a jackass again. I looked at Louie and nodded. "Do you have a good recipe for humble pie?"

CHAPTER FOUR

ONDAY ARRIVED WITH A JOLT. Literally. The convulsive eruption of my bed knocked me into consciousness at seven a.m. My house was in the midst of a grand mal seizure. I grabbed onto Lex who, thank God, was right beside me howling his defiance at the Fates. At least that's what it looked like. I couldn't hear a thing over the deafening rumble of my quivering neighborhood.

Theories and counter-theories of what one should and shouldn't do during an earthquake raced through my mind. Stand in a doorjamb—get under a heavy desk—stay indoors—go outside. Needless to say, it wasn't the best time to start sifting through them. I stayed put with Lex.

After what seemed like an eternity, the shaking stopped. The sound of roaring destruction was replaced with an annoying cacophony of thousands of car alarms, accompanied by a wailing chorus of house alarms, store alarms, fire alarms and smoke alarms. Just when things quieted down, and I felt brave enough to make the obligatory damage assessment tour, the phone rang.

"Hello."

"Did you feel that?" screamed the panicked voice at the other end of the receiver.

"Even the dead felt that one, Louie."

"Did you die?" he responded in a frantic stupor.

"Calm down. I'm fine and so is Lex. I wouldn't be talking to you if I was dead."

"You could be a ghost. It happened so suddenly, you might not realize you're dead yet."

"Are you okay? We shouldn't be tying up the phone lines unnecessarily. They may be needed for a real emergency."

The earth shifted some more. Aftershocks—the flashback legacy of earthquakes. Nature's little reminder (in case you had forgotten in the past ten minutes) of what a really bad trip you've just been on.

Louie screamed.

Lex howled.

And the alarms resumed their dissonant symphony.

"I knew this was going to happen," Louie screeched, trying to be heard above the din. "Damn earthquake weather!"

"That's an old wives' tale. There's no such thing as earthquake weather."

I've heard people proclaim this theory regardless of it being hot, cold, wet or dry. With those odds, when it comes to earthquakes in Southern California, the door's always open and the welcome mat is out.

"Are you hurt?" I asked Louie, again.

"I don't think so."

"Have you checked the condo out yet?"

"No."

"Why don't you go do that? I'll do the same here and then get back to you. Okay?"

"I guess so." Louie sounded uncertain. "The power's out here. Maybe I'll listen to my car radio and find out more about what's going on."

"Good idea. You know you should keep a transistor radio in the house for emergencies like this."

" 'Que Sera, Sera.' "

A song title. He was feeling better.

"Louie, be careful. I love you."

"Ditto. Speak to you in a few."

I hung up the phone and looked at my alarm clock. It was still seven a.m. *Power's out.*

Lex and I took a look around the property. We got off easy. Some broken dishes, a few fallen books and a couple of pieces of overturned furniture. Other than that, everything seemed to be in order. In the backyard, behind the pool, it looked like part of a brick wall separating my property from my neighbor's had come down. I was on my way to investigate the extent of the damage when the phone in my office rang.

"Hello, Roberta Law speaking."

"Hello, Roberta. It's Sharon, LaVonne's mother. I'm going to have to reschedule our appointment with you today."

"Is everything okay? Were you hit hard by the earthquake?"

"Yes, I'm afraid so. No one was hurt, but we lost part of our chimney. It fell onto my car. I'm going to need a few days to get everything sorted out with the insurance companies. And I'm expecting to be putting in some overtime at the hospital because of this."

"I understand completely. How's LaVonne doing?"

"Considering everything she's been through in the past little while, I think she's doing quite well. Her sleeping patterns improved over the weekend. She's still waking up, but not as frequently or violently. This earthquake has shaken her up a bit though. She's going to stay with her father for a few days until everything settles down here. This one didn't affect Orange County. Can she get through a few more nights without another session?"

"It's hard to say. She seems to be responding well, but post-hypnotic suggestions can be tricky things. Consistent application and reinforcement aids their effectiveness. Make sure you thoroughly go over the triggers with her father, and give him my number in case he needs to reach me for anything."

"I'll do my best. Frank isn't the most open-minded person in the world. He wasn't fond of this hypnosis idea in the first place."

"So I've heard. He thinks I'm a witch doctor."

"Oh, LaVonne shouldn't have told you that. I apologize."

"It's all right. I'm used to it. Perhaps he should attend one of our sessions. It may help to demystify the whole process for him."

"We'll see. I'll call you when LaVonne's back home."

"All right. Take care of yourself, Sharon."

As soon as I hung up the phone, it rang again. This pattern repeated itself until my appointment slate for the day was cleared, giving me a chance to tidy up the house and review the notes I had made about my brother's book.

First things first though, it was time for my morning cup of coffee and Lex's bowl of breakfast kibble. I poured water in the coffee maker and then remembered the power was out. After rustling about the cupboards under my kitchen sink, I dragged out my dusty French press. Kettle filled with water, I set it down on top of the gas stove and turned the dial for the front right burner. Nothing. I tried the others. No success.

Earthquake must have triggered the emergency shut-off valve on the meter. It was encouraging to know that something was working.

On the gas company's line a prerecorded message announced, "Due to a high volume of calls, please try back later."

Doesn't look like I'll be doing any cooking for a while. My focus shifted back to Lex's breakfast. *Kibble scooping seems like an earthquake neutral activity.*

Bowl in hand, I reached into the large bag of diet dog food stored in the laundry room. The small hard nuggets clanging against stainless steel served as a dinner bell for Lex. I put the doggie delicious meal down on his official Beagle Brigade placemat in the kitchen.

"Lex! Lex!"

He was nowhere in sight. Highly unusual behavior for this beagle. I called his name a few more times. No response. Something was wrong. Lex never missed a meal. I searched every room. Not a trace. The last time I had seen him he was headed for the backyard.

I stepped onto the patio. The earth let out another unnecessary reminder of its power. The rumble was brief but strong. Horrified, I watched the rest of the back wall come tumbling down.

Oh God, I hope he isn't near there.

Blinded to everything but my rescue mission, I raced past the pool to the back of the yard. Failing to notice a small branch from a nearby orange tree had fallen to the ground, I tripped; my brief air flight destined for an inevitable and wet crash landing. The chilling cold of the unheated water did not faze me. Emotions numb, I swam to the side of the pool and dragged myself out.

Reaching the wreckage that was once my wall, I dug through assorted pieces of brick and piles of rubble. Soaking wet, covered in dirt and mud from my efforts, the good news was the same as the bad news—no Lex.

Just when it seemed like all hope had been lost, a beagle howl came from my front yard. I rushed along the side of the house, swung open the redwood gate, and crashed right into Ben Cohen.

"I believe this vagabond belongs to you," he said, handing me a rope with the unabashed Lex attached to the other end.

Ben stood there in his khaki pants and yellow sports shirt looking as cool, calm and collected as Jeff Probst at Tribal Council.

Barefoot and filthy, with a wet tee shirt and panties clinging to my body, I looked like a contestant from *Survivor: Black Lagoon.*

"Where did you f-f-f-f . . ." I stammered. *Why do I always get so nervous and worked up around this guy?*

"Find him?" Ben asked.

"Yeah, that's it."

"I was driving over here to see if you were okay, when I noticed my beagle friend scrounging around a dumpster a few blocks away. His tag confirmed my suspicions."

"You were checking to see if I was okay, after the way I treated you the other night?"

"Forget about the other night. It's history. I tried calling a few times before coming over, but I couldn't get through."

"Sorry about that, I was dealing with a lot of client cancellations today." *C'mon ... swallow the humble pie.* "I also want to apologize for the way I acted on Friday."

"Apology accepted. So you're free for breakfast then?"

"Sure," I said, accepting his surprise invitation. "If you don't mind waiting while I shower and change."

Smiling, Ben scrutinized me. "Other than the dirt, I think the outfit is quite flattering."

Feeling like I was suddenly standing there stark naked, I tugged at the tee shirt clinging to my body.

Maybe I should invite him to join me under the steaming waters.

Then I remembered—no gas = no hot water.

Just as well, I need to cool down a bit.

We went inside and I fed Lex before jumping into the ice cold shower.

Why does the guy affect me this way? ... maybe there really is something to this twin flames malarkey ... no more being so close-minded and judgmental ... that's my vow from now on ... today I start afresh.

I stepped out of the shower.

I'm a blank slate … and Ben Cohen's the chalk.

Dried myself with a towel.

I'm just a little bare slate … and Ben's a big hard piece of chalk … that I'm going to let write all over me.

My body dampened with perspiration. I stepped back into the cold shower.

* * *

None of the restaurants in Valley Glen, Studio City, Sherman Oaks or Van Nuys were open that morning. They were all closed for repairs and cleanup. We were going to check out North Hollywood, Toluca Lake and Burbank, but after hearing on the radio the epicenter of the 5.0 quake was in Glendale, that appeared to be pointless. Since we weren't having much luck finding a place to eat, Ben asked if I'd mind making a quick stop at his office.

We headed over the hill via Beverly Glen. Damage and traffic lessened once we crossed over Mulholland Drive, leaving The Valley behind us. Lex took up residence in the backseat. I didn't want to leave him home alone, in case there were more aftershocks. Besides, how a man behaved with a dog in his car told you a lot about his inner nature—that, and his taste in shoes. Tobacco-colored suede Skechers on his feet and a slobbering beagle's head resting on his shoulder, told me everything I needed to know.

The offices of the California Center for Parapsychology & Paranormal Research were in Westwood Village, a stone's throw from the UCLA campus.

"Roberta Law, this is Nancy Perkins," Ben said, introducing me to the stunning twenty-something blonde sitting at a desk outside his office.

I didn't realize it's Take a Supermodel to Work Day. I shook the perfectly manicured French-tipped hand. "Pleased to meet you." *Did that sound convincing?*

"We spoke on the phone the other day," she replied. I detected a stifled giggle in her voice.

"You must be the receptionist," I said, countering the giggle with a patronizing tone.

Ben corrected me. "No, she's my personal assistant."

"Oh, I'm sorry. Please excuse me."

"It's okay. His personal assistant also answers all the phones around here. As you can see, we're not that big an operation." Nancy gave Ben an admiring look. "At least, not yet."

Damn it ... there's something I like about this woman ... what's not to like? ... she's warm ... friendly ... self-effacing ... gorgeous ... obviously thinks the world of Ben ... it's definitely those last two I'm having trouble with ... come on Roberta ... you're a bigger person than this ... be nice. "We must get together for lunch sometime. I'd love to hear more about your work here." *That's for sure ... watch it ... you're stepping out of bounds again.*

"Great idea. Nancy, why don't you join us?" Ben glanced at his watch. "We were planning on breakfast, but it's starting to look a lot more like brunch."

Just say no, Nancy ... it's easy.

"It's only ten-thirty. My lunch hour isn't until one."

That's what I like to see ... a conscientious young employee.

"I'm shutting down the office early," Ben said. "Take the rest of the day off."

Bad boss ... is this any way to run a business? ... I don't want a chaperone on our first date.

"How bad was the earthquake at your place?" Ben asked.

Perhaps she should skip lunch ... get home to clean up the mess.

"It shook a little bit, but I rode it out like a wave."

"Nancy lives in Venice Beach, Roberta. She's quite the surfer."

Figures.

"Call Inn of the Seventh Ray. See if they're open today. Make a reservation for three at eleven-thirty." Ben looked down at Lex. "Make that for three and a quarter. It's all outdoor seating. I'm sure they won't mind."

"Don't worry about Lex. We can park in the shade and leave a window rolled down for him if there's a problem. He's good in the car."

"The restaurant's open and management doesn't mind dogs, but the Department of Health does," Nancy announced without even bothering to make a call. "Sorry, Lex. Looks like it's the car for you."

Ben turned to me. "I forgot to tell you, Nancy's psychic."

I laughed, pretending to enjoy their little joke.

"No, I'm serious. That's how we met. She took part in one of our studies."

"Ben exaggerates." She stifled another giggle. "I'm more of a mind reader than a predictive psychic."

"Give me five minutes to do a quick check of my e-mail," Ben said, walking into his office.

"So you read minds." *I feel like a total ass.*

"I know," Nancy smiled. "Don't worry; I'm not interested in Ben—not romantically. I could never come between twin flames. That would take real supernatural powers, which I don't have."

"When I'm around Ben I just don't know what comes over me." Nancy looked into my eyes.

A strange sensation spread through me. It felt as if both our bodies melted away and we became two thoughts in a single mind, then a single thought—a pair of flickering flames. Then poof, I popped back into awareness of my physical body. "What was that? A Vulcan mind meld?"

"In a way. Did my twin flames image come through?"

"Loud and clear—and creeeepy."

"I wanted to show you that what I do, you can do. Everyone can. Some of us just need a little practice. As a courtesy, I'm going offline with you. I do that with all my friends and family, unless of course an emergency should arise."

"Thanks," I said, even though I didn't quite believe her.

"Excuse me, I better call and make those reservations."

While she busied herself on the phone, I decided to test the line between us. *Okay, missy ... I better not catch you messing around with my man ... or there'll be hell to pay ... just kidding ... did you get that?*

"She didn't, but I sure did," Ben said, walking out of his office. He came up behind me and whispered in my ear. "Nice to know you care."

"Not you, too?" I turned to face him. "How about a courtesy offline?"

"Don't worry, I'm not very good at it."

"Let's keep it that way."

"Doesn't every woman dream of finding a man who reads her every thought?" Ben goaded.

"Yet another idea that works better in theory than in practice." I assured him.

"I'll make a note of that."

Nancy hung up the phone. "Reservation's all set. Ready to roll?"

* * *

Ben took the scenic route to the restaurant, traveling down Sunset Boulevard to the ocean. Nancy followed in her red Miata convertible. Far enough from the epicenter, there was little or no visible earthquake damage along the way.

The day was warm and sunny until we reached Pacific Coast Highway, where things turned cool and foggy. For a place where the weather never changes much day-to-day, it does manage to have some wild fluctuations from one part of the city to the next.

We hugged the coastline for a few miles before turning onto Topanga. The sun made its gradual return as we headed up into the canyon. The roadside was littered with tie-dye shirt vendors, head shops, organic produce stands, yoga studios, an outdoor amphitheater, a former nudist colony, and hitchhikers. If anyone's in search of the sixties, it's alive and well in Topanga Canyon—the land that time forgot.

Inn of the Seventh Ray was located at a crossroads smack dab in the middle of the canyon. A cluster of rustic wooden buildings, the place was rumored to have once been Aimee Semple McPherson's private mountain retreat. At the front, The Spiral Staircase, a combination New Age bookstore and gift shop beckoned to all wayfaring seekers and shoppers—communalism meets capitalism.

"We can check out the store after we eat," Ben said. "Maybe pick up a couple of books on twin flames for you."

Whoopee… just joking, anyone who's listening.

We walked under a filigree archway, down some stone steps and into the restaurant. The term "into the restaurant" is figurative, as most of the tables were—ahem, shall we say—en plein air. You know. Outside. Like at a picnic.

The hostess, a warm earth mother type wearing an elegant purple caftan, seated us at a small table situated above a dry creek bed. Encircled by an abundance of sycamores and oaks, chirping blue jays and robins idyllically coexisted with laid-back diners seated on wrought iron chairs, noshing at lavender clothed tables—I couldn't help but wonder about the sanitation of such an arrangement. Though there was a sublime tranquility about the place, it was a bit unnerving.

"I hope you like the menu," Ben said. "There's a little something for everyone on it."

"They have a great raw foods selection," Nancy piped up. "I'm trying to transition from vegan to Natural Hygienist."

"Fantastic," I said, wishing I could figure out what in the world she was talking about. *Where's that mind meld when you need it?*

I pored over the menu. It featured all natural meat, fish and poultry items alongside vegetarian and vegan fare. Everything was free-range and hormone free. For "free" food, it was awfully expensive.

All I'm in the market for is a couple of high cholesterol fried eggs ... crispy nitrite-filled bacon ... some toasted Wonder Bread ... and a high-test coffee.

"They used to list all of the dishes by their vibrational frequency," Ben said.

"Guess there's not much demand for that," I said.

"One day there will be though," Ben predicted. "They were ahead of the paradigm."

Blatantly aware I was in over my head, I agreed with Ben. *These people are operating on a different plane than me ... possibly a different planet ... this girl's a "Broadway Baby" ... not a "Black Magic Woman" ... oh, no ... I'm starting to think like Louie ... Louie! ... I was supposed to call him back hours ago ... he'll be beside himself with worry.* I got up from the table. "Will you two excuse me for a moment?"

"Everything okay?" Ben asked.

"Yes, fine. I just remembered a call I forgot to make earlier. I'll take my cell into the store over there. Be right back."

"Should we order for you?" Nancy asked.

"Sure, I'm feeling adventurous today. Why don't you surprise me? I never met a meal I didn't like." *Though today that record could be broken.*

The eclectic store was filled with all the prerequisite items: crystals, tarot cards, candles, esoteric books, and blank greeting cards with momentous, meaningful cover art. Strains of world music floated through the pungent aroma of this month's featured incense—hemp. A scent that was sure to be popular with the sixties peace and love hippie—turned eighties politically correct liberal—turned twenty-first century neoconservative crowd.

Slipping into a quite corner near the front window, I placed my call to Louie's cell.

He answered before the first ring had ended. "What's going on? I've left about a hundred messages on your cell, at your home and on your office line."

"Sorry, Louie. I lost track of time."

"I'm headed over to your place, as we speak."

"But, I'm not there."

"Where are you?"

"The Inn of the Seventh Ray restaurant."

"In Topanga? What are you doing there?"

"Having brunch with Ben Cohen."

"Ooh, girlfriend, you certainly know how to get around. Am I hearing 'I Feel the Earth Move' segueing into a rousing 'Afternoon Delight'?"

"Not exactly. His assistant, Nancy, is with us."

"Don't tell me your man is 'Torn Between Two Lovers.' "

"Enough. I just wanted to let you know Lex and I are okay. However, I am in need of a new brick wall in my backyard."

A chartreuse Rolls-Royce pulled up in front of the restaurant, catching my eye. The passenger door opened and out stepped Lori Taylor, flanked by a man and a woman fitting the description of the people my brother had seen her with. She moved cautiously, as if they were helping her to walk.

Is she ill?

"Hello, hello. Anybody there?" Louie called out. "Can you hear me? Can you hear me now?"

"Lori Taylor's here. She's headed into the restaurant."

"Are you sure it's her? How does she look?"

"Older and heavier. Sort of like the missing link between hippies and grandmas."

"That's her. I'm on my way over there."

"What for?"

"Her autograph, of course. What is wrong with you and your brother?" Louie's voice went into a fever pitch. "I have to go back home first and get my copy of her *Caged Songbird* album. Whatever you do, do not—I repeat, <u>do not</u> let her out of there without getting an autograph for me. I'm serious. This could make or break our friendship."

"Danny was right. The guy with her does look familiar. I can't place the face either."

"I bet I can. Take his picture."

"With what? I didn't bring a camera with me."

"You have one in your phone?"

"I do?"

"Don't you remember when I talked you into upgrading?"

"I thought it was just a PalmPilot.

"Baby, that phone is a day timing, address booking, web browsing, net surfing, photo snapping, video shooting wonder of the modern world. If you treat it right it'll even make you a cappuccino and vibrate you to sleep at night."

I looked upon the unassuming gizmo in my hand with a new-found respect and, perhaps, a slight fear. It truly was an amazing gadget. However, I was still trying to figure out how to store phone numbers and use the voice activated calling feature. Deep down I knew I was unworthy of this phone.

"All right, Louie. Wish me luck."

I returned to the table, but was distracted in my conversation. The Lori Taylor party was within eyeshot and my attention kept drifting in their direction.

Who is that man with her? ... do I know him? ... where have I seen that face before?

"Something the matter, Roberta?" Ben asked.

"Did you notice Lori Taylor's seated over there?"

"Who's Lori Taylor?" Nancy asked.

"One of the greatest singer-songwriters who ever lived," Ben replied.

"Like Aimee Mann?"

"More like Aimee Mann, Björk, Avril Lavigne, Sarah McLauglin and Alanis Morissette all rolled into one," I said.

"Even then you'd come up short," Ben added.

Whadda ya know ... Ben Cohen and I are on the same frequency ... we actually have something in common. Granted it was a mixed blessing, bestowed on us only because we were both graying boomers. But, it was a start. "Do you recognize the guy who's with her?"

Ben glanced over at their table. "Hard to tell, he has his back to us."

"I need to get a picture of him. Do either of you know how to work a phone camera?"

"I do," Nancy said.

"If I distract them by getting Lori's autograph, can you snap his picture without their noticing?"

"Sure. Why do you want his picture?"

"Maybe my pal Louie can put a name to his face. The picture's insurance, in case they leave before he gets here."

"Louie's coming here?" Ben looked surprised.

"Oh, did I forget to mention that?" I said sounding sheepish. "I hope you don't mind?"

"Not at all," Ben said. "I'm dying to meet my old friend, Louie. We have so much to catch up on."

Is he amused or upset? ... I didn't complain about Nancy joining us ... at least not out loud. "Once he heard Lori's here, there was no stopping him. He's a big fan of hers. The autograph is for him." *I sound like some sort of celebrity stalker ... alerting fellow crazies to random star sightings around town ... I'll make one last stab at explaining this ... before sinking under the table.* "Lately, Lori Taylor's name, voice, and now the lady herself keep popping up in my life." *That doesn't even make sense to me.*

"Synchronicity," Ben said. "Like the way Louie keeps popping up in my life."

Touché, sir. "Can we continue this discussion later? I need to get this picture."

Nancy took my cell phone and I flagged down a passing waitress for a piece of paper and a pen. When I reached Lori's table, Nancy continued past me pretending to be on the phone.

"Sorry to bother you, but … aren't you Lori Taylor? I'm a big fan. Could I trouble you for an autograph?" I held the pen and paper out to her.

The aloof trio sat in silence behind their shiny black Hollywood shades. Glasses designed more for hiding one's eyes from other people, than from the sun.

A moment or two passed before the man nodded his head, signaling Lori to take the paper and pen from my hand. He was undoubtedly running the show.

She hesitated before signing, then scrawled something on the paper and hastily pushed it back at me.

My fingertips barely grazed the edge of the paper, when the man lurched forward and snatched it away from me.

He took one guarded look at the contents, crumpled it, and threw it on the table. "That one's not acceptable. Do it again," he said in a dictatorial tone.

I tried to place his face again. He appeared to be in his late fifties or early sixties. Balding, salt and pepper hair. His harsh, lined, boyish face sported a scraggly gray goatee.

Is he an agent or manager I've met? … he's certainly obnoxious enough to be one.

I caught sight of Nancy rejoining Ben at our table. *Mission accomplished.* I reached for the reject paper. "This'll be fine."

The man clamped down on my wrist. "She'll do another one." He glared at the younger woman. "Get a fresh piece of paper, Vanessa."

The woman looked to be about my age, but—judging by her Botox-swollen face—having some difficulty coming to terms with the fact. A copycat version of Lori Taylor, minus twenty years. Finding some paper in her purse, she gave it to Lori.

Hand trembling, Lori rewrote her autograph and handed it to the man for approval.

He inspected it before allowing me to take the paper.

Though I only caught a brief glimpse of the previous autograph, I could tell something different had been written the first time. "Thank you, sorry to interrupt your meal." I turned to leave.

"Wait," Lori called out to me in an urgent, desperate voice. "You never told me which song of mine is your favorite."

"That's tough," I answered. "There are so many to choose from. I don't think I could pick just one."

"My favorite's, 'Ill Deceived,' " she said.

I shook my head. "Don't think I know that one."

"She means 'Ill Conceived,' " the younger woman interjected. "From her first album. You'll have to excuse my mother. She hasn't been herself lately. Guess the sixties are catching up with you when you can't recall the titles of your own songs." Her tone was flippant and dismissive.

The waiter arrived with their food. I excused myself and returned to my table.

"Nancy showed me the picture she took." Ben passed me my phone. "I can't quite make out his face. The sunglasses don't help much either."

"I'm not the greatest photographer," Nancy apologized.

Squinting at the digital image captured on the screen, I wasn't about to disagree with her. The man's face was out of focus.

"I got a better picture of the autograph then I did of that guy," Nancy said.

She was right. It had photographed well. I could even make out the ink on the paper. *Too bad I can't read what it says.* "How about trying to get one more picture?"

"I would if I could," Nancy said.

"What do you mean?" I asked.

"They got up and left the moment you walked away from their table," Ben said.

"Why would they do that? Their food had just arrived." I looked back at the table. A busboy was removing plates full of food. "Excuse me, again."

I rushed over to the busboy. "Did you happen to find a crumpled up piece of paper here?"

"Basura?" the boy asked in a Mexican accent, seeming unsure if he understood me correctly or not.

"See, me basura," I replied in pidgin Spanish, patting my chest with my right hand.

The boy gave me a bemused look and continued clearing the table.

Did I just call myself garbage?

Moving right along to the universal language of charades—I reached into the back pocket of my jeans, pulled out the paper with Lori Taylor's autograph, crumpled it up and threw it onto the table.

The boy picked up the discarded paper and added it to the teetering pile of dirty dishes in his gray plastic busing tub.

"No," I shouted, and retrieved the freshly soiled piece of paper.

This last move caught the attention of one of the waiters. "Is there something I can help you with?" the young man asked.

"Yes. A few moments ago, I was speaking to the people who were seated at this table and I left behind a piece of paper. It was all crumpled up and could be mistaken for garbage."

The waiter communicated this to the busboy.

"Nada, señora," the busboy replied.

"Thanks," I said to the waiter. "No translation required."

"I saw the gentleman pick up a piece of paper," the waiter said. "Right after I arrived with the food."

"Do you know why they left so suddenly? Was Ms. Taylor taken ill? She seemed a bit shaky."

"Which one was she?"

It's amazing how quickly one can be forgotten when out of the public eye. "She was the older woman."

"No, I don't think so. It seemed like she was the only one who didn't want to go. I offered to wrap up the food, but the man didn't want to wait."

"Do they come here often?"

"I've never seen them before, and I've worked here three years."

"Thanks for helping me out." I slipped him five dollars for his trouble and rejoined my party.

"What was that all about?" Ben asked.

"Don't quite know. For some inexplicable reason, I think it has something to do with one of my clients. Actually, I was hoping to get some professional advice from you."

"From me? I'm flattered. You're the expert on hypnosis."

"This case is a little out in left field for me. When I visited my brother at the Zen Center yesterday, he suggested I get your input. What do you know about past life regressions and reincarnation?"

"We've conducted a number of studies on that topic at my center." Ben placed his hand on mine in a gesture of trust. "I'd be willing to open my files to you."

Taken off-guard by the warmth of his touch, and at a complete loss for words, I sat gaping at him. *Did he say what I think he said?* "You meant to say 'files,' right?"

"I did say 'files.' "

Then why did I hear fly? "Okay. Never mind."

"What did you think I said?"

I looked at Nancy to make sure she still had me on a courtesy offline. "Fries." She didn't flinch. "Boy, I must really be hungry."

"Help is on the way," Nancy said. "Here comes our food."

"Good thing I ordered you the special—scrambled tofu with parsnip home fries," Ben said.

I surveyed the foreign specimen set in front of me. *Why can't these people read my mind when I need them to?*

Gingerly, I picked up my fork. *Looks edible.*

I braced myself for the first bite. *Smells good.*

Deliberately chewing, I tried not to grimace. "Delicious."

"Surprised?" Ben asked.

"No, I love tofu."

"That was a parsnip you just ate," Nancy said.

At that very moment, my knight in shining armor arrived to liberate me from the epicurean hot seat. Brandishing a plethora of record albums, Louie Lopez galloped to my rescue.

"Where is she?" Louie asked, oblivious to everyone and everything but his prime objective.

"You just missed her," I said.

"Did you get me an autograph?"

"Yes." I handed him the paper.

He held it away from his body—pinching a corner, between his right thumb and index finger. "Ooh, icky. Why's it stained with mustard?"

"Long story," I said. "Louie, let me introduce you to Ben Cohen and Nancy Perkins."

"Enchanté." Louie proffered an outstretched hand.

Ben stood to shake it.

And Nancy gave him a hug and a peck on the cheek.

I sat there suspecting Louie secretly wished their choice of greetings had been reversed.

Ben pulled an empty chair to the table. "Please, join us," he said to Louie.

"Well, if you're inviting ..." Louie played the coquette. "I wouldn't mind some huevos rancheros, but I am watching my figure. Just a coffee, perhaps."

We spent the next hour chatting about Broadway and Hollywood, Louie's favorite topics. Still a performer at heart, Louie loved to entertain an attentive audience. He dazzled us with an array of trivial tidbits about movies, television, music and celebrity gossip.

I'd heard most of it before, but Ben and Nancy seemed to be enjoying the show. By the end of the meal we'd come full circle, returning to the topic of Lori Taylor.

"Did Roberta tell you about the murder we're trying to solve? It has something to do with Lori Taylor," Louie said, throwing a verbal hot potato in my lap.

"I haven't had a chance to get a word in edgewise since you arrived. And don't go starting rumors, someone may overhear you."

"Is that the synchronicity you were referring to earlier?" Ben asked me.

"Yes. A young client of mine, a ten-year-old child, spontaneously regressed into what appeared to be a past life while we were doing trancework for insomnia. The sleeping disorder seems to have been triggered by recurring nightmares of a murder. She claims to have been stabbed to death in an alley somewhere. While under, she uttered the words 'Father' and 'Lori Taylor Singer.' What it all means, I haven't a clue. She's only been in hypnosis twice."

"Sounds like you've had two very productive sessions," Ben said.

"It's nice to hear that because I feel rather stuck at the moment. Danny gave me some advice, but I'm a little stymied on how best to apply it."

Ben feigned a bow in my direction. "The services of the California Center for Parapsychology & Paranormal Research, and Dr. Benjamin Cohen are at your beck and call."

Louie shot me a suggestive look, and I gave him a playful kick under the table.

Nancy giggled. I still wasn't fully sold on this "courtesy offline" business.

Time to acquaint Louie with the special powers of my new superhero friends ... before he has a chance to get us into any real trouble.

A zealous howl rang out from the car.

"I hate to break this up, but my master calls," I said.

"Show Louie the picture before you leave," Nancy said. "I want to see if 'Mr. Show Biz Trivia' can recognize the guy."

"Praise the Lord, you used the phone camera," Louie said.

I handed him the phone. "Nancy took the picture for me."

Louie examined the image.

"It's not the best photo," Nancy said.

"Doesn't matter." Louie pressed a few buttons on the phone before giving it back to me.

"What did you do?" I asked with piqued curiosity.

"Sent a copy to my e-mail. I'll run the image through Photoshop. If we're lucky, I'll be able to clean it up enough to make a positive ID."

"Very impressive, Detective Lopez. Looks like watching all those TV crime dramas has paid off. Let's go." I grabbed Louie's arm. "You're giving Agent K-9 and me a lift back to headquarters."

Ben picked up the tab and the four of us walked back to the cars.

"I'm going to run by the office and put that past life research material together for you," Ben said. "Call me later on, let me know when would be a good time to drop by with it."

Now it was my turn to play the coquette. "Oh, you don't have to go to all that trouble. I can pick it up."

"Okay, if you prefer."

Hey! … that's not what you're supposed to say.

"I live in Studio City," Ben continued. "We're practically neighbors. My place it is then."

That's more like it.

Ben dangled his car keys. "Let me get Lex for you."

"Darn, I forgot Lex's doggie bag. Louie will you take Lex for me, please? Nice meeting you, Nancy. Speak to you later, Ben." I hurried back into the restaurant.

The busboy from my earlier encounter was clearing the table. I could have sworn I heard him mutter, "Señora loco," under his breath before escaping to his kitchen refuge.

Grabbing my little white bag of leftovers, I started for the parking lot. Out of the corner of my eye, about ten yards from where I stood, I saw a beagle scramble down into the dried-out creek bed.

Louie rushed in, yelling. "Lex ran away! He was acting really weird. I couldn't restrain him."

"He's down there," I said, pointing below. But he was no longer anywhere in sight. "Let's hurry. He's moving fast. Something must have spooked him."

We barely took a step when the earth shifted below our feet. It was another aftershock. Not as strong as earlier, but unsettling nonetheless.

"Shit!" Louie cursed. "I hate those things."

"Lex must have sensed it coming. That's why he ran away. Come on, we've got to find him before he gets too far."

With Louie following my lead, we set off on foot in search of Lex.

Only one thought crossed my mind. *Where do you find safety ... when the world is crumbling beneath your feet?*

I was about to find out.

CHAPTER FIVE

W E FOLLOWED TOPANGA CREEK for about half a mile or so, shouting out Lex's name and rattling the bag of leftovers—using it as beagle bait.

"He's got to be around here somewhere," I said. "How far could he get on those fat little legs?"

Louie looked above. "Maybe he climbed up to one of those houses."

Old Topanga Road bound the creek on one side; an odd assortment of houses bordered the other. There were shacks, teepees, old railcars, ranches and mansions peppered in hodgepodge fashion. Some places were almost hidden, as if not wanting to intrude on the natural splendor surrounding them. Others were sitting on clear-cut acreage, crying out their self-importance to every passerby—here more because they could be, rather than because they wanted to be.

"I doubt he got any farther than this; let's head back to the restaurant by road," I said. "We'll be able to get a better view of the houses from up there."

About halfway along the road, I spotted something I had missed from below. "Louie, look over there."

"Where? I don't see Lex."

"Not Lex. Do you see that Rolls?"

"A blind man could see it."

"That's the car Lori Taylor got out of earlier."

"Well, that makes sense. I know she lives somewhere in this canyon."

"Let's check it out. Maybe the guy will be there and you can get a good look at him. Just knock on the door, say you're looking for a lost beagle."

"Me? Why me?"

"Because they already saw me at the restaurant and it may seem suspicious."

"I have to go back to the car and get my albums."

"You can't do that. Then you'll look suspicious. Who goes out looking for a lost dog carrying old records they want autographed?"

"Where are you going to be during all this?"

"I'll continue looking for Lex down in the creek."

"I don't know about this."

"Remember Antonio Banderas? No mystery solved, no movie made. If you want first dibs on those film rights, you're going to have to help me with this."

"Fine, I'll do it. Chalk it up to one more case of my people doing your people's dirty work."

I gave him a peck on the cheek. "Thank you, Louie."

We climbed back down into the creek and Louie scrambled up the other side. I perched myself on one of the many boulders dotting the landscape—waiting for Louie and searching for signs of Lex.

Waiting was never one of my strengths. It was a major catalyst for my leaving performing. Actors were always waiting for the next audition, the next job, the next call from their agent.

I looked around the dusty creek bed with its dry trees and brown brush, ready to combust at any moment. A profound sense of peace engulfed me. In this most unlikely of places, I felt like I was in the right place, at the right time. Taking in a long deep breath, I filled my being with the moment. Holding the air in my lungs— hoping this feeling would never leave me—startled back into real time by the blaring of my cell phone.

"Hello."

It was Louie. "Get up here right away and don't forget the doggie bag. I've found Lex, but he's not coming in without ransom."

"Did you see the guy?"

"Nobody's home. Hurry!" He hung up.

Where the heck did I put that bag?

Behind me, I heard the sound of ripping paper. Hesitant to move, not wanting to look back and discover what I had been so oblivious to a moment ago, thinking happy thoughts of cute little raccoons and harmless baby possums—all animated of course—I took a quick peek over my shoulder.

Rats! I hate rats!

That was all the motivation this girl needed. I shot off the boulder and out of that creek faster than Janet Jackson's costume-popping breast at the Super Bowl.

My sudden burst of adrenalin came in handy when I joined Louie in the great beagle chase. Lex could really haul ass when he wanted to.

"Where's the food?" Louie shouted at me.

"Rats!"

"Oh, that's not right. This nature stuff is highly overrated."

"Wait, wait," I panted to Louie. I looked up at the big, barn-red house as we ran by it for what seemed like the hundredth time. *Is someone peeking at us through the second floor curtains?* "He thinks were playing. If we stop, he'll stop."

Sure enough, the moment we stood still—so did Lex. He was about five yards away from us, tail wagging, trying to predict our next move.

I grabbed onto Louie. "Let's sit down and wait him out." We fell in a heap to the ground, our backs to the house. "I'm sure he's exhausted by now."

Lex watched with suspicion, cautiously moving in our direction. When he got within arm's length, I reached for his brown leather collar. He ran right past me toward the house.

Louie started after him.

"Let him go. He'll come back," I said

"I don't know about that," Louie said. "He just went into the house."

"What?" I bolted up from my spot and faced the house. "I thought you said no one was home."

"Well, no one answered the door when I rang. I think Lex pushed it open."

Back door slightly ajar, we peered into the kitchen—Lex was nowhere in sight—a surprising revelation, this being his favorite room in any house.

"Lex ... Lex ... I pushed the door open a little farther. "Come on ... time to go home, boy."

"Let's just go in and get him," Louie said, stepping onto the worn oak floor of the canary yellow kitchen.

"Wait," I said, pulling him back. "I think I saw someone watching us from one of the upstairs windows. Maybe we should announce our presence before barging in."

"Isn't that what Lex is doing?"

"Hello ... hello ... anybody home?" I called inside.

"Yes," a deep voice resonated behind us. "May I ask what you're doing here?"

Letting out a couple of startled yelps, Louie and I turned around and found ourselves face-to-face with Lori's mystery man.

"Hey, weren't you the autograph hound at the Inn of the Seventh Ray?" the man asked in an unpleasant tone. "What are you, some kind of stalker?"

"No! I can explain. My dog ran away from the restaurant and I followed him here. The door was open and he went inside. He's a beagle hound. They're very curious types."

"He must take after you," the man said. "Is he a liar, too?"

"I beg your pardon?" I said, amazed by his nerve.

"You didn't have a dog with you in the restaurant."

"He was in the car, so you wouldn't have seen him. They don't allow dogs in the restaurant. Which is kind of funny I think, since the entire place is outdoors."

He was not amused. "So where's your car now? I didn't see it outside." He took out his cell phone and started punching in numbers. "Maybe I should call the police for you and report it stolen ..."

"Aren't you Paul Graham?" Louie interjected.

The man stopped what he was doing.

"I'm a huge fan of yours," Louie gushed. "Could I bother you for an autograph?"

He put the phone down. His entire demeanor changed—a smile broke across the stern face, his steely gray eyes lost their bitter edge. "Why yes, I am."

"I knew it," Louie said. "Too bad I don't have my albums with me."

"You have my records?" He seemed surprised.

"Of course. I have all of them—your two Graham & Taylor albums and the two solo ones you released."

Now I remembered him, too. He and Lori Taylor were a duo in the mid-sixties. After their split, Lori skyrocketed to fame and he dropped off the radar.

"I don't run into many people who remember my solo work. That was a couple of lifetimes ago," he said wistfully.

"Are you and Lori planning a reunion? That would be amazing. I'd stand in line to buy a ticket," Louie said, sounding like a concert promoter pitching an idea.

"Why would I do that?" Paul snapped back.

"You'll have to excuse him. He's a talent manager," I added in an attempt to smooth things over. "That kind of thinking is an occupational hazard."

"I'd like you two to get out of here now." Paul's voice was terse and abrupt.

This guy's a regular Jekyll and Hyde. "If I could just get my dog, we'll be on our way. Lex! Lex!" *Where the hell is that pooch?* "Louie, are you sure you saw him run in here?"

"Positive. He pushed open the door and went inside. Maybe he's hiding."

"Do you mind if we take a quick look for him?" I asked Paul. "He thinks we're playing a game."

"Wait here," Paul commanded. "I'll look for your stupid dog." He exited the kitchen and disappeared into the house.

"What a jerk," I muttered to Louie under my breath.

"It's my fault. I ..."

"Shh! Tell me later."

I could hear the creak of footsteps as Paul made his way up the stairs. A series of doors opened and closed. At the last room, he knocked. The door unlocked—opened—and closed again. The sound of muffled arguing drifted down through the kitchen ceiling.

"There's someone in there with him," I said to Louie.

"I know," he replied, straining to listen to the voices above.

"So there <u>was</u> someone looking out at us before. Why didn't they answer the door when you rang earlier?"

"Shower?" Louie surmised.

"Can you make out what they're saying?"

"Not really, just bits and pieces."

"What happened to that bionic ear you had up at Mount Baldy?"

"Works better when I'm not trying so hard."

"Then don't try so hard." I gave him a mock slap with the back of my hand, but it was already too late.

The door opened—closed—and locked again without delay. The returning footsteps were accompanied by the clicking of nails on hardwood.

"Here's your dog." Paul reentered the kitchen holding a long tie-dye silk scarf with Lex attached to the other end.

"Thank you." I reached down to remove the expensive looking scarf from Lex's collar.

"Keep it," Paul said.

"Oh, I couldn't possibly. That wouldn't be right."

"Never mind." Paul seemed anxious and uneasy. "I'd rather lose the scarf than see this nosy beast make his way back here."

"Hope he didn't disturb anyone?" I was fishing. *Maybe I can find out who else is here . . . and why they had Lex locked in a room with them.*

"No. No one's home," Paul insisted.

I cast my line once more. "Sorry, I thought I heard voices."

"Radio was left on upstairs," he replied, pushing us outside.

Louie shouted back at the door rapidly closing in our faces. "What about getting those albums autographed?"

The door halted midway. "I'll let you know," Paul said, hidden from view. Then the door slammed shut.

Good ol' Louie. When in doubt, play to this man's ego.

"But you don't know how to reach me," Louie called out.

"Don't worry, Louie. He may not know where to find you, but we know where to find him. Something tells me we'll be back here sooner than we think."

I looked up at the draped second-story window.

Was Lori Taylor the one watching us? ... if she's in trouble ... why didn't she cry out for help? ...how does LaVonne Jefferson fit in? ... is this serendipity? ... or is my imagination working overtime? ... no one at the window now ... was there ever?

* * *

The trip back to the San Fernando Valley was welcome in its uneventfulness. There were no discernable aftershocks; it's often hard to detect smaller shakes while driving. We arrived at my house near three o'clock.

"Do you want to come in?" I asked Louie, before getting out of the car.

"No, thanks. I'm going to head over to In-N-Out Burger. I'm starving."

"Why didn't you eat something at the restaurant?"

"All that healthy organic stuff doesn't agree with me."

"I could use a Double-Double, myself. Scrambled tofu doesn't stick with you very long."

"That's my girl," Louie said with a big smile, and then serenaded me with a raucous rendition of Jimmy Buffett's, "Cheeseburger in Paradise."

We ate in the car so we could keep an eye on Lex; his Uncle Louie treated him to a cheeseburger.

93

"You really shouldn't be encouraging him in his bad behavior," I said, watching Louie feed Lex.

"What bad behavior? Thanks to Lex, there are no more degrees of separation between me and two very important autographs for my collection."

"Is there anything you don't collect?"

"Yes, garbage."

"That's debatable. What were you going to tell me about Paul Graham?"

"Whadda ya mean?"

"You said it was your fault he suddenly got so upset. In my opinion, the guy has some kind of serious personality disorder."

"I shouldn't have brought up that business about a reunion with Lori. They had quite an ugly break-up."

"Then why are they palling around together?"

"I don't know. Maybe they patched things up and I reopened an old wound. Or he doesn't like the fact I'm a talent manager."

"Why's that?"

"He and Lori split because she signed with a manager who was only willing to handle her as a solo act. The rest of course, as they say, is history."

"If my client is having a valid past life experience, somehow or someway that life must have intersected with Lori Taylor's."

"Or Lori Taylor Singer's, whoever she is," Louie added, taking the last bite of his burger.

"Right. But it will be a whole lot easier for me to start with the first assumption, then confirm or rule it out before moving on. Do me a favor. Can you get together some kind of background history on Lori Taylor? Put in everything you know or ever heard about her."

"Will do. Ready to go?"

"Looks like it," I said, finishing off my Diet Coke.

We drove back to my place.

While getting Lex out of the backseat, I noticed one of the Lori Taylor albums Louie had brought from home. "Which one of her albums is this?"

"*Caged Songbird,*" Louie answered.

"I can see that, but which one is it? When did she record it?"

"It's her solo debut."

"Do you remember the song, 'Ill Conceived'?"

"Sure. It's the one about putting her baby up for adoption."

"Can I borrow this?" I reached for the album, scarcely managing to touch it when Louie grabbed onto the other end.

"Don't scratch it on that shitty turntable of yours."

"I'll only put one penny on the needle arm."

The color drained from Louie's face. He looked like he was about to have a stroke or a heart attack.

"I'm kidding. I'm kidding. I'll tape it, that way I won't have to play it more than once."

"Let me come in with you and supervise the taping. Why jeopardize our friendship over a scratched LP? I'd never forgive myself."

"You're crazy, you know that?"

"I prefer to think of it as obsessed—it's sexier."

I escorted beagle Lex into the house, while Louie escorted vinyl Lori.

Once inside, Louie prepared the turntable to receive his offering. "Do you have a brush to clean the stylus?"

"My hairbrush is in the back bathroom," I said, trying to remove the silk scarf from around Lex's collar. "Whoever tied this knot took it seriously."

"You use a hairbrush to clean this thing? No wonder your stereo is in such a sorry state. If there was someplace to report this kind of abuse, I'd be making a call right now."

"I don't use a brush. I just flick it a couple of times with my index finger. That seems to do the job just fine." Still no luck with the knot and Lex was getting impatient. "Can you come here and help me untie this?"

"Step aside woman, this is gay man's work."

Louie was right. He had set Lex free before polishing off the first two bars of "I Feel Pretty." Singing and swaying, he wrapped the long, flowing material around himself.

I yanked the scarf away. A piece of paper fluttered to the floor.

"Hey, where'd that come from?" Louie pinched my right cheek. "First a hypnotist, now a magician. Your comadre's impressed, mija."

"It fell out of the scarf. It must have been pressed between the folds and tied in around Lex's collar."

"Looks like part of a piece of sheet music." Louie said.

I picked it up off the floor. "Ever hear of a song called, 'Rock and Roll Hades'?"

"You mean 'Rock and Roll Hell,' the BTO and KISS tune."

"Nope. That's not what it says here. Look."

Louie took the paper from me. "Hmmm, must be new. It's credited to Lori Taylor, but I've never heard of it."

"I thought she had retired from the music biz."

"She did. And as my dear Martha would say, 'It's a good thing.' Definitely not her best work, listen to this." Louie sang the lyrics written on the sheet, "Trapped in a prison of my own faking. Reached for heaven, now in hell I'm baking. Soul from a past long forsaken, says it's time to take what's taken."

"Do you think it's a message?"

"For who and about what?"

"That's what I can't figure out," I said with an exasperated sigh.

"Answer me this: If she has something to say, why the hell doesn't she just come out and say it?"

"Maybe she can't. Suppose this is the only way she's able to communicate."

"By wrapping a note around the collar of an unknown passing beagle? Either you or she has watched one too many *Lassie* reruns."

I nodded in agreement. "Never thought I'd live to see the day when you'd be the rational one in our relationship."

Louie checked his watch. "I can't stay much later. Let's get this recording done."

Surveying the album cover, it was difficult to reconcile the image of this fresh budding flower child with the broken and weary-looking woman I met today. An old Peggy Lee tune played in my head as I asked myself, "Is that all there is to being a rock and roll legend?"

It didn't take long to make the tape. Our voyeuristic glimpses into Lori's hopes and dreams, heartache and loss, played out in a scant forty minutes.

"My work here is done." Louie removed his record from the turntable.

"I haven't heard that album in years. It's funny, I never really paid much attention to the lyrics."

"You were always more a 'disco baby' than an 'earth mother' type."

"Guess so. It's going to take me a few replays to try and figure it out.

It'll be easier when I get the background info to you. So let me go and get started on it.

I gave Louie a hug and walked him to the front door.

"One more thing," I said as Louie stepped outside. "Did I mention Lori referred to the song 'Ill Conceived' as 'Ill Deceived'?"

"No, you didn't. Why?"

"Maybe she was trying to tell me something."

"Conceived? Deceived? Could have been an honest mistake. Is that it?"

"Seemed funny she wouldn't remember the name of her favorite song."

"That's not her favorite song."

"According to her it is."

"Then she must be losing her memory because her favorite song is 'Caught In Your Trap.' It's on her fifth album, *Tune In Gemini*. She mentioned it when she was inducted into the Rock and Roll Hall of Fame, a couple of years ago. Case closed."

Louie headed down my front walk. He came to an abrupt stop about halfway to his vehicle. "Oh, my God! Oh, my God! It is a message! She knows any real fan would know it's not her favorite. We really are solving a mystery. I've got to get home and listen to that tune right away."

Louie rushed to his SUV.

"I want to hear it, too," I called out to him.

"I'll make an mp3 and send it to you." Peeling away from the curb, he tore off down the street—leaving me with one more mystery to ponder.

What's an mp3 and how do you play it?

* * *

Tidying up what remained of the mess inside, I was pleased the aftershocks were dwindling in frequency and intensity. The power was back on and the gas company promised to put in an appearance the next day. As a precaution, I locked the gate leading to the pool to prevent further beagle escapes.

I thought about Sharon Jefferson. The sooner her life was back on track, the sooner I would be able to pursue some of these clues with LaVonne.

Finding the best way of doing that was a matter for discussion with Ben Cohen. We had a date to meet at his place that evening and I still needed the exact time, his address, and something stunning to wear.

Maybe I should make an emergency run to Victoria's Secret.

Somehow my one hundred percent cotton Hanes Her Way didn't seem to fit the bill. It had been a long time since I had to worry about making that first vital undergarment impression. Sure, Lex liked them, but what did he know. He also liked sniffing out and eating old pizza scraps from the garbage. The ring of my office phone snapped me out of my lingerie reverie.

"Hello."

"Hi, it's Ben. I think it's about time we moved our relationship to the next level. Don't you?"

"I'm not quite sure I know what you mean."

"Your home phone number. You never gave it to me. All I have is your business line. I mean … I've already seen you in your underwear, so I'm sure you can trust me with it."

"Why are you bringing up my underwear?" *Has he been reading my mind?* "When did you see me in my undies?"

"This morning on your front lawn. Remember?"

Talk about a selective memory … I expect a ten-year-old to have accurate recall of a past life … when I can't even remember what happened to me a few hours ago.

"We can talk about that later." Ben continued, "I've dug up some very interesting research that should help with your case."

"You are reading my mind!" I said with an indignant shout.

"Just for a nanosecond. I told you I'm still not very good at it. It controls me more than I control it."

"Shut it down."

"Sorry, I have to get much better at it before I can do that. Let me practice on you tonight."

An erotic shiver passed through my entire body.

Don't think about it ... not now ... not with him on the other end of the line ... quick, think about something else ... empty the mind ... start over ... sing ... what should I sing? ... I can't think of anything ... great ... when I need to think about something ... I can't ... got it!

" 'O say, can you see, by the dawn's early light, what so proudly we hail'd at the twilight's last gleaming ...' " *Why'd I pick that? ... no one ever remembers the words.*

"Are you all right, Roberta?"

"Proud to be an American."

"Good to know, I guess?"

He must think I'm one crazy chick ... no ... stop thinking ... stop thinking ... "I've gotta go! There's someone ... at the door ... must be ... the gasman."

"Wait—dinner at eight, my place."

"See ya later."

"The address is ..."

I disconnected the call.

Seconds later, Ben rang back.

I didn't dare pick it up.

He left the info on my answering machine.

Have to find a way to block him from reading my thoughts ... how would I look in a lead hat?

CHAPTER SIX

T HE DRIVE TO BEN'S PLACE took all of ten minutes. His condo was situated on a quiet little street in Studio City, not far from Ventura Boulevard—the main drag in The Valley. Nothing was far from The Boulevard in Studio City. What mattered, in terms of prestige, was whether you were north or south of that demarcation. My house was two miles north; Ben's condo was two blocks south.

So he's higher up the real estate food chain ... location-wise ... my house still trumps his condo ... in the long run ... what am I doing? ... we're not in competition ... I'm seeking advice ... one professional to another.

I rang the bell outside the entranceway to his building.

Why do I have these feelings of inadequacy? ... because my only credential is a certificate ... and his is a doctorate ... shouldn't make me feel inferior ... it's only paper.

"Can you hang on a moment?" Ben's voice spoke from the small black box next to the buzzer.

"Sure. No problem." *Why doesn't he ring me in? ... I'm only a few minutes early ... what's the matter?*

A kaleidoscope of images rushed through my mind. I saw Ben in a panic, racing around, throwing things into closets and behind furniture. A smoke detector sounded in the background, I smelled burning food.

"I'll be right down," Ben called out from the box, a beeping sound pulsing underneath.

Right down? ... thought we were eating at his place ... guess that was before he burned dinner ... I've been reading his mind! ... it's incredible! ... so easy ... like I've been doing it all my life ... reminds me of those flying dreams ... there's a trick to it ... you only remember how to do it when you're asleep ... am I awake?

Ben appeared from behind the lobby door. "I burned it, all right. Is Casa Vega okay with you? I feel like Mexican and they make a great mole. We may have to wait to get a table, but it's worth it."

"I love the mole sauce there. Is that what you were making?"

"As you may have noticed, my culinary skills aren't that highly developed. You were reading my mind, weren't you?" Ben gave me a knowing glance. "How does it feel to have the shoe on the other foot?"

"Wonderful, until you take it from me and put it back on your foot."

"I prefer to think of it as karmic."

"Do unto others?"

"Right."

Out of sheer impulse, I threw my arms around Ben and kissed him with a deep and revealing intensity.

"Owed you that one," I said, lingering in the embrace. "For karma's sake." *Let's save dinner for later ... get a good appetite going first ... have something sent in for a late night snack.*

"Are you up for a little workout before eating?" Ben asked.

See we've flipped to the same page in the cookbook. "Sounds like a great idea." *Whisk me away to your den of iniquity.*

"Then what are we waiting for?" He broke free of my hold. "Let's get power walking, I'm starving." Ben dragged me away from his doorstep, in the direction of Ventura Boulevard.

Clearly, we'd planned entirely different menus for the evening.

∗ ∗ ∗

As usual, Casa Vega was packed. Always a popular neighborhood hangout, but when Brad Pitt pronounced it one of his favorite spots, the place became a bit of a zoo. We made our way through the throng. Ben put his name on the waiting list and was given a pager to signal when our table would be ready.

Back outside, we chatted while waiting. I brought him up to speed on my further adventures with Lori Taylor. " ... The question that remains to be answered is how do I go about integrating this into my work with Lavonne? Where do I start? What do I ask? Any ideas?"

"I've been involved with a lot of past life research, but never in the capacity of crime solving. Your background in acting may come in handy for this one."

"How did you know I was an actress? I wasn't even thinking about that. Did you see me in something?"

"No, your brother mentioned it. He's really quite proud of you."

"He's proud of <u>me</u>? I'm not the genius in the family. That's why I need his help on this case. Did he mention anything to you, anything I might be able to use? He said the two of you had a long discussion about his work."

"That's why I brought up the acting. Danny thought it would be the most accessible point of departure for you."

"You know my brother has some mental deficits, don't you?"

"What appears to be a deficit in one state of consciousness is often an asset in another. Many of our greatest scientists and visionaries were regarded as madmen in their day and age. Use your natural creative abilities, if you were playing the part of a detective in a play or a TV series what would you ask? Go with your gut." He unclipped the pager from his belt. "And my gut tells me it's time to eat."

We reported back to the hostess. Though jam-packed with tables, the darkness of the place created an atmosphere of seclusion—usually.

"Ben! Ben! Over here," came a shrill cry from the back of the room.

I looked past the paintings of bull versus matador, past the intertwined strands of red chili pepper lights, past the señors and señoritas—waiting hand and foot on margarita-guzzling conquistadors—to a booth in the far corner. A lone woman sat there waving, signaling us to approach.

"Who's that?" I asked Ben.

"I think it's my wife."

"Your wife?" *Twin flames, my eye ... more like candelabra.*

"Soon to be ex."

Where haven't I heard that one before?

"Do you want to meet her?"

Do I have a choice? ... can't pretend we don't notice her ... the entire restaurant is watching this spectacle. "Sure. Why not?"

We walked over to the frenetic female.

Glad I didn't sleep with this guy ... obviously still have a great deal to learn about him.

"Hi, Trixie," Ben said. "How are you doing? This is Roberta."

Trixie? With that name and those looks—platinum blonde coif, double-D's oozing out of a silver spandex mini-dress—I was willing to bet she was a former Vegas showgirl or, at the very least, an exotic dancer from a local Spearmint Rhino club.

She held out her hand—ruby red nail extensions aimed in my direction. "Pleased to meet you, Robert."

"It's Roberta," I said, giving her claw a tight squeeze.

"Excuse me. It's so difficult to hear over all the noise."

Maybe you should invest in a hearing aid.

She turned to Ben. "How are things in *The Twilight Zone*?"

"Work's fine. Roberta's a colleague of mine. I'm advising on one of her clients."

Colleague, am I? ... why's he playing it so cool? ... are they really getting a divorce?

Trixie looked me over. "What do you do, honey? Work for one of those psychic hotlines?"

Is Anna Nicole Smith deriding me? "No. I'm a hypnotherapist."

"I tried that once. Didn't do anything for me. Frankly, I doubt I was even hypnotized."

Half-wits can't be hypnotized.

"Roberta, that's cruel."

Is that you Ben?

"Who else would it be?"

You're right; I apologize. It's not her fault the silicone leaked into her brain.

Ben took my hand. "We better sit down before we lose our table."

Every time he touches me . . . I go weak in the knees . . . that's why he took my hand . . . he's afraid I'm going to belt her one.

"I was just leaving," Trixie said. "My date's having the car pulled round. Don't want to keep him waiting." She slipped out of the booth. "It was a pleasure."

Standing high atop a pair of silver stilettos, she wiggled her way to the front entrance. All that was missing was her showgirl headdress of rhinestones and feathers.

Ben and I sat down, straightaway ordering a couple of much needed drinks.

"A lime margarita on the rocks with salt, please," I said to the waiter.

"The same. Only make mine a double," Ben added.

"So how many kids do you have?" *Enough with the surprises ... I want all the dirt.*

"None. That I know of."

"Too bad, she seems like the maternal type—would have made a champion breast feeder."

"There's a lot more to Trixie than meets the eye."

Now that's a scary thought.

"She's a top-notch therapist," Ben continued.

"Therapist? She's a therapist?"

"I said you were underestimating her."

"What's her specialty?"

"Sex."

Why am I not surprised? "How long have you two been married?"

"Twenty years."

"That's a long time. Why the split?"

"Clichéd as it may sound, we've been growing apart over the last ten years. I left a lucrative Marriage and Family practice in Beverly Hills to pursue my growing interest in the paranormal. Trixie thought the move was crazy. She's a very practical person. If she can't see it, touch it or taste it, she's not interested in hearing about it."

"So I guess she's not a big supporter of the twin flames theory?"

"She doesn't know anything about it."

"Is that why you introduced me as a fellow colleague?"

"Does that bother you? It wasn't worth getting into with her. Besides, it's still only an academic theory. Until you help me prove it to be otherwise."

"I'm still waiting for you to explain exactly what I'm getting myself into here."

Ben raised his water glass. "Let us toast fire with water—feet firmly planted on the earth—glasses meeting in the air—we call on the four elements to ignite our hearts, cleanse our souls, ground our bodies and let our spirits soar."

Can't say I've ever heard that toast before. It was enthralling in a bizarre sort of way.

That evening we clicked—we bonded—we joined forces—call it what you will, something <u>began</u> between us. According to Ben and his twin flames research, something <u>resumed</u>. We were ancient souls reuniting in time and space. An unseen force or energy pulsated between us.

After dinner we went back to Ben's place and chatted into the wee hours of the morning. The perfect gentleman, Ben acted like we were long lost buddies playing catch-up.

Should I make a move? ... didn't work earlier ... though he seemed to be into that kiss as much as I was. "I should get going," I said, glancing at my watch.

"So soon?" Ben replied.

There may still be hope.

"If you consider two in the morning soon. My first client isn't until eleven, but I'd still like to get in a few hours of sleep before seeing her. It's not good form to put yourself into trance with the client." *Ball's in your court, mister ... it's now or never ... make it worth my while to stay.*

"It can be done though. There's some interesting research out there on how shamans perform their work in an altered state of consciousness. You may want to keep it in mind, as another possibility for your sessions with LaVonne."

More shop talk ... obviously, you haven't been reading my mind in the last few hours. "The only altered state I'm willing to entertain involves a pillow and a bed."

The humiliating seconds inched by. Nothing.

See 'ya. I got up from the sofa.

Ben caught my arm. With a show of territorial force, he pulled me back down onto the sofa and into his body.

Bingo! ... that's more like it, fella.

"I'll call you tomorrow," Ben said, releasing me. "It's not that I don't want to," he added.

"You <u>have</u> been reading my mind all night."

"On and off. Mostly on."

"What are you? Some kind of tantric sex tease?"

"I think that may be an oxymoron."

"It's getting to be awfully clear, I'm the only moron around here."

Jumping up from the sofa, I made a dash for the front door. He wasn't going to have the satisfaction of seeing me cry.

Ben ran after me. "I don't want to see you cry, Roberta," he whispered, taking me in his arms. "There's nothing wrong with you. It's me."

He's impotent … even his bombshell sex therapist wife couldn't help him.

"Wrong. I'm a celibate."

"Celibate?" *That's easy to fix.*

"I can't fix it."

"Sure you can. Eunuch's the one you can't fix."

"What if I don't want to fix it?"

"I thought you didn't want to see me cry?"

"It's important we wait. We have to be ready. The coming together of twin flames makes nuclear fusion look like a fireworks display at Disneyland. If we're not careful, we could implode rather than explode. It was a combination of celibacy and contemplation that brought you to me. Once I reached a state where I no longer felt the need for a partner, that was the precise moment you appeared in my life."

"Let me get this straight. You're telling me I'm attracted to you because you don't want me?"

"No. No. You've misunderstood."

"Good. I've already been in enough of those relationships."

"You're attracted to me because I don't need you."

"Funny, you're not making me feel any better." I placed my hand on the doorknob. "I've really got to go."

Ben jammed his foot in front of the door. "Can't you give it more time? We've waited this long, what's a little while longer?"

Good point … it's not like there's anyone else on the horizon … wouldn't hurt to get Trixie completely out of the picture first. "All right, I'll go along with you—under one condition."

"Whatever you want. Just ask."

"You've got to spill all the beans about this so-called 'reunification' process we're going through."

"I promise to tell you about each stage of the process as we prepare to go through it. You'll have the choice of opting out whenever you choose."

"This isn't some kind of cult you've gotten involved with, is it? Because I'm not a cult kind of girl—no X's on the forehead—no Kool-Aid in the cupboard—no burning compounds. Not my style."

"I'm researching this as I experience it. It's new to me, too. If anything looks the least bit suspicious or doesn't feel right, I'll be bailing right alongside you. First and foremost, I'm a scientist."

"So were Dr. Jekyll and Dr. Frankenstein."

"Yeah, but they didn't have the help of a beautiful partner." Ben moved his foot away from the door. "I have something for you." He went to retrieve his surprise, returning with a blue folder in hand. "These are some articles on past life research I've come across over the years. Never know, there may be something worthwhile in here for you."

I thanked him, though I was hoping for something a tad more romantic. We left his condo and went downstairs.

"Call me when you get home." Ben closed my car door and motioned for me to roll down the window. "I won't be able to sleep until I know you arrived safely."

When did any guy I ever dated say that? ... never ... he's as endearing as he is infuriating ... a modern day Don Quixote ... and I'm his Dulcinea ... hmmm ... interesting choice of characters ... means he's old and delusional ... and I'm a whore ... better revise ... how 'bout colleagues? ... like Clark Kent and Lois Lane ... he had secret powers ... they spent years in a sexually frustrating relationship ... perfect!

* * *

I arrived home exhausted and exhilarated. After calling Ben, I took Lex for a quick walk prior to going to sleep. Once in bed, I tossed and turned for about an hour before giving in and getting up.

Can't sleep ... may as well work.

Lex mustered up the energy to open one fatigued, droopy eyelid and watch me walk past his bed on the way to my office.

Waiting for my computer to boot up, I opened the blue folder Ben had given me. Rifling through the series of articles on past life phenomena and the work of various promising researchers, a few notable pieces jumped out at me.

There was a story about Carol Bowman. Inspired by the vivid past life recollections of her own children, she wrote the book, *Children's Past Lives.*

A fascinating *Washington Post Magazine* piece concerned Dr. Ian Stevenson, author of *Children Who Remember Previous Lives: A Question of Reincarnation,* and *Reincarnation and Biology: A Contribution to the Etiology of Birthmarks and Birth Defects.* Using spontaneous, non-hypnosis induced, recollections of children, he's pieced together a compelling array of evidence. He compares current birthmarks or birth defects with autopsy photos of the supposed body from the previous incarnation. Over a forty-year period, he has documented more than twenty-six hundred cases with impressive and astounding correlations.

The never-ending debate over the famous, or infamous— depending which side you're on—Ruth Simmons (a.k.a. Bridey Murphy) case was examined and re-examined in a number of different publications. I even came across an old clipping about Danny's groundbreaking discoveries in the field.

The material validated my work with LaVonne and laid out a rough roadmap for our upcoming sessions. I was on the right track; all I had to do was follow it back to the beginning.

I logged into my e-mail account.

Louie had sent me a preliminary report on Lori Taylor, a thumbnail sketch of her life and career highlights to date. He was still in the process of deciphering her song lyrics. There was a lot of material there and it would take a while.

The instant message window popped onto my screen.

Who's knocking on my cyber door at this time of night?

"☺ u r up," wrote screen name, LouieLouie.

"Can't sleep," I typed back.

"u alone? can u talk?"

"If I wasn't alone at four in the morning, I'd be stroking something better than a keyboard."

" ;) cleaned up photo nancy took of paul graham. not much improvement on face, can read scrap of paper in his hand—HELP! CALL POLICE."

"Something weird is going on. I think they're holding her hostage. Don't you?"

"4 what reason? wouldn't media b all over it? why would daughter & 4mer partner do this & b stupid enough to b seen out in public? what's 2 gain?"

"All good questions needing to be answered. We can't involve police without some solid evidence a crime is being, has been, or will be committed."

"what next, sherlock?"

"We have to go back to Lori's house. Do some snooping around. Watch the comings and goings."

"what if we get caught?"

"That's where your record collection comes in. Dig out those old albums you want autographed. If anything happens, we'll use them as our alibi."

"sounds like a plan. when do we start?"

"We both have day jobs. I guess we're going to have to do this at night. That may work in our favor. Make it easier for us to watch them, while going undetected ourselves."

"(channeling pointer sisters & singing) i'm so xcited."

"(channeling Fifth Dimension and yawning) Last night I didn't get to sleep at all."

"10-4, see ya later," Louie signed off.

I shut down my computer. It was almost four-thirty and I had no business being awake, not with the day and evening I had ahead of me. Getting up from my desk, I knocked the blue folder onto the floor. Papers flew everywhere.

An article I hadn't noticed before caught my eye—"JANE DOE FOUND STABBED TO DEATH IN ALLEY." I scanned the brief report: "A Caucasian female, five-feet, six-inches tall, approximately thirty years of age, with blonde hair and blue eyes, was found brutally stabbed in the chest early this morning. Her body was discovered in a deserted back alleyway near the downtown core. The victim's face had been beaten beyond recognition. No motives, suspects or witnesses have been identified. The police are seeking the public's help in identifying the body."

I looked at the date on the yellowing piece of newspaper. It was almost twelve years old. The story was in the *Chicago Tribune*; on the backside was the article about my brother.

Random coincidence? ... or serendipitous clue?

The rush of anticipation had me pumped. I wanted to call Danny, or instant message Louie, or rush over to Ben; but I needed sleep and so did they. Switching off the light, I headed back to my bedroom guided by the comforting snore of a beagle.

* * *

The ringing of my doorbell, at the ungodly hour of seven a.m., jostled me from my slumber. I entertained the idea of ignoring the unwelcome pest, before recalling I was the one who had extended the invitation.

Must be the gas company.

My appointment was on a four-hour window—anywhere between seven and eleven.

Why don't they ever show up early when you want them to?

Wearing my usual uniform of white tee shirt and panties, I searched for a bathrobe. The best I could come up with was an old tan trench coat. With tired bloodshot eye, I peeked through the peephole in my front door.

A balding man in a gas company uniform was walking away from my house.

I had the door open in a flash. "Yoo-hoo!" *Yoo-hoo? ... of all the things I could have shouted ... why pick that? ...I sound like Aunt Bea from Mayberry.*

"Sorry, ma'am," the gasman said, turning back.

Ma'am? Now I feel like Aunt Bea.

"I thought nobody was home."

He didn't look too shabby when you saw him head on. Kind of sexy—in a bad boy biker way. Thinning hair, slight hint of a paunch, fiftyish. He reminded me of Jack Nicholson circa *Terms of Endearment.*

Leading him into the house, I caught a glimpse of myself in the foyer mirror.

Yikes! ... forget about Aunt Bea ... I'm a dead ringer for Otis ... should be happy he guessed my gender correctly.

"You expectin' rain or just hopin'?" he asked, eyeing my garb.

"Neither. This is my bathrobe. It's the latest rage in France. What do you think?"

"You know those French, never been quite the same since the war."

"Which war?"

"All of 'em. Let me make sure your appliances are shut off before I go out and turn the main line back on. When I'm done I'll relight your pilots for you."

"Thanks. If you need me for anything, holler. I'll be in the back of the house getting ready for work."

By the time I had washed and dressed, the gasman was waiting for me in the kitchen.

"You're all set," he said.

"Great. Just in time for breakfast. Would you like a coffee or anything?"

"No, I better get goin'. This earthquake has my schedule packed tighter than a virgin on her weddin' night."

Interesting analogy.

"Can I get you to sign this work order?"

"Sure," I said, taking pen and paper from him.

"Can't believe I'm turnin' down a cup of coffee with a beautiful young lady."

There's something I like about this man.

"The guys in the band'll never believe this one."

"Is that what you gasmen call yourselves? The band?"

He laughed. "No. I'm talkin' about a rock 'n' roll band. Do you remember the Sound Squadron? I was their bass player."

"Didn't you work with Lori Taylor?"

"Yeah. We backed her up on a couple of her albums in the seventies."

"What happened to you guys?"

"We Double D'd."

"Double D'd?"

"Drugs and disco. Did in a lot of bands back in the day. Still keepin' my hand in it, though. Sometimes I gig with Hell's Papas. We're playin' a club in Reseda this weekend."

He knows Lori Taylor ... a man I should stay in contact with ... might come in handy. "Do you have a card?"

"Matter of fact, I do, sweet miss. Being a bass man never fails to attract the ladies. There's magic in these fingers." He pressed his card into my palm. "Stop by the club Saturday night. Catch a coupla sets." He clasped my hand shut over his index finger, then slowly pulled it out.

Thanks, but no thanks. I read the crushed card; looks weren't the only thing he shared with Nicholson. "I'll see what I can do, Jack."

"My turn."

I gave him a quizzical look. *His turn for what?*

"Your card?"

"Oh, let me get you one." *What difference will it make? ... he already knows my name, address and phone number.* "Here you go," I said, returning from my office.

"Hypnotherapist. Interestin'. I once saw a guy bring a woman to full climax usin' hypnosis. He was sittin' in a chair across the room from her, talkin'. Didn't lay a hand on her. Most unbelievable thing I ever saw."

Where'd he see that show? ... Times Square in the seventies?

"Guess it's sorta like phone sex without the masturbatin'. Have you tried it?"

I was taken aback by his brashness. "Phone sex?"

"No, everybody's done that. I mean hypnotic sex."

"Can't say I have." *How'd we get onto this topic?*

"Man it would be amazin' to combine trance sex with actual sex. I'd really love to try that some time."

If he's making a request, I'll have to refer him out ... maybe Trixie can help.

"On second thought," Jack looked from my card to me, "I might be able to slip in a quick hot breakfast. If you catch my drift?"

More like a blizzard than a drift ... I'm attracting some interesting types ... the one I want *to sleep with is on a sex free kick ... the one I* don't want *to sleep with is a free sex zone.* "Darn, I'm going to have to skip breakfast. Completely slipped my mind, I have an early appointment scheduled."

"Most important meal of the day," he said, eyeing my crotch. "Is it too late to cancel?"

"Afraid so," I said, hustling him out the door.

"Come by for the last set at midnight. I might not be able to concentrate on my music if a hot babe like you is sittin' there watchin' my moves all night. Of course, I'll be savin' my best moves for your personal post-concert pleasure." He traced the outline of my face with his fingers.

No matter how I tried to deny it, he was attractive in a purely physical—please don't talk, let's just do it—kind of way. Even if he was stringing me along with a bunch of cheap lines, it felt better than to be left hanging high and dry by an avowed celibate.

It may help speed things up a bit if Ben sees his twin flame attracting some moths. "Do you mind if I bring a friend along?"

"Ooh, a lady after my own heart. The more, the merrier."

By the orgasmic sound of his response, I knew he wasn't picturing the type of friend I had in mind. It was comforting to be around a guy who didn't have a clue about anything I was up to.

CHAPTER SEVEN

E VENING ARRIVED with more of the same hot, dry weather. I missed the usually cool California nights. Exhausted as I was, I made it through all my clients without falling asleep in the middle of their sessions. By the time Louie came to pick me up, I looked like a bit player from *Night of the Living Dead*.

"Maybe we should do this tomorrow?" he said, staring at the dark circles under my eyes.

"No. If something sinister is going on we can't afford to wait. I'll catch a nap on the way over there."

"Is that what you're planning on wearing?"

I looked down at my blue jeans and yellow tee shirt. "Yeah."

"Do you consider it appropriate?"

"Would you prefer I wear pajamas?"

"Only if they're black. This is a surveillance mission."

"I'm too tired to change; this will have to do. It's so dark in Topanga at night; I'm sure this will be fine."

"There are a couple of stops I need to make along the way."

"Fine by me, I can use the extra sleep." That's the last thing I recall until being shoved back into consciousness by a man wearing a black facemask. "What the fu …"

"Shhhh." He clasped a leather-gloved hand over my mouth. "Put this on." Removing his hand from my mouth, he stuffed some clothing into my lap.

"Who are you?" I asked with a startled gasp.

"Who am I? Who is Jack? I want to meet him."

"Louie! What are you doing in that get-up? You scared me half to death."

"Be quiet," he whispered. "The windows are rolled down. I've been listening for any unusual sounds. So far they've all come from you. You and some guy named Jack—getting down and dirty. I didn't mean to scare you, but we can't risk blowing our cover. Put your outfit on; it matches mine. Everything should fit. To be safe I picked it up in two other sizes."

In my lap sat a pair of black pants, a black long-sleeve turtleneck and a black wool cap. "Not planning on doing any skiing tonight, thanks." I passed the clothing back to Louie.

"My, aren't we testy? I thought your tumble in the hay with Mister Jack would've put you in a better disposition. Why'd you tell me you were alone last night?"

"I was."

"What happened to your date with Big Ben? Did you get stood up?"

"In a way, and he's not Big Ben."

"That's why you're so crabby. Lover boy came up short in the package department."

"No ... he's suspended deliveries."

"Why?"

"He's celibate."

"He's still a virgin?"

"I hope not, he's been married for twenty years."

"You're having a platonic affair with a married man?"

"He's getting a divorce."

"Why bother?"

"It's part of this twin flames research he's doing. He asked me to bear with him."

"Bear with him?" Louie said, laughing.

"What's so funny?"

"I have the perfect nickname for him—Gentle Ben."

"Ha. Ha. Ha. Thanks for the moral support."

"With a boyfriend like him, you have all the moral support you need."

"Let's drop it. How long have we been here and what have I missed?"

"Not long and not much. We've been here about half an hour. The house is in total darkness; either they go to bed early or no one's home. My vote's for the latter, since I don't see the Rolls anywhere. I think we should move." Louie had parked the SUV on the side of the road, next to the creek. "Even though we have a great view of the house from here, it's too exposed."

"Where do you suggest we go?"

"Let's pull onto the private road that runs alongside the house. If we park half a mile past here and hike back through the brush, no one should notice us. At least not those of us wearing basic black; I can't vouch for the safety of the canary yellow crowd."

"Enough, you win," I said, grabbing the bundle of clothes back from Louie. "I was hoping we wouldn't have to get out of the car. Groping around in the dark has never been a favorite activity of mine."

"No wonder you're having man troubles."

"Drop it," I warned.

Louie started the engine and headed for the private road fifty yards ahead of us.

"Aren't you going to turn on the headlights?"

"Too risky. If someone's home they may notice the reflection as we drive past."

"Don't you think the sound of us crashing into the creek will tip them off? There are no street lights anywhere around here and barely a sliver of a moon's out tonight."

"Not to worry. I'm wearing infrared goggles under this mask. Yours are in the Spy Works bag on the backseat."

"You've given this caper a lot of thought."

"I've never been one to do anything half-assed."

Resisting the urge to comment on his last remark, I held my tongue for the remainder of the short trip.

Louie found us an inconspicuous parking spot behind an old abandoned shack.

"This looks good," he said, opening his door. "I'll get the rest of the gear together while you change."

"What gear?"

"You'll see."

Even the canyon felt hot that evening. My commando outfit only made matters worse.

"Aren't you hot?" I asked, approaching Louie at the back of the vehicle.

"Mine are a hot-blooded people, gringa. From heat we draw our passion for life. The sweat of our brow anoints us on our noble mission."

"Are they rerunning *Zorro* on Nick at Nite?"

"Here, this should help." Louie passed me a small, battery powered, pen fan. "Cool off a bit, I'm going to need a hand carrying the rest of this stuff."

He shut the back door. On the ground sat two bulky knapsacks and an ice chest.

"What's all this for?"

"As we used to say in Boy Scouts, 'Be Prepared.' "

"If I'd known we were going camping I would have brought along my guitar. Of course, you probably have one packed in there somewhere."

"These are just a few essentials: infrared binoculars, remote listening device, water, a few snacks. Throw one of these packs on your back and pick up the other handle on the cooler."

"This chest weighs a ton." We struggled to make our way through the parched and brittle brush. "What types of snacks are in here?"

"It's mostly ice. Sushi and chardonnay should be well-chilled."

"When did you become James Bond?"

"Don't even go there. I've been dying to sing 'The Spy Who Loved Me' all night."

"So where'd you put the record albums?" I asked, about halfway to Lori's house.

Trudging along like a loyal burro, I awaited a reply. None came.

"You forgot them, didn't you?" I halted in my tracks.

Acting coy, Louie batted his eyes. "Are you mad at me?"

"Can't say I'm looking forward to walking back to the car to get them."

"It's okay, you don't have to."

"Should I wait here for you?"

"No ... I ... left them ... back at my place."

"Louie!" I let go of the cooler.

"I didn't do it on purpose," he said, scrambling to balance the load. "There isn't any need to take it out on innocent fish and wine. I've had a lot on my mind. It's not easy to assemble a half decent spy kit at the local mall."

"That's supposed to be our cover story in case we get caught."

"Don't worry, I'll think up something else."

A pair of headlights flashed into view, followed by the sound of gravel crunching under tires. We ducked behind what smelled like an old outhouse.

"You didn't happen to bring along any gas masks did you?" I whispered to Louie, clutching my nose.

We were still a good distance from the house; it was difficult to make out who was there and what was going on.

Louie removed the pack from his back. "Look through these binoculars. Tell me what's going on while I set up the equipment."

"A man and a woman are getting out of the car. I can't quite make out the faces. My guess is it's Paul, with Lori's daughter. Did you find out her name?"

"Karen. Karen Hall. It's in the preliminary report I e-mailed you. Haven't you read it yet?"

"I took a glance ... Ben gave me a folder containing some interesting articles on children and reincarnation ... oh, my God ..."

"Is someone coming?"

"No," I said, putting down the binoculars. "They've gone inside. I almost forgot to tell you about this old article I came across in the *Chicago Tribune*—about a Jane Doe who was stabbed to death in an alley. I have this strange feeling she may be the same woman my client is seeing in her nightmares. What do you think? Talk some sense into me."

Louie was preoccupied with his elaborate doodads. "You'd think they could throw in a battery after you've gone and spent three hundred bucks."

"You wasted three hundred bucks on this junk?"

"Only for this long range microphone." Louie stood behind me wearing a set of headphones, and holding out what looked like a small satellite dish on the end of stick. "How do I look?"

"Like a boom operator on a location shoot."

"I was hoping for *The Man from U.N.C.L.E.*"

"Will you settle for Maxwell Smart?"

"Do you mind waiting here while I check if I have any batteries in my glove compartment?"

"What choice do I have?"

"None, really. Why don't you crack open the wine while I'm gone? When I get back we'll have some sushi and you can tell me about the Jane Doe murder."

"I'm not going to eat dinner behind this cesspool."

"Okay, we'll move in closer. What about over there?" Louie pointed out a clump of pines. "We'll still be far enough away from the house to go undetected."

We moved the cooler and packs over to the trees. After Louie left I set up our late night picnic. Opening the bottle of wine, I heard the faint sound of my ringtone coming from behind the outhouse.

Damn … dropped my cell phone.

Fingers pinching my nose, I dashed back to pick it up. It was Ben.

"Hello," I said in a nasal whisper. "Can I get back to you?"

"Where are you? Why are you disguising your voice?"

"I'm behind an outhouse holding my nose.'"

"What are you doing there? Never mind—get out fast! You're in danger. Call back when it's safe."

What was that about? I put the phone on vibrate, then looked back at the pines. *I can't carry all that stuff on my own … should I wait for Louie?*

Stepping into the open, I decided to make a run for one of the knapsacks. It was too late. Two flashlight beams were headed in my direction. Trapped, not knowing where to go or what to do, I ducked into the outhouse. Praying I hadn't been spotted and hoping the smell wouldn't kill me, I held my breath as angry voices approached.

"Where the hell can she be?" A man's voice boomed within a few feet of me. "We weren't gone long?"

Paul Graham.

"How did she manage to get out of her room?"

"I'm sure she didn't get far," a woman replied. "She's afraid of the dark,"

Karen Hall?

"What isn't she afraid of?" The irritation rose in Paul's voice.

"This is getting ridiculous," the woman said. "We have to do something soon. You said we'd commit her when she got this bad. I'm calling a nursing home tomorrow."

Something brushed my leg. I jumped, knocking my foot on the wooden wall I was pressed up against.

"Did you hear that?" Paul asked. "She's in this old outhouse."

"Not in a million years, it's filled with rats. She's not that crazy."

Rats! I never wanted to scream more in my entire life. *Run outside … so what if I get charged with trespassing … big deal … Ben warned me I was in danger … but of what … rats? … the police? … Paul and Karen? … Lori?*

"There's an abandoned shack up the road a bit. Let's look in there. I'd like to avoid calling the police. All we need is to have the media all over this ..." Paul's voice faded as they moved past me.

When it sounded like the coast was clear I ran outside, past the main house to the road.

What if they bump into Louie? I called his cell. "Hide yourself right away. Paul and Karen are headed for the shack."

"Don't worry, I'm safe. I drove to the store for batteries. Where are you?"

"They didn't see me. I made it to the private access road."

"Go down to Old Topanga Road. I'll meet you there."

Propelled by adrenalin, I headed farther away from the house. It didn't take me long to reach the main road. Judging by the far-off shouting, Paul and Karen were still knee-deep in their search.

A pair of approaching headlights blinded me. The vehicle slowed to a stop. It was Louie. I hopped in beside him.

"Are you okay?

"Now I am." I reached for my seat belt. "Let's get out of here."

The SUV peeled away from the side of the road, picking up speed. Out of nowhere, a figure bolted in front of us. Blaring his horn, Louie slammed on the brakes. Swerving to avoid the pedestrian, we smashed headlong into a tree. Dazed and shaken, but still in one piece, we climbed out of the vehicle.

A pained voice cried out in the darkness. I tracked the sound to the creek bed. About halfway down I discovered a filthy, disheveled woman crawling around on her hands and knees.

"My baby! My baby! Please, someone help me find my baby," she wailed.

"Did I hit her?" Louie asked in a state of shock. "Was she carrying a baby?"

"I didn't see a baby. It all happened so fast." I touched the huddled woman on her shoulder. "Ma'am are you hurt?"

Desperately clutching my arm, she pulled me down to the ground. "Have you seen my baby? I need my baby!"

I was close enough to see her face. "We hit Lori Taylor."

"No, you didn't," spoke a familiar male voice. "We saw the whole thing. She threw herself down there after you avoided hitting her."

Standing on the road above me were Paul Graham and Karen Hall.

"She's looking for a baby," I said, attempting to pull both Lori and myself up from the ground.

"Where's my daughter?" she asked, as I helped her out of the creek.

"Right here, Ma." Karen scrambled toward us. "Thank you, I think I can manage her from here," she said, taking Lori from me.

The women walked away toward the house.

"Fancy running into you two again." Paul stared at Louie and me. "Do you live around here?"

"No, just out for a drive," I said.

"Awfully dark for a drive, not much to see," Paul said, probing.

"Well, to be perfectly honest, I was planning to drop by and see if you would sign those albums for me," Louie explained. "Problem is once I got here, I realized I'd left them at home. That's what we were doing when Ms. Taylor ran out in front of us, turning around and heading back home. I would have called first, but you never gave me your number."

Paul seemed to be mulling over Louie's story. It sounded quite convincing and was sort of true, in a covert kind of way.

"I can't believe I forgot them," Louie continued. "Sometimes I get flabbergasted when I know I'm going to see one of my idols. If I'd remembered them, it would have made cracking up my car a lot easier to take."

The last part seemed over the top to me, but it was enough to convince Paul. This guy's ego had a serious appetite. "Sorry about your car, buddy. I'll make sure Lori takes care of it. It was her fault, after all."

"Would it be all right if we called for a tow truck from the house? My glove compartment got jammed shut in the accident and I can't get at my cell phone."

Quick thinking, Louie ... get us into the house ... maybe we'll get a better idea of exactly what's going on.

"Sure, it's the least I can do." We followed Paul back to the house. "In a way, I'm kind of glad it was you who ran into Lori," he said, putting his arm around Louie. "As you can see, she's not well. If we can keep this out of the papers, I'll make sure those albums of yours get signed."

"You have my word," Louie said. "Nothing serious with Lori, I hope."

"I'm afraid it is." Paul stopped walking. "Lori has Alzheimer's. This is a very delicate situation for the family. We'd like to be able to handle this in our own way and in our own time. Under the circumstances, I'm sure you can imagine how difficult this has been for my wife."

"Your wife?" I asked.

"Karen. Lori's daughter is my wife. I was the one who brought them back together. That event helped bring a lot of healing into our lives, but it also makes the current situation all the more tragic."

So much for the big mystery I'm solving ... whatever's going on with LaVonne ... real or imagined ... has nothing to do with Lori Taylor.

"Paul, I don't think we'll be needing to use your phone," I said. "In the excitement I forgot about my cell. It's on the floor of the SUV."

"Are you sure it's working?" he asked.

"If it isn't we'll be back to take you up on your offer."

Louie gave me a confused glance; I returned an assuring nod. We had intruded enough in these people's private lives.

"Here's my number." Paul handed Louie a card. "Give me a call and I'll arrange for those albums to get autographed for you. Don't forget our deal."

"Oh, we won't. My brother suffers from schizophrenia. I know how trying it can be to help a loved one through a mental illness under the glare of a spotlight."

"Your brother's well-known?"

"In some circles. His name's Dr. Daniel Law."

"I remember him. He was one of the guests on an *Oprah* taping I attended. Interesting guy, don't know if I agree with his theories." He offered his hand in a welcoming gesture. "You know, I never did catch your names,"

"I'm Roberta Law," I said, shaking his hand. "And your number one fan here is my best friend, Louie Lopez. We won't keep you any longer. The sooner we call triple A, the sooner we'll be out of here. I hope the rest of your evening is a lot less eventful."

"Me, too. Good night, folks." Paul continued on toward the house.

When we got back to the SUV, Louie gave me an earful. "Why'd you go and tell him our real names? What if he comes after us next?"

"It's over, Louie. LaVonne's mystery is not about to be solved here. Lori's illness accounts for her strange behavior and our supposed clues. Everything fits. It all makes perfect sense. We're looking for someone named Lori Taylor Singer, not Lori Taylor—the singer."

"Isn't she too young for Alzheimer's?"

"It happens. Look at Rita Hayworth. The tabloids had a real field day with her. I don't blame them for wanting to protect Lori. That's probably the real reason behind her sudden retirement. Let's call for a tow and get of here."

"What did you do with my gear? Since the case is closed, I may as well return it and get my money back."

"It's right where you left it."

"Back in the trees?"

"I was scared out of my wits. How was I supposed to run for my life hauling that load?"

"Why were you running? I thought you said they didn't see you? That spot is fairly well hidden."

"Ben called and told me I was in danger. Oh, I never got back to him." I reached for my phone. "He must be worried."

Louie grabbed the cell from me. "No calls till you help me get my stuff back. Since it doesn't look like we're going to be selling any movie rights, I can't afford to be out a thousand bucks."

"You're on your own. I'm not going near those rats again."

"Rats! How come you keep running into rats?"

"Don't know. I'll look up the symbolism when I get home, if I ever get there."

"Fine. You leave me no choice." Louie got out of the vehicle. "I'll do it by myself, even though it'll take much longer." He slammed the door shut; it fell off its hinges and crashed to the ground.

I wanted to laugh, but didn't have the heart. He'd gone out on a limb for me with this one and I owed him. "Wait. I'll come, but not all the way."

"You remind me of a girl I dated in high school."

"If you bring the stuff back to the shack, I'll carry it down the road."

"Deal."

"Let's still be careful though. I don't want to have to explain this to Paul."

Louie and I parted ways at the shack.

I put in a call to Ben. While waiting for him to pick up, the call waiting tone beeped in my ear.

"Ben," I answered. "I apologize for taking so long to …"

"Sounds like we have more players in this game than I realized."

I looked at my phone, the blue digital display read "PRIVATE CALLER."

"Excuse me? May I ask who's calling?"

"Playin' hard to get. That's cool. I like it when it gets a little rough. So tell me, what are you wearin'? I'm lyin' here with a firm grip on my tool belt. If you catch my drift?"

"Jack, why are you calling me on this number?"

" 'Cause your sweet voice on the answerin' machine told me to."

"Only in the case of an emergency. Do you have a professional emergency requiring my services?"

"Now that you mention it, somethin' requiring your special touch just popped up."

Oh, brother … this guy's a real piece of work … I'm done with this Lori Taylor business … cut him loose … look out world … here he comes! "Perhaps I gave you the wrong impression earlier today."

"Ooh, sexy. I like that. Keep talkin'."

"You find a wrong impression sexy?"

"The only way I know of makin' any kind of impression is by takin' somethin' hard, and pressin' it into somethin' soft." His breathing grew faster, more intense

This guy must have done some really great drugs in the sixties. "Let me try this again, Jack …"

He let out a loud moan. "Jack: a female socket designed to receive a male plug," he panted.

Two can play the dictionary game. "How about—jack: a small metal object with six points." *Try that image on for size.*

"Kinky. I like that one. This hypno-sex is killin' me. You're incredible!"

Afraid to say more, I dropped the call before reaching its inevitable conclusion.

My phone rang again; "PRIVATE CALLER" flashed across the screen.

Enough is enough. "If you don't knock it off, I'm calling the police."

An angry male voice barked at me. "If you don't do something about my daughter soon, you'll be speaking to the police!"

This is not my night. "Calm down. I think you have the wrong number, sir."

"Is this the number for Roberta Law?"

"Yes, it is."

"Then I have the right number. I'm only calling you because I made a solemn promise to my wife."

"There must be some sort of misunderstanding."

"Maybe this will help you understand."

A child wailed in the background. "Please don't make me go to bed. I don't want to sleep …"

I called out, "LaVonne, what's the matter honey?"

"What do you think is the matter? She's having those god-damn—excuse me, Lord—nightmares again. I told Sharon she was wasting her money."

"Have you been using the triggers?"

"I'm not one for spells and incantations."

"This has nothing to do with witchcraft, Mr. Jefferson."

"It's Reverend Jefferson and I refuse to do the work of the devil."

"Could you put LaVonne on the phone for a minute? I think I can calm her down."

"You better, if you know what's good for you, miss."

"Are you threatening me, Reverend Jefferson?"

"If you call a lawsuit a threat."

LaVonne's protests grew more hysterical.

"For your daughter's sake, I suggest we both let cooler heads prevail here for a moment. She may be reacting more to your state of panic than she is to her own fears."

He let out an exasperated sigh and put LaVonne on the phone.

"I'm sorry I made my daddy get mad at you, Roberta," she said, gulping back tears.

"It's not your fault and your daddy's not really mad at me. He's just tired and worried about you. Remember how much fun you had playing and dreaming with Lex when you were at my house?"

"Yeah." Her tone brightened. "Can I say hi to Lex?"

"Lex isn't with me right now, sweetie. But I know a way you can visit him if you want to. Would you like to do that?"

"Uh-huh."

"Okay, I want you to sit down in the comfiest chair you can find. Let me know when you've done that." I listened as LaVonne relocated herself.

"Ready," she announced.

"Where are you sitting?"

"On the sofa."

"Are you comfortable?"

"Yes."

"All right then, let's find Lex. He's waiting for you in your secret room. Close your eyes and I'll take you there." I counted her down into trance.

It was awkward working with clients over the phone. Something was lost when you couldn't rely on any physical cues as signposts to guide you along the way, but this was an emergency situation. My only objective was to take her into a deep enough state to allow her to feel safe and sleep through the night.

"Are you in the playroom, LaVonne?"

"Yeah," she replied in a distant, drowsy voice.

"Do you see Lex?"

"Uh-huh."

Her voice grew weaker with each response. She trusted me. We had built a good rapport during our sessions, allowing her to swiftly move into a state of total relaxation.

"I'm going to leave you there to play with Lex for a while. The TV in the room is broken; you won't be able to see anything on it tonight. It's just you and Lex having fun together. You can stay there for as long as you wish. When you're ready to leave, all you have to

141

do is open your eyes and you'll be back at daddy's house. It will be morning. You'll feel rested and refreshed."

Reverend Jefferson came back on the line. "I don't know how you did it; she's fast asleep. Praise the Lord."

"That should hold her for tonight. It's imperative I resume my one-on-one work with her as soon as possible. Can you bring La-Vonne into my office tomorrow?"

"What time?"

"I'm attending a conference for most of the day. How about four o'clock?"

"I was planning on bringing her back to her mother's house to-morrow evening."

"Would you prefer a later appointment?"

"No. The sooner I find out what you're doing to my daughter, the better." His tone was harsh and filled with accusation.

Not an easy man to please. "You're more than welcome to sit in on the session."

"Don't worry. I will." He hung up in my ear.

"You're welcome," I said into the night air.

Louie appeared from out of the darkness wearing one of the knapsacks, and dragging the ice chest behind him. "Who were you talking to?"

"No one you want to know. Where's the other backpack?"

"In the chest. Broke my heart to have to dump all that wine and sushi."

"You smell like you drank the entire bottle of wine."

"I had a glass or two before one of those rats of yours appeared, and made me spill the rest of it all over myself. Who knew rats liked sushi?"

"Can we get out of here now?"

"I wonder what's inside this old shack." Louie mused.

"More rats, probably. Let's just leave. We've done enough trespassing for one evening."

"A little peek won't hurt anyone."

"Tell you what, I'll take the pack in the ice chest and meet you back at the car. While you're peeking, I'll call triple A. You can fill me in on your findings while we wait for the tow."

"Chicken."

"Yes, and darn proud of it."

I took the pack from the chest and set off for the car. Halfway down the road, a winded frenetic Louie caught up to me.

"Why are you running? See a ghost?"

"Close enough. I think I found a body."

CHAPTER EIGHT

I SHRIEKED, "A BODY!"

Louie put his hand over my mouth. "Not another word," he whispered in my ear. "Got to keep moving. Someone may be following me."

We reached Louie's wreck of an SUV and continued past it without stopping.

"Where are we going?" I whispered.

"I don't know. It doesn't matter. Anyplace far away from here."

"What about your car?"

"I'll get another one."

"We can't walk all the way home."

"Let's try."

Nothing more was said until we reached the empty parking lot at Inn of the Seventh Ray. It was one in the morning; the restaurant was closed.

"I'm calling Ben to come and get us," I said, dialing his number.

"Hello, Ben Cohen's residence," a female voice answered.

"Sorry, wrong number," I replied, and quickly hung up. *What a childish overreaction … should I call back?* My heart pounded in my throat.

The low battery indicator beeped.

Call back.

The phone rang. "PRIVATE CALLER."

Not now, Rev. Jefferson. "I'm sorry, but I can't talk long my battery is going."

"You're not mad at me are you, babe?"

Jack.

The warning beeps grew more insistent.

"Did you hear that?" Louie asked.

"Low battery," I said.

"Not that. Listen carefully."

Closing my eyes, I pulled the phone away from my ear. Crunching leaves and cracking twigs, accompanied by a lonely whistle, echoed from the creek below.

"It's him," Louie whispered.

"How can you tell?"

"He was whistling the same tune near the shack. I bet the guy's a serial killer." Taking me by the arm, Louie hurried us farther down the road. "Let's head for the ocean; it's downhill from here, we'll be able to move faster."

"Hello! Hello!" Jack shouted over the phone. "Did you hang up again?"

I was almost out of power—battery and leg. "Louie, do you have your phone?"

"No, it really is stuck in my glove compartment."

"Wonderful."

Two choices remained, Jack the Pervert or Jack the Ripper.

Why am I hesitating?... desperate measures are called for. "Jack, I need you. Come and get me right away."

"I'll throw on a robe and be right over."

"Wait! Wait! I'm not at home. Meet me on Topanga Canyon Boulevard. I'll be on the side of the road, somewhere between Pacific Coast Highway and Old Topanga Road."

"Yeow! You hypno chicks are hot!" The last words I heard before my phone went dead.

Louie and I made tracks for about half an hour, feeling assured we had lost the whistling killer.

"I'm going to call him The Stranger." Louie took off his pack and rested against a large rock. "Want to know why?"

I leaned next to him. "Because we don't know who he is."

"No. Because that's the song he was whistling, Billy Joel's 'The Stranger.' "

"Precisely what did you see?" Reflecting on Louie's somewhat melodramatic nature, I had some justified reservations.

"Well, it was dark and it happened so fast. After you left I reconsidered my idea about checking out the shack. I picked up the cooler and was about to follow you, when I heard someone coming from farther up the road. He was whistling that tune. It was spooky. Not wanting to be seen, I ducked into the shack and tripped over the naked body of a headless woman. Before I even had a chance to scream, the door flew open. Standing in the doorway was the outline of a figure in a hooded robe holding an ax. He would never have noticed me, except for the fact that I knocked him over running out of there."

Even the stifling heat couldn't stop a chill from running down my spine. Dumping bodies wasn't uncommon behavior around LA, finding them was. "An hour ago I was standing outside that shack, waiting for you."

"Yeah, it could have been you I was tripping over."

"What a comforting thought."

"Are you sure you're not letting your imagination run away with you?"

"You heard the whistling, didn't you?"

"It doesn't prove he murdered anyone."

"Robe, ax, decapitated body is all I need to know."

"We've got to report this to the police right away.

A pair of headlights passed by on the other side of the road.

"Maybe we should flag a car down," Louie said.

"I'm not getting into a car with someone I don't know after what you just told me. Let's wait for Jack."

"Hey, isn't he your 'Dream Lover'?"

"Don't you dare start singing. This is neither the time nor the place."

"I was thinking more along the lines of The Beatles' *White Album*—side two, track seven—'Why Don't We Do It in the Road?'"

"What you bring that up for? 'Helter Skelter' is on that album. Now all I can think about is Charles Manson."

"Sorry."

"Let's try to be quiet for a few minutes. It wouldn't hurt to say a prayer right about now."

The welcomed tranquility gave me a chance to do some deep breathing and let my irrational fears subside.

"The Manson Family killed a guy in Topanga," Louie said, breaking the silence.

"Can we change the topic?"

"You're the one who brought it up."

A vehicle appeared from around the bend. Slowing as it passed, it pulled over and stopped about twenty-five feet in front of us.

"Here's our ride," I said, running ahead, glad to be free of our macabre musings.

"That looks like a gas company vehicle," Louie said, following after me.

I reached the van and the passenger door opened. The cab light revealed a strange man seated inside. Shaven head, tattered clothing, he looked like a drifter or a paroled convict.

"Oh, excuse me," I said, stopping in my tracks. "I thought you were someone else."

The man sat there staring straight ahead.

"It's me." Jack leaned forward in the driver's seat. "This here's an ol' buddy I ran into. He needed a ride. Scooch on in."

"I don't think there's enough room. Someone's with me."

Louie stepped forward and waved at the two men.

"You must be Ben," Jack said.

"Nope, I'm Louie."

"How many of us are ya' plannin' on reelin' in on that line of yours, Red? Hop on in. I'm sure Louie won't mind havin' that sweet ass of yours rubbin' up against him. If this wasn't a company vehicle I'd trade places with him."

Jack's mute friend slid over into the middle and Louie squeezed in next to him.

Getting in last, I positioned myself on Louie's lap. "Thanks for coming out here on such short notice."

Jack gave me a lascivious glance. "I'll think of some way for you to return the favor."

"We need to see the police," I said.

"Sorry, babe. That band's long gone."

"I know that. We need you to take us to a police station."

"No can do. Can't risk gettin' caught joy ridin' with a bunch of friends in a company vehicle. Besides, I'm holdin' some X for when we get back to your place. Sorry fellas, have to catch you next time; there's only enough for the lady and myself."

"You don't understand." I attempted to impress the seriousness of the matter upon him. "We found a dead body."

"You sure it's dead?" Jack asked.

"Positive," Louie answered.

"Then what's the rush? It's not goin' anywhere. It'll keep till mornin'. Hey, I haven't even introduced you to my ol' pal. Well ... not a pal ... really. Sorry, man. But you were a bit of an asshole back then. This is Richard, a.k.a. Ritchie Rich, a.k.a. Sir Richard the Dick-hearted, a.k.a. ... I forget ... we had a million nicknames for him back in the day."

"All deserved, I may add," were the first words the peculiar man spoke.

"Anyway, we were just catchin' up before I caught sight of you two. What was that Billy Joel tune you were whistlin' before man?"

" 'The Stranger.' "

Louie's terror-stricken body stiffened beneath me. "It's him. It's him," he whispered in my ear.

"I know," came my under-the-breath reply.

"Know what?" Richard asked.

"Nothing," I said coolly.

"We don't know anything." Louie added hastily.

"You seem somewhat anxious. I have a special method that never fails to help people relax." Richard reached for Louie's neck. "May I?"

"Don't touch me." Louie twisted beneath me, pushing his body against the door. "Relaxing makes me tense."

"That's unusual," Richard said, intently massaging his hands.

"Maybe I should give him my X," Jack chuckled.

"Drugs are a temporary escape. There is only one permanent way out of this earthly cycle." Richard patted Louie's knee. "I've decided to dedicate my life to helping people get there."

"I'm out of here!" Louie shouted, opening the door.

I shrieked. The thought of being dragged out of a moving vehicle terrified me, but probably less than the fate of being left behind with The Strange and The Stranger.

"Holy crap, man!" Jack hit the brakes. "Wait till I stop. Are you crazy or somethin'?"

"No, but the guy next to you is," Louie shot back. "He killed a woman and dumped her body in an abandoned shack."

Jack stopped on the soft shoulder. "What the fu ..."

"It's true," I said. Louie and I wasted no time exiting the stationary vehicle. "Run for your life."

"No need for that." Jack reached underneath his seat. "Man ... and I thought you'd changed." He pointed a blue and white striped beach umbrella at Richard's neck.

"I have."

"Yeah, for the worse."

Richard sat there calm, cool, and unfazed. "Is that parasol loaded?"

"Wanna find out?" Jack pressed the pointy tip deep into Richard's throat. "You might have screwed over a lot of people in the past, but you never used to kill 'em."

"Tell that to the skeletons rattling around in my closet," Richard murmured.

"Serial killer, I knew it," Louie said.

"What were you doing in my cabin?" Richard asked Louie.

"You live there?" I asked.

"Not anymore. Too many old memories."

"And old bodies," Louie added.

"That wasn't a body in there. It's a mannequin. A prop from an Alice Cooper tour I booked."

"You booked Alice Cooper?" Louie asked with peaked interest.

"Richard was his manager. He handled all the top acts at one time or another," Jack informed us.

"You're Richard Baxter," Louie said in awe.

"I was until I entered a Buddhist monastery. The only thing I was trying to lay to rest tonight was my past. All that's left of my former existence is the memorabilia I have stored in my cabin. It's time to let go."

"If there's anything I can take off your hands, just let me know," Louie offered.

"How about getting this thing off my neck?"

Louie took the umbrella from Jack. "I'll take over from here, Mary Poppins. Do you have a license for this?"

"Don't make fun. It's saved my life more than once. You try readin' a backyard gas meter when there's no one home but a pack of rabid pit bulls."

I resumed my grill. "Why the ax?"

"I picked it up when I heard Louie inside. It was the first thing handy."

There was something I didn't quite buy about his story. "Aren't you monks pacifists?"

"I'm not a monk until I take my final vows."

"So you still have some leeway," I continued.

"Come back to my cabin. See for yourself."

Louie came to his defense. "I believe him."

"You're the one who saw the body," I said, affronted by his sudden backpedaling.

"Thinking back on it, the body didn't feel very fleshy."

"Forget about the body." Something still nagged at me. I looked back at Richard. "Why go there in the middle of the night?"

"Shouldn't I be asking you that?" Richard said, turning the tables on me.

He had a point. We were the ones who were trespassing.

Do I want to make him privy to my folly? ... I liked him better when he was a serial killer.

"We were doing surveillance on a case," Louie offered.

"Don't the police usually carry guns?" Richard said with a note of sarcasm.

Jack looked bewildered. "Hey, you told me you were a hypnotist. I was just kiddin' about that X before," he hastened to add.

"I am a hypnotist. We were there because of one of my clients."

"You make undercover house calls?" Richard jibed.

This would-be monk could give Columbo a run for his money. "Due to confidentiality codes I'm not at liberty to say any more."

"We were investigating Lori Taylor's connection to ..." Catching hold of Louie's forearm, I gave him a good pinch. "Ouch! I'm not at liberty to say anymore."

"Something's wrong with Lori, isn't there?" Concern crept into Richard's voice. "She always had a lot of quirks, but this is different. I had hoped reuniting with our daughter would bring her some peace."

"You're Karen Hall's father?" I said in surprise.

"Yes. She doesn't have much to do with me though. Not that I blame her, I was the one who talked Lori into putting her up for adoption back in Chicago. I was married and Lori's career was on the verge of taking off; a baby didn't fit into the plans."

Karen Hall was born in Chicago ... the same town Jane Doe was murdered in ... coincidental? ... or providential? ... maybe Jane Doe is the woman LaVonne keeps seeing ... did I throw in the towel on the Lori Taylor connection too soon? ... could Karen Hall be the missing link between Jane Doe and Lori Taylor?

"I'm tired," Richard yawned. "Can we call a truce? No harm, no foul, as they say."

I seconded. "Sounds like a good idea. I'm exhausted. This has been a very long day."

"Jack would you be kind enough to drop me back at my cabin? It's too late to head back up to Mount Baldy."

"I still have to call for a tow," Louie remembered.

"You're welcome to spend the night at my place," Richard offered.

Louie perked up at the possibility of getting first dibs on the shack's hidden treasures; Jack perked up at the possibility of getting first dibs on me.

"Don't forget you promised to help me sort out that other situation back at my place," I said, locking arms with Louie.

"There's another situation?" Louie asked, perplexed.

"Yes." I shifted my eyes in Jack's direction. "You know the one I mean."

"Oh, yeah ... of course, I do?" Louie stumbled.

"It'll probably keep us busy for the rest of the night," I said, offering Jack an apologetic look.

"I'm game. Tomorrow's my day off," Jack replied obtusely. "I haven't done a three-way in years."

Grateful as I was for his coming out late at night to rescue my stranded ass, I wasn't about to give it to him as a thank-you gift. Before I had an opportunity to set my rock 'n' roll Romeo straight—once and for all—the wailing and flashing of bright red sirens making their way into the canyon pierced the still night air. A police car and a paramedic unit whizzed past us.

"Let's hustle," Jack said. "I don't wanna draw any unwelcome attention bein' parked out here by the side of the road."

"Do you mind if I make a rest stop before we leave?" Richard asked.

"No, man. Just make it quick," Jack answered, waving Louie and me back into the van.

Five minutes later, we were still waiting for Richard to return.

"What's takin' him so long? Don't tell me he's havin' a dump." Jack went outside to look for him.

Another police car sped by.

"Richard, come on man. Where are you?" Jack called out into the darkness. "We've got to get goin'."

"Louie, don't you dare leave me alone with Jack."

"I'm not in the mood for a three-way this evening."

"You know what I mean."

Jack got back in the van and started up the engine. "How do you like that? He up and took off on us. Where's your car, man?"

"On Old Topanga Road," Louie said. "Down the way from Richard's shack, in front of Lori Taylor's house."

"Not possible," Jack said, making a U-turn and heading back up into the canyon.

"What do you mean?" I asked.

"I've been to both their places. They don't live that close to each other. Not while Richard's wife has any say in the matter. She hates Lori."

"Are they still married?"

"He said they were. No big surprise there, she swore she'd never divorce him while Lori was still around."

Near Inn of the Seventh Ray we discovered where all the police vehicles were headed. A roadblock had been erected and traffic was being diverted away from Old Topanga Road.

"Looks like there's been an accident. You'll have to get your car towed in the morning, buddy," Jack said to Louie.

A body on a stretcher disappeared into the back of a paramedic unit.

"Someone's been injured," I said.

"That's my SUV being dragged out of the creek!" Louie shouted. "Pull over!"

Leaving Jack behind, Louie and I scuttled out of the van and ran up to the police barrier.

"Hang on," Louie hollered. "I'm the owner of that vehicle."

"May I see some identification, sir?" a policeman said, holding us at bay.

Louie pulled out his driver's license.

"Louis Lopez," the officer read. "Stan," he called out to his partner. "What name was on the registration you found?"

"Louis Lopez," Stan answered.

"Was your vehicle stolen, sir?"

"No, I had an accident."

"You do realize it's a crime to leave the scene of an accident."

"Yes. I was trying to get to a phone."

"An operational cell phone was found in the vehicle. Why didn't you use that?"

"It was stuck in the glove compartment."

"We found it on the passenger seat, sir.

"This isn't even the accident I was in."

"Have you been drinking, sir?" he asked, taking a whiff of Louie. "I'm going to have to give you a breathalyzer before taking you down to the station."

"Down to the station?" Louie asked, stunned.

"Yes, sir. You're under arrest. The woman you hit is in critical condition."

"I can vouch for this man, officer," I interjected.

"Were you with this man tonight, ma'am?"

"She's with me," Jack's voice answered from behind. "We picked him up halfway down the road and gave him a lift. He's tellin' the truth. When we passed by here earlier there was no sign of an accident."

"All right," the officer motioned to Jack. "I'm going to have to ask you to step over here and give a statement to my partner before you leave."

"What's going to happen to Louie?" I asked, feeling helpless.

"I'll read him his rights and then take him down to the station for booking." He hauled Louie away and put him in the back of a cruiser.

Jack gave a brief statement to the other officer, after which we were free to go.

"Why'd you do that?" I asked walking back to the van.

"I know a frame-up when I see one, babe. You'll be a lot more useful to Louie out of jail than in."

"Thanks." When he wasn't busy being crude, there was something appealing about this guy.

"Whatever you two have gotten yourselves into has managed to upset somebody."

Yeah ... but who ... and why? "What are we going to do about Louie?"

"You look beat, Red. Better get some sleep." Jack turned the key in the ignition. "I'll check out the bail situation in the mornin'."

That's the last thing I remember until being awakened by the sound of Ben Cohen's voice. "Is she all right?"

"She's asleep. It's been a long night. Who are you?"

"Ben Cohen. Who are you?"

"Jack Hensler."

"I didn't realize the gas company had a pick-up and delivery service."

"Looks like I'm gonna have to get back into shape. There's a lot of competition for this little lady."

"So I'm learning."

"Ben?" I uttered, peering out from my drowsy fog. "Where are we?"

"Home," Jack answered.

"Jack? Why can't I feel my feet?"

" 'Cause I'm carryin' you in my arms, babe."

Riveted back into full consciousness, I tumbled out of Jack's arms.

"I should get going," Ben said. "Just wanted to make sure nothing had happened to you. Nothing life threatening that is."

I do declare ... Mr. Ben Cohen sounds jealous.

"Why didn't you call me back? I've been up all night worrying."

"I did call you back."

"When? I never spoke with you. There wasn't any message."

"A woman answered the phone."

Jack interceded. "Now, Red, be fair. I just met the guy, but you can hardly blame him. From what I've seen so far, he's not the only weenie you invited to the roast."

"Who asked you to butt in?" I said with irritation.

"We've got us a real mustang on our hands, buddy. May the best cowboy win," Jack said, shaking Ben's hand. "I'm givin' the lasso a rest for tonight. She's all yours." Jack walked to his van. "I'll stop by in the mornin', babe, with the name of a good bail bondsman," he called back before driving off.

"Trouble with the law?" Ben asked.

"Louie's in jail. The police think he hit a woman with his SUV and fled the scene. He didn't do it, but it may be hard to prove."

"Guess I was wrong. You weren't the one in danger after all."

"I'm not so sure about that. It's been quite the bizarre night all round—Jack's only the tip of the iceberg. If it wasn't for him, I'd probably be sitting in jail with Louie right now."

"Then I should be grateful he was able to come to your rescue—though for some reason, I'm not."

"Jack's harmless. I met him for the first time this morning. He came by to turn my gas back on and relight my pilots."

Ben looked at me with an air of curious suspicion. "That's what I call service," he said, looking at his watch. He wasn't buying what I was selling.

"I meant that literally, not figuratively." *This would be an ideal time for you to read my mind.* "Can I fill you in on everything tomorrow? I'm beat," I said, unlocking my front door. "Thanks for checking in on me. That was a sweet thing to do."

"Good night, then." Ben reached over and kissed me on the forehead.

Excitement ignited my entire body. My gasman was cute, but he didn't pack quite the same charge.

I have all day tomorrow to be exhausted … why waste whatever possibilities tonight may still hold. I wrapped my arms around Ben's neck; hopeful we could get past this pesky phase of our relationship. "Have you considered revising that celibacy policy of yours?"

"Every time I'm near you," he said, seductively, before pulling away from me. "There's someone waiting for me at home."

Come again?

"Remember the woman you spoke with earlier? I'll introduce you to her tomorrow. We'll do lunch."

And I want to meet her because?

"She's going to be staying with me for a while."

Staying where? ... you live in a one bedroom. "Where's she going to sleep?"

"My bed."

Comfy.

"What kind of son would make his mother sleep on the couch?"

"You really think you're funny don't you?"

"I try. You'll like her and so will Louie. Her name's Barbara; she's an attorney."

He was right. I already loved her.

CHAPTER NINE

DAWN BROKE—hitting me in the head like a ton of bricks. Somehow, someway, I vowed to get some rest today. If I kept up this kind of pace, I was sure to be out of business—or dead—or both, by the weekend.

Dragging myself into the kitchen, I decided to forgo the coffee pot and headed right for my espresso maker. Three double shots and a bowl of cereal later, the previous night's fiasco gradually came into focus.

About an hour after I got home, Louie called to let me know he was all right. The California Highway Patrol had brought him to the Malibu Sheriff's Department for processing. He flunked the breathalyzer (thanks to the wine he chugged back at our Lori Taylor stakeout) and they wanted to run some further tests—blood and urine. The additional tests had been prompted by what they termed his "strange" behavior. God help us on that one, Louie's behavior had always been strange. They were going to hold him overnight for observation. Bail had not yet been set.

Instead of expanding my professional knowledge at a hypnotherapy conference as planned, I now found myself enrolled in "Bail 101." Informative as it might be, I wasn't expecting any continuing education credits. People "made bail" in movies all the time. Of course, they never show you how to do it. I was glad Jack was coming by to hold my hand through this one. What was uncharted territory for me seemed like known terrain for him.

From the dining room window I watched a classic red Thunderbird convertible pull up in front of my house. The driver's door opened, and out stepped Jack in a skintight pair of black Levi's, black leather cowboy boots, and black satin shirt.

That gasman sure cleans up nice.

The doorbell rang.

"Just a minute," I called through the door, "I'm not dressed."

"I don't mind," Jack called back.

Nevertheless, I threw on some jeans and a baggy shirt.

"What's up?" I asked, opening the door.

A hungry, carnal look flashed in his eyes.

Wrong question. "Let me rephrase that," I said, not giving him a chance to reply. *I've never met anyone with such a grammatical libido.* "Why are you here so early? Any news about Louie's bail?"

"I see you haven't listened to the radio or watched any TV this mornin'." He bent over and picked up the *LA Times* tossed on my front lawn.

Nice tush for an old rocker. "Would you like to ..." *How do I ask him in without using the word "come"?* "Shall we step inside?"

Handing over the newspaper, he followed me into the living room.

I flipped through the paper. "What am I looking for?"

"It won't hit the papers till tonight. Look for a headline that will read somethin' like, 'RECLUSIVE POP ICON'S DAUGHTER IN CRITICAL CONDITION AT LOCAL HOSPITAL.' Louie was identified as the suspect arrested at the scene."

"Poor Louie," I groaned.

"You can say that again. That bond's gonna cost him plenty. High profile victim translates into high price bail in this town."

"He's innocent. You know that."

"Doesn't mean anybody's gonna believe it though. Lori Taylor's reunion with her long-lost daughter was the feel good story of a lifetime. Someone's gotta pay for destroyin' it."

"I've set up a meeting with a lawyer at lunchtime. Did you follow up on the bail for me?"

"I'll call from here. Once we know how much it's gonna cost, it shouldn't take long. You can't spit in Van Nuys without hittin' a bail jockey in the eye. Maybe we should go with Bail Bond Girl. She's hot lookin' in that superhero outfit of hers."

"You said you were going to find somebody good."

"Oh, I'll find out if she's good, but first I want to find out if she's bad. If you catch my drift?"

"Is that why you're all decked out?"

"Don't go gettin' jealous. You're the one who wants the open relationship."

"I never ..."

"Hush now." Jack smiled. "Don't worry, Red. I'm still squirmin' on the end of your hook. The band's havin' some new publicity shots taken. Just remember—a fish can only squirm for so long, and then you either have to let 'im go or eat 'im up."

I wasn't going to touch that one with a ten-foot fishing pole. When dealing with Jack Hensler, I was quickly learning no response was often the best response.

"Here's the phone." I handed him the silver cordless. "The number's on the coffee table. He's in Malibu."

"Not too shabby. That's a nice little jail they've got over there."

"What were you doing in the Malibu jail?"

"Much as I hate to admit it, I was a bit of a wild man in my younger days." Judging by the smirk on his face, he was managing to successfully cope with his past indiscretions.

"I'll be ready in no time," I said, exiting into my bedroom.

By the time I returned Jack had made all the necessary calls, and his prediction had come true. Setting Louie free was going to cost, and it looked like I would be the one footing the bill.

"We're lookin' at fifty grand here. They've charged him with a DUI, hit and run involvin' a pedestrian injury, failure to report an accident, and ... oh yeah ... drivin' with an expired license. The last one doesn't matter much because they've suspended it. They're holding him at the courthouse for us. It should take about an hour to spring him."

"It's going to take me longer than an hour to come up with fifty thousand dollars," I said, dumbfounded. "I don't have that kind of money."

"Don't worry, babe. That's where the bail bondsman comes in. You give him ten percent and he puts up the rest. Louie is just fifty Benjamin's away from freedom. They take Visa, MasterCard and Amex."

Ten percent ... these guys sound like agents ... except in their case ... it's the clients who are the crooks. "I should be able to swing that. Let's go get this done."

"Ah ... one more thing ... you own these digs ... right?"

"Why?"

"To secure the fifty G's they're postin' on your behalf. And you need to bring along the title deed for this property. To be used as collateral, in case your boy tries to make a run for it."

"Louie's not going to do that. He's not guilty of anything."

"Sweetheart, it takes a lot more than that to beat a bad rap. There are plenty of innocent people servin' time, and plenty of guilty ones roamin' around out here with the rest of us. If Lori's daughter doesn't pull through, he's lookin' at vehicular manslaughter. That lawyer you found better be good."

What did I know about Barbara Cohen other than the fact that she was Ben Cohen's mother? Let's face it; I didn't know that much about her son. She was offering her services gratis, which was awfully generous.

She may have a lot of free time on her hands ... especially if she's never won a single case in her entire career ... that would put a dent in one's client pool ... a celebrity case is guaranteed to drum up oodles of free publicity ... maybe get interviewed by Barbara Walters ... that's sure to impress the ladies at her B'Nai B'Rith meetings.

As much as I liked Ben, it would be hard to forgive the fact that his mother was responsible for sending Louie up the river.

* * *

After signing my life away to a short, fat, bald, bail bondsman in a gray seersucker suit, Jack and I headed for Malibu. Putting down the top of his car, he took Topanga Canyon to the Pacific Coast Highway to, as Jack put it, "maximize ocean breeze time through our hair."

The scene of the previous night's incident was crawling with reporters, cameras, and satellite news trucks. I thought about Lori Taylor and wondered if the media had laid siege to her home.

She must be aware of what's happened to her daughter … being capable of understanding it is another matter … where's Richard Baxter? … why'd he skip out on us last night? … he was supposed to meet with his daughter, Karen … is he by her hospital bedside now? … does he even care? … he seems cold and distant … Zen has not brought him the inner peace I see in my brother.

We picked Louie up at the Malibu Courthouse.

"Jack's dropping us off at Geoffrey's," I informed Louie. "We're meeting with an attorney over lunch."

"I can't go to Geoffrey's dressed like this. What if one of my new clients sees me?"

"What new clients?" I asked.

"I opened negotiations with a couple of people last night."

"What are you talking about? You were in jail; you must have been dreaming."

"That jail is one of the best places I've ever been to for networking. How do you think the name Robert Downey, Jr. will look on my roster?"

"Like you're running a rehab center."

"Rehab—now that's the place to find a lotta talent," Jack interjected. "We formed the band there."

"Which band?" Louie asked with piqued interest.

"Hell's Papas. The hell we're referrin' to is rehab."

"I haven't heard of them," Louie replied.

"You will if we can get a recordin' deal in place. The business has changed a lot since the seventies. There's not a big market out there for real hard drivin' rock 'n' roll, unless you're a nostalgic favorite like the Rollin' Stones or somethin'. I think that's why Richard Baxter got out of the business. He might have been a real bastard, but he knew talent. Now it's all about cookie-cutter looks and manufactured sound."

"Louie, Jack was the bass player for Sound Squadron."

"So that's how you know Richard. Weren't you also involved with Lori Taylor at one time?" Louie inquired.

"Everybody was screwin' everybody back in the day. The Pill was on the scene and HIV wasn't. It was a sexual free-for-all. If you weren't gettin' some you were dead, or your last name was Osmond."

We pulled into Geoffrey's, an upscale open-air eatery on a cliff overlooking the Pacific. After assuring Louie for the hundredth time that the "scruffy look" was sexy, we exited the car and headed for the bar to wait for the rest of our party. Arrangements had been made with Jack to pick us up after he finished his photo shoot in Santa Monica. We ordered two Arnold Palmers and rehashed the previous night's events.

"Sorry I involved you in this foolishness, Louie."

"Forget about it. My life needed some excitement. Things have been a titch dull since Danny and I split."

"How are you going to get around if you can't drive? Do you want to stay at my place for a while? I can take you wherever you need to go."

"God, no!" Louie was aghast at the suggestion. "If I'm going to be stuck, I'd rather it be in BoysTown than Burbsville. My office is close by. The walk will do me good; I could stand the extra exercise. My preliminary hearing is scheduled for next week. I was barely over the legal alcohol limit. Once a judge hears my side of the story and realizes I wasn't the one who hit that woman, they'll give me back my license."

It looked like I was going to have to be the one to break the bad news to Louie.

"Karen Hall is the woman who was hit last night. It's all over the news."

"Am I mentioned?"

"Yes, as the suspect arrested at the scene."

Louie took a moment to absorb what had just been said. "Can I borrow your phone?"

"Sure," I said, handing him my cell. "Who are you calling?"

"My office. Hi, Ed. It's me … I'm okay; you're the one I'm worried about. How's it been? … Just as I suspected, can you handle it by yourself? … I'm meeting with a lawyer first … If you need any help, call in a temp … Hang in there, I'll see you later." Louie handed the phone back to me.

"What was that about?"

"My office has been flooded with calls from actors, writers, producers, reporters, you name it. Your friend, Louie Lopez, is the hottest thing in town."

"That's sick."

"That's show biz. So fill me in on this lawyer you found. He should pay me for the exposure this case is going to give him."

"He is a she, and has agreed to handle this pro bono."

"There's a smart cookie. Who is it? Leslie Abramson or Gloria Allred?"

"It's Ben's mother."

"Was his cleaning lady busy?" he said with a disbelieving laugh.

"I'm not joking. She offered."

"What! Are you out of your mind?"

Louie's rising volume attracted the unwanted attention of some nearby onlookers.

"Calm down. Let's not get kicked out of here before she arrives. If you don't like her, we'll find someone else. At least give her a chance. What have you got to lose?"

"How 'bout my freedom for starters? My poor little grandma didn't swim across the Rio Grande so that I could end up in San Quentin."

"Your grandmother didn't swim across any river. She was born in San Diego."

171

"Close enough."

"Roberta," Ben's voice called out. He joined us at the bar.

"Where's your mother?" I asked.

"She's running a little late. Her press agent overbooked her."

"See, I'm already making her famous," Louie piped in.

"Is your mother prepared to handle a case like this, Ben?" I said with concern. "It might have been more appropriate for her to have met with Louie before going out and hiring herself a press agent."

"You know how moms are—always craving attention, wanting to feel loved. Can't really blame the poor woman, not after the way dad ran off with his secretary. Something like this could prove to be the perfect confidence booster for her. Just what the doctor ordered, so to speak. Dad's a doctor."

I was taken aback by Ben's callous disregard for his mother.

Ben turned to Louie. "How are you holding up?"

"Check back with me after I meet your mother." Louie nodded toward the reception desk. "There's a lawyer I wouldn't mind having,"

A stunning looking woman in her mid-sixties was talking with the hostess.

"Who is she? I asked. Where have I seen her?"

"*60 Minutes*, Court TV, the evening news," Louie responded. "You're looking at one of the best criminal lawyers in the country, Barbara Goldberg,"

"She's also my mother," Ben stated matter-of-factly. "Gotcha!"

"You set me up." I gave Ben a playful slap. I wondered why you were talking about your mother that way. You never said you're related to Barbara Goldberg."

"Never said I wasn't. Shall we join her?"

Quick introductions were made all round and we were seated for lunch.

"So my Benny tells me you two are a regular Nancy Drew and Frank Hardy."

I didn't know her well enough to say she was being patronizing, but she did seem to be sizing us up.

"Not really. I'm a hypnotherapist."

"And I'm a talent manager," Louie added.

"Exactly how did two fine upstanding citizens like yourselves get into such a mess?" A touch of condescension colored her remark. "From what I've heard from my sources, they've arrested the right person."

"I'm innocent," Louie beseeched.

"That's your story," Barbara snapped. "Can you prove them wrong?"

I rushed to Louie's defense. "There are witnesses to back up his story. And whatever happened to innocent until proven guilty?"

"How nostalgic of you, my dear. This is the era of trial by media. His best friend's testimony's not going to cut it," she fired.

"Fine," I fired back. "Jack can testify."

"The gasman? Maybe. Considering his past record, I wouldn't call him the most credible witness. What was he doing out in a company vehicle after hours? Topanga Canyon isn't even part of his territory."

"Then we'll get Richard Baxter to testify," I said. "He passed by there before the accident and was in the van when Jack picked us up. He's a Buddhist monk, why would he lie?"

"There was someone else? Why didn't the police get a statement from him?" Barbara demanded.

I held my ground. "Because he disappeared shortly after we heard the sirens go by."

"Then we need to find him and see what he has to say. Where's our waitress? I'm famished." She sat back in her chair, draped in serenity and Donna Karan. Not a trace remained of the vicious jackal that had just gone for my jugular.

"We? Does that mean you're taking the case?" I asked in confusion.

"Of course, I'm taking the case. Isn't that why we're having this meeting?"

"The way you were grilling me, I thought you were getting ready to have me arrested, too."

"It's my lawyer act. If you can stand up to that, you'll have no trouble on cross-examination. You passed with flying colors."

"The last time I felt like this was at a Hal Prince audition."

She let out a hearty laugh. "Goodness, I'm flattered. No lawyer's that tough. Glad to see you found yourself someone with a sense of humor for a change, Benny. Have you met Trixie?"

"Yes, once."

"Well, once is enough."

"All right, Mom. Let's leave Trixie out of this."

Sensing Ben's discomfort, I attempted to shift the direction of our conversation. "You sure had me going, Barbara. It's nice to know the real you isn't, if you'll pardon the expression, such a ball-buster. For a minute there," I laughed, "you almost had me believing Ben's cockamamie story about your husband leaving you for his secretary."

A sudden pall fell over the table.

Barbara's body tensed, her back as rigid and upright as a steel rod.

Ben cleared his throat and fidgeted uncomfortably with his tie.

Louie sat there looking like a scared kid wondering if he'd done something wrong.

"See Benny, I'm not the only one who wants to talk about Trixie." Barbara's tone was falsely sweet. "That's no story, dear. First she ran off with my husband, then a few years later she came back for my son. One Cohen man wasn't enough for her, she had to have them all."

I looked over at Ben for confirmation. The stupid guilty look on his face said it all.

Why didn't he say anything about this the night I met Trixie?

Louie tried for a last ditch rescue from out of left field. "When did you audition for Hal Prince?"

"About twenty years and twenty pounds ago," I said without missing a beat.

Barbara's laughter brought some much-needed relief to the proceedings.

"You and I are going to get along fabulously, my dear."

The rest of lunch went by without a hitch. I liked Barbara. She wasn't afraid of being tough when she had to be; yet, underneath the hard veneer, there lurked a wicked sense of fun. Most important of all, she was going to be a big help to Louie. The plan was to avoid a trial by having all charges dropped at the preliminary hearing. A key element to this strategy's success was locating Richard Baxter. The most logical place to start looking was the Mount Baldy Zen Center. Louie promised to put in a call to Danny as soon as he got home.

We waited for our respective rides at the valet station. Barbara's dark green Jaguar was the first car brought round. After her departure, Louie stepped away to use the men's room, leaving me alone with Ben.

"How could you let me put my foot in my mouth that way?" I chastised.

"It's not my fault. I told you my father left her."

"You also made it sound like your mother was some poor little hausfrau in desperate need of a self-esteem boost. I assumed the whole thing had been a joke."

"A good therapist never assumes."

"A good mind reader knows when to interrupt."

"That I apologize for. No signals were coming through. Blame it on the fact I get too uptight around her."

"Was it her or because she brought up the topic of Trixie? You married your father's mistress? *There I said it … his dirty laundry was out there … hanging on the line … blowing in the wind.*

"Here comes my car. Can we get into this at a later date?"

If Ben's car hadn't arrived, I suspected he would have come up with some other way to avoid the topic.

"Fine by me." I spotted the red Thunderbird pulling into the lot. "I wouldn't want to keep Jack waiting."

"I don't blame you. The last thing the ozone layer needs is his gas guzzler idling away for any longer than needed." And with that parting barb, Ben pulled away from the restaurant, throwing Jack a half-hearted wave as he passed.

Louie riffed upon his return. "Talk about still waters. That boy of yours is a daytime soap opera wrapped in a primetime package. You know, like a gringo starring in his own novella—Telemundo meets PBS."

"Enough, already. I get the picture."

We seated ourselves in the Thunderbird.

"So how's dear ol' Mom?" Jack asked, as we climbed the road leading back to the Coast Highway.

Louie was in the mood for being a smart-ass. "Which one? He has two. The one he's married to or the one he isn't married to?"

I glowered at him sitting there smugly in the backseat.

"Why are you giving me that look?" he asked.

Jack merged into traffic. "Is he a Mormon or something?"

"No, they're the ones with all the wives," I said.

"Same diff. If your dad has a bunch of wives, by default you'd have a bunch of moms."

Convoluted as Jack's logic was, it did make sense.

"I stand corrected, but that's not what happened in this case."

"Kinky."

Once again, Jack had managed to bring the conversation back to his favorite topic.

"Look, it's simple." I attempted to put the subject to rest. "There's nothing kinky about it. His soon to be ex-wife, from his first marriage, is the same woman as his father's ex-wife, from his father's second marriage."

"Right." Jack seemed perplexed. "So who was his father's first wife?"

"His mother," Louie and I said in unison.

"His father was married to his grandmother and you don't think that's kinky? Whoa, Red—you really are a wild thing!"

"Does she make your heart sing?" Louie quizzed.

"She makes everything groovy." Jack played along. "Great song, man. Did you know it took The Troggs only twenty minutes to record?"

Jack and Louie bonded over sixties music trivia all the way to West Hollywood; their retro lullabies serenaded me to sleep.

* * *

Warped notes of psychedelic music wafting on a gentle, marijuana-scented breeze nudged me back into awareness. Jack had promised to drop me back home in time for my appointment with LaVonne. My ears and my nose were sending my brain advance notification of a change in plans. Peering cautiously through a semi-closed eyelid, I attempted to identify my surroundings before jumping headlong into God knows what with God knows who. Based on my recent experiences falling asleep in moving vehicles, this would be the wisest course of action. Problem was, nothing was identifiable—not even me.

My feet—clad in leather Jesus Christ sandals—displayed ten strange filthy toes. *There goes the pedicure I had last week.*

On my legs—a pair of mud-caked, orange paisley, corduroy hip-huggers. *Hip-huggers? ... what was I thinking?*

My bare midriff was much tighter than I remembered. *All that abs work is finally paying off.*

My top was ... *Hey! Where's my top?*

The initial knee-jerk reaction to cover my chest was waylaid by my fascination with these firmer, fuller breasts. Gravity had reversed its earthward pull. I fully opened my eyes for a better view. *These are great looking tits.*

"Come on in," a faraway male voice beckoned.

Looking up, I saw I was in a meadow near a pond, surrounded by young people—hippies to be precise.

Am I at some sort of themed costume party? "Where are we?" I called out to the young man in the pond.

"In heaven," he replied.

Have Jack and I been in a car accident ... if we're dead ... where is he?

A sudden image of fire and brimstone flashed through my mind. *Poor Jack ... on the other hand ... poor me ... except for the body makeover ... this isn't exactly my idea of heaven ... maybe hell's the place to be.*

Another possibility dawned on me. *Jack's still alive.*

The welcome procedure at this place sucks ... no meet and greet ...

no orientation ... is this any way to run an afterlife? ... soon as I'm settled in ... I'm lodging a complaint.

"Are you coming in?" the young man called to me again.

May as well head over to the pond ... clean up a bit ... introduce myself to the other corpses ... scratch that last word ... they probably prefer "souls" ... don't want to start off eternity on the wrong foot.

I waded naked into the murky water. *If you've got it ... flaunt it.* "How long have you been dead?" I asked the fellow who summoned me.

"I was dead until I arrived here," he said with an ecstatic look on his face.

Religious type ... this is the place for it.

A teenage girl with an Afro floated by us. "We were all born dead."

This must be Limbo ... I need an upgrade. "They sent me to the wrong place; I was baptized a long time ago."

"Nothing that happened before counts in here," a redheaded boy with acne said.

"You don't understand. It was a Roman Catholic ceremony. They created Limbo, so my baptism should be recognized here. It works like a fast pass to the pearly gates." *After a brief stopover in purgatory for an eon or two.*

"We'll limbo with you, sweetie pie," a horny-looking older couple offered.

These dead babies are getting on my nerves. "Excuse me! Are there any baptized Roman Catholics here?" I asked the others standing round me.

"What's she on man?" A gorgeous looking hunk with long dark hair stood at the edge of the pond. "I wanna get me some of that shit."

I recognized the voice. "Jack? Is that really you?"

"You bet it is, babe." Within seconds he had stripped down to nothing.

Wow! ... the secret allure of bass players revealed to me at last.

"Get ready, 'cause here I come." He charged into the water like a runaway bull, and I do mean bull.

A dappled mix of sunlight and water rippled over his sinewy body as he swam. Stunning to behold, he disappeared beneath the water before reaching me. From below my waist, he slowly resurfaced. His glistening body caressing me as it deliberately glided over mine.

"I don't believe we've met," he said. Then he took me in his arms and kissed me with a burning intensity.

Okay ... maybe this is heaven. "Jack, you look so young and virile. Aren't these new bodies terrific?"

"Fantastic. Why don't we give each other a tour of the grounds, if you catch my drift?"

"Why not? We've certainly got a lot of time to kill."

"Yeah, we're still a ways away from Hendrix."

"Where's that at?" I asked.

"On the big stage."

"Stage? Is Hendrix a play?"

"Sure he's gonna play. This is Woodstock. The tribes have gathered and the gods shall speak."

"What year is this?"

"One of my faves, babe. Good ol' sixty-nine."

"That's impossible!"

"It's easy." He lifted me out of the water and started for the shore. "Let me show you how easy."

"We passed sixty-nine a long time ago."

"I love you Kama Sutra chicks. Before this festival's over we'll work through the entire book together."

"Is Lori Taylor here?"

"Naw, she couldn't make it. Wanna meet her? My band's got an audition lined up in LA with her manager. Come along, maybe she'll be there."

"Sure, if I don't wake up from this dream first."

"Stick with me and you'll be California dreamin' before you know it."

Dizzy and overwhelmed, I closed my eyes. The soothing harmonies of The Mamas & the Papas coasted through my mind.

* * *

"Wake up, Red," Jack said, gently shaking me. "We're here."

"Is Hendrix on?"

"No, babe. It's The Mamas & the Papas."

"Were they at Woodstock?" I opened my eyes and found myself back in the Thunderbird, parked outside my house. "We're you at Woodstock?"

"Sure, I was there. John, Denny, Michelle and Cass weren't though."

"I was just there. I heard them."

"You fell asleep. They were singin' on the radio."

"No, no. It was different from a dream, more vivid."

"You know what they say—if you remember Woodstock, you weren't there."

"But I was there. With you. We were working through the Kama Sutra together."

"No way, Red. You'd have been a little kid back then. Not my style."

"I was a young woman with a very hot body."

"You still are, babe. But if you don't get that tail of yours cookin' pretty damn soon, you'll be late for your appointment. I promised to get you back in time and, as a man of my word, I did. The rest's up to you."

Reality check, Roberta ... you're a hypnotherapist ... not a hippie.

"What time is it?" I fumbled with the car door handle.

"Quarter to four."

"Thanks for everything, Jack," I said, hurrying out of the car. "Sorry to dash."

"No prob. I'm takin' a rain check on that Kama Sutra tutorial though."

Amused by his relentless tenacity, I turned toward my walkway. Then something occurred to me. "When did you first meet Lori Taylor?"

"In LA. I think it was nineteen sixty-nine. Yeah, it was sixty-nine. A few days after Woodstock. Why?"

"Just wondering. Do you have any pictures of yourself from back then?"

"Some publicity shots."

"I'd like to take a look at them. Bring them by next time." *Who knows ... maybe I'll make good on that rain check.*

Whatever had happened, I knew it wasn't an ordinary dream. Call it what you will—lucid dreaming—time travel—or what have you; I'd been through some sort of out-of-body experience. Out of my body and into someone else's.

CHAPTER TEN

THERE WAS NOT MUCH time to prepare for my appointment with LaVonne. I was barely through the door when my cell rang. It was Sharon Jefferson.

"Sorry to bother you, Roberta, I had to speak with you right away."

"I'm glad you did; that's what this number's for. Is there a problem?"

"Yes. I just found out LaVonne has a session booked with you today. Have they arrived yet?"

"No, but I expect them any minute."

"Whatever you do, don't mention anything about past life regression to Frank. He'll hit the roof."

"That's going to be rather difficult. He made it clear he intends to sit in on the session."

"Don't let him."

"I can't do that. She's a minor and he's legally entitled."

"He's so narrow-minded and suspicious. I don't want to go to battle with him over this."

My office doorbell rang.

"I've got to go; they're here. Don't worry, Sharon. I won't lie to him, but nothing prevents me from being creative in my explanation of what's happening."

This case was certainly putting my abilities to the test. My training as an actor was coming in as handy as my training in hypnosis. I never realized they were complimentary skills.

Frank Jefferson was a short, stocky, African-American man in his mid-to-late forties. What he lacked in warmth, he made up for in officiousness. "How long will this take?" he asked, brushing past me and taking a seat in my office.

LaVonne trailed behind him. She was shyer, more reserved, in the company of her authoritarian father. It was easy to see why Sharon Jefferson had left him, albeit the initial attraction was much harder to perceive.

"The session lasts about an hour, with thirty to forty minutes spent in trance," I said.

"It's this trance business I don't care for. If you ask me, there's something downright unchristian about the whole thing. My wife gets a lot of crazy notions."

"Last night you saw for yourself how well LaVonne responds to this modality. It has nothing to do with religion; her pediatrician referred her to me. I'm sure you'll feel differently after you witness what goes on here today. Do I have your permission to proceed?"

He looked over at his daughter sitting in the recliner. "What do you want to do, baby?"

"I want to say hi to Lex."

"Who's Lex?"

"He's my dog. May I let him in?"

"Does he bite?"

Of course … that's why he's so popular with kids … who can resist a vicious dog? "No."

"All right," he said apprehensively. "Put him on a leash, just in case."

I rounded up Lex and brought him into my office. After a brief visit with LaVonne, he took up his usual position on the oval rug in front of the recliner and we were ready to begin.

"Okay, LaVonne. Do you want to go play with Lex in your secret playroom?"

"Uh-huh," she nodded.

"Excuse me, when are you going to hypnotize her? I have to be back in Orange County for a church meeting."

"That's what I'm trying to do. The playroom is an imaginary device used to assist her in relaxing. I'll have to ask you to reserve the rest of your comments and questions until the end of the session."

He seemed embarrassed by the gaffe. "Oh, right. Sure." It was obvious humility was not a customary state.

"Now let's prepare to travel to your special place. I'm going to count backwards from twenty down to zero. With each and every number your eyelids will grow heavier, your breathing will become deeper, and your mind will drift further away from where you are on the outside, and closer to where you want to be on the inside. There is nothing to worry about on this journey. You are safe and protected at all times. As a matter of fact, you won't even remember anything that happens here today. When it's time to come back, you'll awaken relaxed and refreshed like you do after taking a very long nap.

I want you to visualize or imagine yourself standing at the top of a staircase with twenty steps leading downward, and two strong, sturdy handrails on either side. This staircase will lead us to your special secret place. At twenty, you start down this staircase—step-by-step—at nineteen—eighteen—seventeen. Going deeper and deeper—ten times deeper—with each and every count. The deeper we go, the calmer you become."

I continued counting in a slow, deliberate manner—hypnotizing and deepening her simultaneously. It was my intention to carry on with our work at the deepest level possible. I had some probing questions to ask that unidentified woman in the alley, the woman who's murder LaVonne kept witnessing in her nightmares.

Could she be the Jane Doe stabbing victim I read about in the Chicago Tribune article Ben gave me?

Once I found out exactly who she was, where she was, and when she was, it would be possible to determine if she was real or imaginary—a child's invention or a window into another dimension.

"Two. That's right, keep on going you're almost there. One—let go of the present and step into the past. Zero—deep sleep!"

Her body was limp and motionless.

"Where are you?"

"In an alley," LaVonne responded in a woman's far-off voice.

"At Boy Scout camp," Frank Jefferson answered in the cracking voice of an adolescent boy.

I swiveled round to face him. He was slumped over in the straight back chair, out like a light.

A somnambulist … just what I need.

Somnambulists are the most suggestible of subjects, the ones lured onstage to make fools of themselves in Vegas. It wasn't worth the risk of breaking LaVonne's trance depth to bring him out. Moreover, my job would be much easier if he remained out of the loop. He didn't appear to be in any distress.

How much trouble can he get into at a Boy Scout camp? "Frank, how old are you?"

"You know how old I am, Ma. Fourteen." He had flipped into an age regression.

"Can I trust you to be a good boy and behave yourself if I leave you here at Boy Scout camp?"

"Does that mean I don't have to go to Bible camp instead?"

"Not if you don't want to."

"Hooray!"

"I'm going to say goodbye now, Frank. The only sights you'll see and the only sounds you'll hear are from your camp. You will not notice anything else until I come back to pick you up."

"Thanks, Ma. Hey, Lou! Wait up! She changed her mind; I can stay."

That should keep him preoccupied for a while. I turned my attention back to LaVonne. "Are you still in the alley?"

"Yes."

"What city are you in?"

"Chicago." The voice was even and steady, helping make up for its inherent weakness.

"What year is it?"

"Nineteen ninety-three."

This <u>could</u> *be the Jane Doe from the newspaper clipping.* "Why are you in the alley?"

"Meeting father. Doesn't know who I am."

"Who are you?"

"Karen Hall."

Karen Hall? ... can't be the same one.

"Karen, who is your mother?"

"Singer."

"Is that her name?"

"No."

"What's her name?"

"Lori Taylor."

If that's true ... who's the woman in critical condition at UCLA Medical's Trauma Center?

Mr. Jefferson moaned.

"Frank, are you okay?"

"Better than okay, I'm in love." The moaning grew more intense and distracting. His hands moved to his belt buckle.

Don't like where this is leading ...last thing I need is a full-fledged hypno-sex demonstration in my office.

He reached for his fly.

I had to end his fantasy camp trip right then and there.

"Frank, it's your mother. I'm back. We have to go home now."

Both hands abruptly fell to his sides. "It's not what you think, Ma. I lost something in the bushes." Frank's voice trembled with fear. "We were looking for it together. Scout's honor."

Yeah ... I bet you lost something in those bushes. Though, I can't deny, my heart went out to him. "I believe you, son."

And with those four simple words, a lifetime of guilt melted away from Frank Jefferson's face. I considered billing him for a double session.

"Does that mean you're not going to whoop me or make me go tell the preacher?"

"Everything's fine, but we do have to leave."

This was taking longer than I anticipated. I needed to check back in with LaVonne and Karen.

"Can I come back again?" he asked.

"Yes, whenever you want, if you come with me right now."

"Let's go!"

A startled LaVonne squirmed in her seat—signs of discomfort evident in her body language.

She was losing depth. Not wanting to risk lightening her state any further, I decided to bring her father back without the benefit of a count.

"Frank, in a moment I will say the words 'welcome home' to you. When I do you will be back in the present, sitting in my office, observing your daughter's hypnotherapy session. It will not be necessary to remember anything that went on here today. However, any positive feelings or helpful insights you have gained will remain with you, continuing to grow and develop in the coming days and weeks. Welcome home, Frank."

He opened his eyes and furtively surveyed the room. "What happened?"

"I was hypnotizing LaVonne and you inadvertently went under, too. As soon as I realized, I brought you back up. How do you feel?"

"Good." He hesitated. "But different." Looking down at his pants, "Is there a restroom I could use?"

I pointed to the door on the far interior wall. "Go through there, you'll find it across the hallway."

Still in a daze, he got up from his seat and stepped over Lex.

"Do you mind if I continue while you're gone?" I asked.

"No, go right ahead."

He left the room. I was thankful to have a few more minutes free of his obtrusive presence. "Karen, are you still there?"

"He's coming." Her steady rhythmic breathing was growing faint and shallow. "Have to go." A sudden powerful frequency surge hit, sending her into overdrive. "I'm breaking off our engagement … Of course I love you … But I can't marry you … Don't hit me." She sobbed. "I'm the one who should be angry … You son of a bitch … The blood tests came back today … You're my father … Why didn't you tell me? … I'm carrying your child." Her tears grew more anguished. "Thanks to you … I'm the bastard sister of my bastard child … My poor sweet baby … I have to abort my poor sweet baby … Stop … You're hurting me!"

"What's all the cussing and crying about in here?" Frank said, bursting through the door.

LaVonne thrashed about in the chair, wailing and screaming "What have you done to my child?" he yelled at me.

I attempted to respond, but was distracted by the marks of discoloration appearing on LaVonne's face and neck.

"Sweet Jesus! Lord have mercy! It's the mark of the beast." Frank tried to yank LaVonne out of the recliner, but was thwarted by a snarling Lex. "Call off your devil dog, lady."

The situation was out of control and deteriorating rapidly. This wasn't something they prepared you for in hypnotherapy school.

"Quiet, everyone!" I screamed at the top of my lungs. To my surprise this technique worked on man, child, and dog. Taking full advantage of the sudden lull, I counted LaVonne out of trance in record time. "Eyes open, wide awake."

"Why are you standing, Daddy?" LaVonne inquired, innocently unaware of what had just taken place. Her body no longer exhibited any physical signs of trauma.

"Because it's time to go now, baby. Wait outside while Daddy settles the bill."

LaVonne rose from the recliner and waved goodbye to me.

"Be careful of that dog," her father warned as she passed by Lex.

Laughing, she reached over and gave Lex a pat on the head and a kiss on the snout before stepping outside.

"I've heard of this sort of thing, though the only place I've ever seen it was in the movies. Stay away from my daughter, I won't warn you again," he dictated, waving an accusatory finger at me.

"You don't understand. Let me explain." How I would do this I hadn't quite figured out, since I didn't completely understand it myself.

"There'll be no need, your work speaks for itself. My suspicions have been confirmed. What I saw here today was a glimpse into the kingdom of darkness."

Bringing up my fee seemed a moot point.

Frank Jefferson opened the door and stomped out of my office.

Without a moment's hesitation I picked up the phone and called Sharon Jefferson. She would need a heads-up on what had transpired here. "Hello, Sharon. It's Roberta, I hope I didn't catch you at a bad time."

"No, you're lucky you caught me at all. I'm on my way home; Frank's dropping LaVonne off before heading back to Orange County. You're finished early. How'd everything go? You didn't mention anything about past life regression, did you?"

"That's what I was calling about. Nothing came out about past life regression, but ..."

"Can you hold for a minute? I've got a 9-1-1 coming in on my pager."

"No problem." *I can use the downtime to figure out how to position my news in a positive light.*

A frantic Sharon retuned to the line. "Roberta, what happened? Frank's taking LaVonne back to Orange County with him. He's ranting and raving about demons and possession."

Missed the window on that positive light strategy. "There was a display of some unusual physical phenomena I wasn't expecting." *How's that for spin?*

"What do you mean?"

Come on, Roberta … get it over with … spit it out. "I think she was exhibiting facial injuries—bruising mostly—from her previous life. LaVonne's fine though, she doesn't feel or remember anything. The effects disappeared as soon as she came out of trance, but not before Frank noticed them."

"It's all my fault. I should never have let him take her to you. That man's mama did a lot of damage to his mind when he was a boy. It's a wonder he made it this far in life, the way she had him believing the seven deadly sins were lurking around every corner waiting to snatch him up. Sad part is, underneath it all, he's really a good man and a great father. He'll come round in a few days, he always does."

"Is there anything I can do?"

"Short of coming to the Lord and letting Frank immerse you in the cleansing waters of baptism? No."

"We had a very productive session. The woman in the alley claims to be Lori Taylor's daughter, Karen Hall."

"How can she be? According to what I heard on the news this morning, she was hit by a car last night and is in a coma."

"If this truly is a past life, one of them is evidently an imposter. There's something suspicious about that accident; it may have been intentional. LaVonne's Karen claims to have been murdered by her father. That same man was in the vicinity of last night's accident. When I track him down, this puzzle should make a lot more sense. This other Karen—the one killed in Chicago—was pregnant with her father's child."

"Did you say Chicago?"

"Yes. I came across an article about a Jane Doe stabbing that took place there a few years back. Based on what I discovered in today's session, they could be one and the same crime."

"What was the year?"

"She said it was nineteen ninety-three. Let me check it against the clipping." I pulled the blue file folder from my desk drawer. "Yep, same year. It says here the body was found in the early morning hours of …"

"February the fourteenth."

"Right. How'd you know? Was LaVonne talking during one of her nightmares?"

"No." Sharon paused. "I was there."

"You were at the murder scene?"

"Yes. I'm the one who found the body," she choked back her words. "No one told me she was pregnant."

"Why didn't you mention any of this to me before?"

"I wasn't sure they were related, and if they were I didn't want to taint your findings. Maybe LaVonne could be of more help than I was. I heard a woman screaming that night. Then I saw a figure run out of an alley. But I was too late; she'd been beaten to a pulp, blood everywhere." Sharon sounded shaken by the recollection. "There I was—an ER nurse—and the sight of it made me want to vomit. I held her in my arms as she let go her last breath."

CHAPTER ELEVEN

ICHARD BAXTER—calculating manager turned disappearing monk—was the person I needed to locate. Last night he was in the vicinity of the accident that put LA's Karen Hall into a coma.

Why the sudden vanishing act when police appeared on the scene? ... had he been behind the wheel of the SUV?

I got Louie on the line. "Did you reach Danny?"

"I left a message. They started a silent retreat at the Zen Center today. We won't hear back from him for another few days."

"So Richard Baxter can't be reached either?"

"Nope."

"My client revealed the identity of the woman who was murdered in the alley. Says her name was Karen Hall. She was stabbed to death in Chicago back in nineteen ninety-three. ID'd her father as the perpetrator of the crime, and says Lori Taylor was her mother. That makes dear old Dad none other than Richard Baxer. Turns out Pops was also her fiancé, and father of the unborn child she was carrying."

"So Lori had twins?"

"Duh. With the exact same name?"

"Identical twins!"

"No. Supposing LaVonne is reliving an actual past life experience, one of them has to be an imposter. In that case, I'm betting it's the Karen who was hit by your car last night, and Richard Baxter is responsible for both crimes."

"Then I was right after all."

"What do you mean?"

"Remember I said maybe her father was also a Father? He's a monk—same difference."

"Your logic is as twisted as Lombard Street."

"Thank you. I'll take that as a compliment. It'll take a few twists to untangle this mess."

"You're telling me. All the people I need to speak with are incommunicado, including my client. Her father whisked her out of my evil clutches and into the safe bosom of that bastion of mainstream conservatism, Orange County."

"Oh, honey, I guess you never watched an episode of *The O.C.* That place puts Sodom and Gomorrah to shame. It's the 'swinging' capital of America. They put on that old-fashioned traditionalist act to keep interlopers out. Damn, I wish my driver's license wasn't suspended."

It was getting close to dinnertime. "Do you need anything?" I couldn't help feeling responsible for Louie's uncertain legal predicament.

"No, I'm going to lay low until I hear back from Danny. Should I tell Barbara Goldberg about this new development?"

"Wait. Let me make sure we're not off on another wild goose chase first."

"How are you going to do that?"

"Perhaps I need to sit down and have a heart-to-heart with Paul Graham. Find out what he knows about his wife's background, and why someone would want to kill her."

"If she is an imposter, do you think he knows?"

"Hard to say. He was the one responsible for reuniting her with Lori. She could be using him as a pawn. We'll see what he has to say for himself."

"We?" Louie gulped. "He thinks I ran over his wife."

"Figurative we. I doubt I'm at the top of his favorites list either. Jack may know him and be able to smooth things over a bit. Do you still have Paul's phone number?"

After getting Paul's number from Louie, I thought it best to put in a call to Jack first.

Not home.

Deciding it was worth taking a calculated risk, I went ahead and called Paul myself.

Also, not home. I left a brief message, "Mr. Graham, it's Roberta Law. Sorry to hear about your wife's accident. I think we both know the person who was driving that vehicle last night, and it was neither Louie Lopez nor myself. I'm prepared to go to the police with information about Vanessa's ..." I was about to say the word "assailant" when his machine cut me off.

199

Who the heck is Vanessa? ... where'd I pull that name from? ... I don't know anyone named Vanessa.

Redialing, I figured it would help if I let him know I meant to say "Karen's assailant" and left him a number where he could reach me. If Richard Baxter was behind this, he might also be after Paul and Lori. I wanted to warn him, plus use the opportunity to do some surreptitious digging to learn how much he knew about his wife's background.

No answer now ... not my day for communication.

* * *

About a half hour later, Lex gave me the look—but the cupboards were bare.

Mother Hubbard has some serious shopping to do.

After a quick doggie pit stop at Sherman Oaks-Van Nuys Park, my car inched its way into the parking lot at Trader Joe's. Crowded Joe's, as I liked to call it, was the preferred grocery store of post-yuppie moderns in search of gourmet fare at near bargain basement prices. Always a beehive of activity, the place was swarming that day. Luckily, I found a shady spot for Lex. Windows rolled down, he could wait comfortably in the car while I and my red shopping cart buzzed alongside the other workers and drones.

Every now and then you might catch a glimpse of a queen bee such as Bonnie Franklin, Mickey Dolenz, Mackenzie Phillips, or some other faded famous face. That day would not provide me with such an auspicious sighting. Reaching for a bottle of Charles Shaw wine—affectionately known in local circles as Two Buck Chuck—I did run into another old bee, however.

"Ben never mentioned you were a wine connoisseur," she pricked with her calculated sting.

Nor did he mention your proclivity for marriage on the family plan.
"Trixie, what a surprise!" *I didn't say it was a pleasant one.*

"How's the mesmerizing business going?"

"It's keeping me busy. What's new in the sex trade?"

Ben turned into our aisle, "I can't find any white sage honey."
The beekeeper had arrived.

"Benny, look who I ran into!" Trixie was far more excited than the occasion merited.

"Roberta?" Ben seemed off his game. "What are you doing here … I mean … I wasn't expecting …"

"When I run out of food, I always make a point of stocking up on more."

"Yes, we can see," Trixie said, purveying the high fat, high carb and high sugar contents of my cart. "I'm more of an Atkins girl, myself. Benny, I don't know how you do it on that vegetarian diet of yours. I'd just die if I couldn't sink my teeth into a big, fresh, juicy hunk of beef."

Her dietary habits are curiously reminiscent of her dating habits.

"What about you, Bobby?" Trixie asked. "Don't you agree?"

"It's Roberta," I corrected her.

"She's definitely a fowl girl. Don't you think, Benny?"

Ben winced at the direction our conversation was taking. "Have you got everything? You promised me this wouldn't take long, Trixie."

"This should do for now. I don't know how to repay you."

I'm sure she'll figure out something.

"How about joining me for dinner?" Trixie purred to Ben.

Is she trying to make me jealous by flirting with her soon to be ex?

"I'd love to," he replied. "But I don't think you'll be serving up anything that appeals to my appetite."

Way to go, Ben!

Trixie appeared taken aback by his uncharacteristically biting repartee.

"Besides, Roberta already invited me over." He put his arm around my waist and gave me a tight squeeze.

This is too good to resist … I have to play along. Picking a package up from out of my cart, I showed it to Trixie. "Potato gnocchi in pesto sauce."

"Sounds delicious," Ben said. "I've been looking forward to stopping by your place for some gnocchi."

Trixie cleared her throat.

"First I have to drop Tixie off at the mechanic's. Her car's in the shop; I'm playing good Samaritan today."

"You've inspired me." Trixie took the package from my hand. "Maybe I'll ask my mechanic over for a hot gnocchi."

* * *

My car was half unloaded when Ben pulled up. "May I help you with that?" he asked.

"You take this good Samaritan stuff seriously." I handed him a paper bag.

"It's my policy to never turn down a dinner invitation from a beautiful woman."

"You were quite deft at extricating yourself from Trixie's offer."

"She's no woman, she's my wife," he said, mimicking Groucho Marx.

We walked into the house and set the bags down on the kitchen counter.

"The way I remember it you invited yourself over," I teased.

"I want to make amends for what happened at lunch today."

"Shouldn't you be cooking me dinner then?"

"All right, I owe you one. How about a compromise? We'll prepare tonight's meal together."

I wasn't opposed to cooking with him—although this wasn't the room I envisioned starting in.

"Deal." *May as well begin somewhere.* "First we take care of Mr. Lex." I handed him the doggie bowl. "At the end of the hallway running past my office, there's a door to the garage. Inside, you'll find a green container filled with kibble. He gets one level cup."

I unpacked groceries while Ben carried out his task.

"It looks like a tornado hit your office," Ben called back to me. "What have you been up to?"

He must be a neat freak ... it's not that disorganized. "What are you doing in there?"

"I'm not in there. You left the door open."

"No, I didn't."

"Go see for yourself," he said, returning to the kitchen.

Entering the hallway, I could see the door to my office was ajar.

"Lex must have pushed it open; I should put a lock on it." I went to shut the door. "Ben, come quick! No, call the police!"

Ben hurried to my side. "What's wrong?"

Filing cabinet drawers were pulled out willy-nilly, confidential client files thrown all over the room.

"I've been burglarized."

"Better check the rest of the house," Ben suggested.

We went from room to room looking for evidence of further disruption. Everything was intact; nothing out of place except for the side window in my living room—it was wide open.

"The burglar entered through here," I said, thinking back to Louie's aborted break-in a few days earlier. "Must have snuck in while I was shopping. Whatever they were after, it wasn't money. My jewelry, TV and stereo haven't been touched."

"They seem to have concentrated their efforts in your office."

"My computer!"

We sprinted back to the avalanche. On the floor, underneath a stack of papers, I spotted my laptop.

"What were they after?" I bent down to pick some folders up off the floor.

"Better not touch anything until after the police arrive," Ben said, intercepting me. "Not even the phone; I'll call them on my cell."

* * *

Though it seemed like forever, a squad car arrived in less than an hour. The officer inside was a fresh-faced young kid who looked like he'd come directly from graduation exercises at the police academy. I told Officer Sanchez everything I knew about what had happened and then he inspected my office. Since it hadn't been determined whether or not anything was stolen, he was reporting it as illegal trespass coupled with malicious mischief.

"Contact me at the station if anything turns up missing." Officer Sanchez flipped his notepad closed.

"Is that it?" I asked.

"Pretty much. Your husband may want to take a look at the window," he said, indicating Ben. "I suggest you repair it immediately."

Husband? My chest tightened. "We're not married."

"Yet," Ben was quick to add.

"You're sure you can't think of anyone who may have a motive for doing this?" Officer Sanchez asked.

"As far as I know, I don't have any enemies."

"Maybe one of your clients does," he said, putting forward a possibility I never considered.

"Blackmail?" *Very sensitive personal material is often revealed in my sessions.*

"Or it may be nothing more than the work of a bunch of destructive kids out on a prank. I'll be on the lookout for any similar incidents occurring in the neighborhood. In the meantime, consider having an alarm system installed." He put away his notebook and looked down at Lex. "Your dog doesn't strike me as the ferocious type."

* * *

I delayed the task of sifting through the mess in my office until after dinner. This would give me an opportunity to fill Ben in on what had happened since lunch.

"I'd say you have a verifiable past life occurrence." Ben poured himself another glass of chardonnay. "How you're going to prove it is the tricky part. You may want to contact the cold case unit of the Chicago Police Department."

"And give them a good laugh?"

"Believe me, they won't laugh. My office has been contacted for referrals to reputable psychics by all levels of law enforcement."

"Yeah, but you want me to contact them. I'm a hypnotist not a psychic. They'll probably tell me to get in touch with a Las Vegas booking agent. I can't see into the past." This brought to mind the Woodstock flashback I'd experienced in Jack's car. *Was it a vivid fantasy … or something more?* "What do you know about lucid dreaming?"

"Lots. Why?"

"I think I was doing it earlier today."

"It's quite common. At its most basic level, one is aware of the act of dreaming while it is occurring. Was there an OBE involved?

"OBE?"

"Out-of-body experience—a compelling sensation that you have left your body."

The muddy nubile form I'd inhabited flooded back into my awareness. "Without a doubt, I was no longer in my body."

"Did you feel like you were floating above your body?"

"No, my body was nowhere in sight; I was in someone else's."

"You were someone else?"

"Inside, I was still myself. Outside, I was some hippie girl at Woodstock."

Ben's brow furrowed. "Sounds more like you were in an RV state."

"Florida?"

"No, a state of mind."

"Right, a New York state of mind." I couldn't resist being facetious. "Woodstock, New York—to be specific."

"Cute. Remote Viewing or Mental Spying, as it was once known, is a form of astral traveling. It was developed during the Cold War. Scientists in the former U.S.S.R. pioneered the early experiments in secret laboratories controlled by the K.G.B. or G.R.U., the military intelligence branch."

"Sounds like something out of a James Bond movie."

"It was. Where do you think Ian Fleming got his ideas? He did espionage work for British Naval Intelligence during World War II. Anyway, these were essentially mind control exercises—the objective being to control people's minds from a distance. Our government was doing most of its research in the areas of hypnosis and mind-altering drugs, such as LSD, before they started playing catch-up with the Soviets' Remote Viewing program."

Beauty __and__ *brains … this guy is quite the catch.* "How does it work?"

"Are you sure you want to know? The answer is long, involved, and rooted in the workings of quantum physics."

Physics ... yuck ... I managed to avoid it in high school ... why mess with it now? "Give me the Cliff's Notes version."

"I'll try. Everything boils down to energy. Nothing is truly solid, not even matter. We only perceive it as so because it's a vibratory by-product of mind. Nothing exists outside of oneself, not even space and time. Hence, separateness is an illusion. In authentic reality, all things are one in the eternal moment of now known as Universal Mind—or God—or First Cause. Doesn't matter which name you use, it's merely semantics.

I'm glad I pushed for the abridged version. "You lost me somewhere after 'I'll try.' Give me the *TV Guide* version."

"*Quantum Leap.*"

Clear as a bell. "I time traveled!"

"In essence, yes; if time actually existed ..."

"Stop right there or you'll lose me again. Don't you think that's kinda crazy?"

"Einstein didn't think so—E equals mc squared."

I'm still figuring out how to balance my checkbook. "He was talking about time travel?"

"Yes, theoretically, among other things."

Guess I proved his theory. "Explain this to me. In *Quantum Leap*, Scott Bakula would dematerialize before he leapt into another body. Why was Jack still able to see me sleeping beside him?"

Ben's intellectual coolness gave way to a much more primitive emotion. "You were in bed with Jack?"

That didn't come out right … though I do enjoy the reaction it triggered … looks like we've moved on to chemistry. "No, I fell asleep in his car."

"Why are you always falling asleep in that guy's car?" His tone was accusatory.

"You're not my husband <u>yet</u>, remember? By the way, what was that supposed to mean?"

"I think the statement speaks for itself."

"Maybe you could consult me first. Or don't I have a say in this cosmically arranged marriage?"

"Don't go flying off the handle. Is the idea of being married to me so reprehensible to you?"

"No." He caught me off-guard. "I don't like rushing into things that's all." *Though not many people would consider marrying in your forties an impetuous act … come clean, Roberta … you have a problem with commitment … you cried yourself to sleep the night of your First Communion … thinking the priest had married you to Billy Wilson, your communion partner.* "I need to take things slow."

"That's a relief. I was afraid the celibacy thing was starting to get to you."

I don't mean a standstill. "How much longer are you planning to maintain this position?" *Or lack thereof.*

"For as long as it takes."

I wonder if it's too late to pick up where I left off with Jack at Woodstock? "How would one induce a Remote Viewing experience?"

Ben seemed relieved the conversation had returned to a more arcane topic. "Do you use self-hypnosis?"

"On occasion."

"You have to take yourself to a deep theta state without falling asleep. I'd advise prerecording an induction with a set intention in mind. That way you won't be distracted while you're in trance. You're not planning a return to Woodstock are you?"

"Why do you ask?" *I thought I'd finally mastered the art of jamming his thought interception.*

"Seems like a waste of energy when you can run over to Blockbuster and rent it on DVD."

Not this version.

* * *

After Ben left I spent what remained of the evening reconstructing my office. Two items were missing—the blue folder containing articles on past life research—and Lavonne Jefferson's file. Richard Baxter was the first name to come to mind.

I was dialing Officer Sanchez when it struck me there was another possible suspect—the Reverend Frank Jefferson. No one other than these two men would be interested in this material. The realization that both of them were her father—past and present— did not get overlooked. One was a Christian minister and the other a Buddhist monk; an *Outer Limits* version of east meets west. This was something to run by Danny; the intricate workings of the laws of karma was out of my league.

"Officer Sanchez, please ... It's Roberta Law calling ... In regards to Case Number 768547-G ... When do you expect him? ... Could you let him know two of my files are missing and I have the names …" *How do I explain the reason for my suspicions without betraying client confidentiality? … or risk sounding like some kind of nutty broad?* "Tell him he has a burglary on his hands … Thank you."

What now? … I could give Frank Jefferson a call … see where that takes me … and if he refuses to speak with me? … I'll ask Sharon to see what she can get out of him … then there's Richard Baxter … he knows I'm a hypnotist … and investigating something to do with Lori Taylor … but knows little else … not even my name … it doesn't add up.

My front doorbell rang; I wasn't accustomed to people dropping by after midnight. I peered out the peephole.

It's Jack … why am I not surprised?

I unlocked the door.

"Hey, babe." Jack handed me a bunch of old black-and-white photos. "Here are those publicity shots you wanted to see."

I recognized him right away. *This is the guy in my dream.*

"Aren't you gonna ask me in? Mighty dry out tonight, I wouldn't mind wettin' my whistle."

Something told me he had more than drinking on his mind. "I don't know. It's late. I was about to go to bed." *Why'd I say that?*

"Would you like some company?"

Yes … I would … but he went home over an hour ago. "Maybe some other time. It's been a long day." *Let's see if you pass your Woodstock tryout first.* "Thanks for stopping by with the pictures."

"Don't thank me, thank Richard. I couldn't find any of my old stuff, so when he called today I asked him if he had any."

"Why did he call?"

"He wants to bring his wife by to see you. She's not dealin' too well with the idea of him becomin' a monk. He thought she'd be more open to hypnosis than meditation. They've been separated for years, you'd think she'd be ready to give up the ghost and let the guy have a divorce. I gave him your address and phone number. You'll probably be hearin' from one of 'em soon."

"Oh, I already have. He broke into my office earlier this evening."

"Why would he do somethin' like that? It's not very spiritual."

"Neither is murder," I said.

"We've been all through that. Louie tripped over a mannequin not a body."

"He murdered his own daughter in Chicago eleven years ago—and he tried to kill her again last night."

"Whoa! What are you on?"

Jack's reaction was to be expected, I was having trouble making sense of it myself.

"I know it's confusing. Believe me, it's even more complicated to explain. Karen Hall is an imposter. The real Karen was killed by her father, Richard Baxter."

"How'd you find this out? It sounds absurd." Jack's skeptical side had finally put in an appearance.

Try this on for size. "From my ten-year-old client who is the reincarnation of Karen Hall."

"Cool."

This he has no problem believing? … he must have burnt a circuit or two back in the sixties.

"I was Nero in a past life. Guess that's why I have an affinity for string instruments and such a hard time quittin' smokin'."

"You've done a past life regression?"

"Naw. I discovered it droppin' acid with The Dead back in The Haight."

There's the Jack I've grown accustomed to avoiding. "You'll have to tell me about it sometime, when it's not so late."

The jarring roar of machinery assaulted the usual peacefulness of my quiet street.

Where's that godawful noise coming from?

A diminutive purple car sputtered to a stop in front of my house. A tall man unfolded himself from the driver's seat.

"Danny," I called. "Am I glad to see you."

"You're givin' me the brush-off for a guy who drives a Gremlin?" Jack griped. "Nice car, man. You might want to invest in a muffler."

"Danny, I'd like you to meet Jack. Jack, this is my brother, Danny."

"In that case, I'm very pleased to meet you." Jack said, shaking Danny's hand.

"Have you seen Louie?" My brother sounded uptight. "I've been looking everywhere for him."

"He told me you were in the middle of a silent retreat."

"I was, but I heard there's been a terrible accident."

"Don't worry, Jack and I were there. We bailed Louie out of a jail. Ben Cohen's mother is a lawyer; she's agreed to take his case."

Danny seemed thrown by this information. "Louie started the fire?"

"The car didn't catch on fire." I hoped my brother wasn't having one of his episodes.

"Louie left an urgent message saying he needed to speak to me about Richard Baxter. The police were up at the Center looking for Richard, to notify him about the fire at his house. I have to make sure he's all right. No one's seen him for a couple of days. He told me he had some personal business to take care of in Topanga."

"Are you trying to protect Richard because he's one of your own?" *The tarnish is showing on my brother's Shangri-La.* "He deserves everything he gets."

"Where's your compassion? The man's wife is in a hospital fighting for her life. He's missing, and may have died in that blaze at his home tonight."

"Sorry, didn't know about his wife," I partially recanted.

"You don't even know Richard." Danny said to me.

"I've known him for over thirty years," Jack interjected. "I introduced him to your sis."

"How long ago?" Danny chastised me with his eyes.

"Just under twenty-four hours," I replied.

"Judgment is a merciless companion," Danny preached. "If you're not careful it will turn your heart to stone, Roberta."

I felt like a petulant child being disciplined in parochial school. "The man's a murderer, Danny. It wouldn't surprise me to find out he's an arsonist, too."

"Richard is a dear friend of mine. He doesn't have it in him to take another's life."

My brother's stubbornness had a way of stirring up my own Celtic pigheadedness. There's a reason we're known as the "Fighting Irish."

"You may want to revise your opinion after I play back the past life regression session with my ten-year-old client today. The same client, incidentally, whose file was stolen from my office within hours of your buddy calling Jack, trying to track me down. The reason Louie's so desperate to reach you is because he needs to find Richard Baxter, in order to be exonerated for a crime he didn't commit. A crime, which I have plenty of reason to believe, was committed by your AWOL cleric."

"I gave him Louie's address, too." Jack said, grimly recognizing the possible consequences of his action.

"Why would he need that?" I asked.

"I don't think he told me." Jack seemed unsure of his response and appeared to be in a fugue state . "You folks'll have to excuse me, my short term memory has more holes in it than a slice of Swiss cheese. You know sometimes I can't even remember whether a red traffic light means 'Stop' or 'Go.' "

Given the fact I had developed a penchant for falling asleep while he was at the wheel, this revelation did not sit well with me. "You drive around all day as part of your job! Where'd you get your license? MacArthur Park?"

"No, I got it at the DMV like everyone else. The problem only kicks in when I'm walkin'." A light bulb flickered on in the cheese factory. "Hold on … it's startin' to come back … he had a big surprise for Louie … and he didn't want me to go and ruin it … by tippin' him off."

CHAPTER TWELVE

DANNY STAYED OVER at my place, neither one of us was able to sleep. After making calls to Louie's home, Louie's cell and Louie's office, we drove over to his West Hollywood condo. No irate voice came over the intercom to curse us out for disturbing him in the middle of his beauty sleep.

"Something's not right about this, Danny. He told me he was going to lay low tonight. I think we should go inside and take a look around. Do you have your key on you?"

Danny reached inside the pocket of his scruffy baggy jeans and produced a ring of at least twenty-five keys. "Hope it's on here, I left the rest back up at Mount Baldy."

"Still collecting keys, I see."

My brother had developed this abnormal obsession during his teens. Our parents wrote it off as an adolescent phase. They had an amazing capacity for tolerance when it came to Danny's eccentricities.

"They remind me to keep seeking, to not give up until I've unlocked every door."

Couldn't you just tie a string around one of your fingers?

"Here it is."

We let ourselves into the lobby and took an elevator up to the fifth floor.

"Did you know there are Five Books of Moses? Jews refer to these books as the Torah and Christians know them as the Pentateuch. There are also Five Pillars of Islam and Five Classics of Confucianism. The number five symbolizes humans and our five senses."

He's on one of his jags … I need to get him home and into bed … pronto.

Stone cold sober, Danny could ascertain deep interconnected meanings the average mortal only noticed when under the influence of a hallucinogen.

"This all relates back to the apple in the Garden of Eden. When cut in half horizontally, the five seeds contained in the core have the appearance of a star. Which is the symbol of the Greek goddess, Kore—known as Persephone, by the Romans. She represents fertility, the primal universe."

Right … and don't forget the Dave Clark Five … and Big Five candy bars … which I believe were made by the Clark candy company … mere fluke? … or cosmic conspiracy? … this must be the slowest elevator in the world.

"The ancient Egyptians painted stars on the ceilings of their tombs to represent the soul. Archetypically speaking, five represents eternity, life and death, the cycle of birth and rebirth, reincarnation."

The elevator came to a stop and the doors opened. Louie's apartment was a few feet away, probably five.

Danny unlocked the door. "I feel funny trespassing like this."

"It's not trespassing if you have a key."

"What if he has somebody in there with him? I don't want him to think I'm keeping tabs on him."

"If he's lying on the floor unconscious I'm sure he'll forgive you for your breach of social etiquette."

Entering the dark apartment, I felt along the wall for a light switch. *Where is that thing?*

Danny clapped his hands together; the place lit up like a Roman candle. "I gave it to him for Christmas."

All I got was a lousy Chia Pet.

We looked in all five rooms; Louie wasn't anywhere to be found.

"If he doesn't show up at work tomorrow morning I'm calling the police," I said in a futile attempt to feel the situation was under control.

Some posters strewn on the coffee table caught my attention. Louie was the tidiest man I ever met. He made Felix Unger look like a slob. When we toured in stock together he'd clean his room before housekeeping arrived. This uncharacteristic oversight told me he must have left in an awful hurry. I went over for a closer look.

The table was covered with autographed vintage posters from the nineteen-sixties, all in mint condition. Blobby psychedelic lettering of Day-Glo pink, yellow, orange and blue spelled out the names of such legendary clubs as the Café au Go Go, the hungry i, The Troubadour and The Fillmore. The lineup of acts they heralded was a who's who of rock and roll history—The Doors, The Byrds, Jefferson Airplane, The Who, Bob Dylan, Janis Joplin, and Lori Taylor. Each and every one of them was inscribed, "To Richard."

"I've changed my mind, I'm calling the pol ..." The sound of someone outside the front door distracted me. Reflexively, I clapped my hands and hid behind the sofa under cover of darkness. "Get down, Danny," I said in an urgent whisper.

"Whatever for?" my brother asked with a nonchalant clap of the hands. His immense intellect hadn't left much room for common sense.

"Because," I replied with an obstinate counter-clap.

The door opened, drawing our ineffectual duel to a close.

There was a new clapper in town. "Danny, what are you doing here?" Louie asked as the lights surged back on.

I emerged from my hiding place. "You had us worried to death."

"Afraid I was going to skip out on my bail?" Louie joked.

"Not funny," I reprimanded. "Where have you been? Why didn't you answer your cell?"

"The hospital prohibits cell phone usage. Guess I forgot to turn it back on."

"Are you ill?" Danny asked, concerned.

"No. I accompanied a mutual friend—Richard Baxter."

I took another quick look at the pop culture kitsch spread out over his coffee table. "Your friendship is going at a very cheap price these days."

Louie reacted defensively. "That collection is a worth a fortune. I think it was extremely generous of Richard to give it to me. The man's a genuine altruist."

"And cold-blooded killer," I added.

"Let's be fair. He should be presumed innocent until proven guilty," Danny weighed-in philosophically.

" 'Presumed' being the operative word here," I said with exaggerated sarcasm.

"No, he's definitely innocent. One hundred per cent, beyond a shadow of a doubt," Louie stated with unwavering certainty.

"Did you arrive at this conclusion before or after he bribed you?" I asked.

"He didn't bribe me. He didn't have to. He's not the father of Karen Hall."

This piece of information threw me for a loop. "Then why did he tell us she's his daughter?"

"Because he thought she was. He only discovered the truth today. His wife spilled the beans while they were in the middle of a heated argument."

"It must have been heated. We heard she nearly died in a fire tonight." I found this series of events to be very convenient.

"That's why we were at the hospital."

"How would his wife know the paternity of a child that isn't hers? He must be lying," I said.

"Richard wouldn't lie," Danny vouched.

"He's planning to take a blood test," Louie added.

"Of course, the blood test will confirm this fact because the Karen Hall run over by your SUV isn't his daughter; she's an imposter." *The man's a diabolical mastermind ... if you _tried_ to break up with him ... he killed you ... if you _wouldn't_ break up with him ... he killed you ... sort of a lose-lose situation for the women in his life ... he was doing the world a favor by becoming a monk ... the only thing I still don't understand ... why the need for an imposter?*

"Speaking of my SUV, Richard promised to talk with Barbara Goldberg and the police concerning my whereabouts on the night of the accident."

It appeared our murderous monk had wrapped everything up into a nice neat little package for himself, with the exception of one key proviso—the entire plan would unravel if either Karen Hall or his wife regained consciousness.

"Where is he now?" I asked Louie.

"I left him at UCLA Medical in the Trauma Center. He wanted to stay by his wife's side in case she came to."

"UCLA Medical's Trauma Center?" A knot twisted in my stomach. "Isn't that where they brought Karen Hall?"

"Yeah, they're in the same unit."

* * *

Danny opted to spend the rest of the night with Louie. Without the foggiest idea of what I planned to do upon arrival, I cruised by UCLA Medical Center before returning home. It was close to two-thirty in the morning when I pulled up to the gate of the visitor parking lot.

Once inside the facility, I checked-in with the staff working the graveyard shift. Those being treated at the Trauma Center may have preferred to call it the overnight shift.

"Excuse me, I'm here to see about Mrs. Richard Baxter. There was a fire at her residence. She was admitted a few hours ago."

The young man looked up from the book he was reading and scanned the list in front of him. "Here it is, Erica Baxter. Are you a relative?"

"No, a concerned friend."

"She's in stable but critical condition."

At least she's still alive.

"Visitation is restricted to family members only."

That doesn't bode well for her continued health. "I understand. Do you know if her husband is still here?"

"He left about thirty minutes ago."

"Do you expect him back tonight?"

"He didn't say."

"How is Karen Hall doing?"

He eyed me with caution. "You're not a reporter are you?"

I may have worn out my welcome. "You must get a lot of media sniffing around this place."

"Sure do," he said, revealing nothing.

Flattery may help oil the gears. "Must add extra pressure to an already trying job."

"Yeah, but no extra cash." He carefully appraised my reaction—waiting to receive an opening bid.

Who said talk's cheap … am I willing to resort to bribery? … sure … though pulling it off successfully requires some actual cash. "Have you ever been hypnotized?"

Looking thoroughly unimpressed, he shook his head.

"So what will twenty bucks get me?"

He picked up his book.

Nothing, I guess.

Foraging through my bag, my wallet, and my pockets, I managed to scrape together one ten, three fives, two ones, four quarters, five dimes, six nickels, and nine pennies.

"Forty-eight, eighty-nine." I slapped my hand down on the counter. "And that's my final offer."

"Hmm …" He carefully surveyed his booty before scooping it up. "All I can say is there was an incident involving the two women's husbands, Mr. Graham and Mr. Baxter."

"What happened?"

"Security was called and they were asked to leave the building."

"Why?"

He returned to his book; the info meter had expired.

Half asleep, I made my way back to the parking lot.

Richard Baxter is up to something … he sends Louie home … saying he plans to spend the night by his ailing wife's bedside … as soon as Louie's gone … he gets into some kind of altercation with Paul Graham.

I was too tired to think anymore. Rather than risk falling asleep while driving, I curled up in the backseat of my car for a short nap.

* * *

Faces known and unknown whirled through my mind. Overlapping sound bites from disembodied voices droned in my ear. I pulled away from my body, watching myself become one of a myriad of fleeting images drawn into the center of a spinning vortex. Growing dizzy, I felt nauseous before completely blacking out.

Reemerging from darkness, I had a sense of being somewhere while feeling like I was nowhere. There was a room—an office— with a large mahogany desk, black rotary dial phone and manual Remington typewriter. A nun wearing a full traditional habit sat behind the desk. A plain, dark-haired young woman of about twenty or so sat on the other side.

"So, Mrs. Baxter, if I understand correctly," the nun spoke to the young woman, "you and your husband are willing to adopt the Taylor baby."

"Yes, if my husband proves to be the child's natural father."

"And if he doesn't?"

"Oh, I never thought about that." She seemed somewhat surprised by the question. "Are the results from the blood test in?"

"Our main goal here at the orphanage is to see the child placed in a home where she is welcomed unconditionally." The nun probed Mrs. Baxter's face. "And, yes, I do have the test results. Was your husband not able to make it to our meeting today?"

"He's on the road." She appeared nervous, on edge. "I'll be taking care of the entire mes …" she caught herself, "matter."

"Richard Baxter is not the baby's father," the nun said.

Mrs. Baxter let out a sigh of relief. "Thank you, Sister." Then under her breath she muttered, "Thank you, God."

"Shall I begin drawing up the papers?"

"Is there a private phone I can use to contact my husband? He's waiting for my call."

"You may use mine. Let me get the operator on the line for you." The nun dialed 9, and then 0, before handing the receiver to Mrs. Baxter. "I'll wait outside," she said, leaving the room.

"I'd like to place a collect, person-to-person call to a Mr. Richard Baxter … He's a guest at the Edison Hotel in New York City … It's from his wife, Erica … Yes, I can hold."

Her face—underscored with a faraway tapping sound—beamed with joy.

"Hello, Richard … They just gave me the results."

She hesitated for a moment, becoming sullen; the aggravating patter grew louder.

"The baby's yours … It's all up to you now."

Her voice turned cruel and bitter.

"Which baby do you want to keep? Your management company or Lori's bastard?"

A self-satisfied aura surrounded her.

"I knew you'd come to your senses. You can always have another child, but my daddy's millions come with only one child—me."

The incessant knocking sound made it difficult for me to stay focused on the conversation.

"Do pass the good news along to dear Lori. Go out and celebrate on me. You've both made your down payment on a successful career in the music business. Just don't forget who the lienholder is ever again."

What's with all the banging?

* * *

"Lady, hello! Hello, lady! Rise and shine or pay the fine."

Is Erica Baxter talking to me? … in a different voice?

"Fork over the loot or I'll give you the boot."

I have to pee like nobody's business. Sitting up, I realized I wasn't at home in my cozy bed.

A large black face pressed up against my window. "Shake it or bake it. Move it or lose it. Let's keep it polite; no need for a fight."

"Who are you?" I asked the mystery rhymer.

The stranger stepped back from my car. I couldn't tell if this person was a man, a woman, or a transitional hybrid of the two. The uniform did manage to communicate that I was dealing with a parking attendant.

I rolled down the window. "Did anyone ever mention you have a habit of speaking in rhymes? I can help you with that," I said, taking out one of my cards.

The attendant eagerly reached through the window. "Are you a talent scout?"

"No. I'm a hypnotherapist."

This bit of news put a damper on the initial excitement of meeting me. Another chance for redemption was offered. "Are you on TV like Dr. Phil?"

"No."

"Then you owe me eight bucks."

The honeymoon was over. I forked over a ten. "Sorry, there wasn't anyone on duty when I pulled in." The balmy evening had given way to another humid day. "What time is it anyway?"

"Eight. Here's your change."

What do you know ... I actually got in five hours of undisturbed sleep ... that's a record for this week. "Thanks."

It was rush hour. My gas tank was low and my bladder full. I pulled into the nearest service station before trekking back into The Valley. While returning the restroom key, my attention was drawn to the TV set behind the counter. A local morning news program was doing an update of late-breaking celebrity gossip around town. Archival pictures of Paul Graham and Richard Baxter appeared on-screen.

"Now to 'the more things change' category," a reporter's smarmy voice boomed underneath the images. "Seems like time doesn't heal all wounds. Ex-music impresario, Richard Baxter, and faded folk-rocker, Paul Graham, were at each other's throats again. The melee broke out early this morning in the Trauma Center over at UCLA Medical. Due to a cruel twist of fate, both men's wives were being treated there for injuries sustained in recent unrelated accidents."

Pictures of Karen Hall and Erica Baxter replaced those of the men.

"The cause of this ad lib performance was none other than their proverbial old sticking point, Lori Taylor."

The camera cut to a split screen of an aging, sun-baked, pretty boy reporter next to a photo of Lori.

"Inside sources inform me that the ever mysterious Ms. Taylor has yet to put in an appearance at her ailing daughter's bedside. Does this behavior have former singing partner turned son-in-law, Graham, in a dither? Not in the least say eyewitnesses. However, he did take offense at Baxter's strident accusation that he was holding Taylor hostage. Neither man has been seen since hospital security shut down the production due to poor public notices. No one could be reached for comment."

Back at the car, I couldn't get Erica Baxter's face out of my mind. *She's older than I remember ... remember from where?*

A gas station attendant rapped on my window. "Hey, toots. I've got other customers waiting here."

I turned the key in the ignition, sparking my engine and my memory.

She was the young woman in my dream.

Though I was beginning to doubt whether it was a dream at all. This occurrence had the earmarkings of a Remote Viewing episode.

Why not run it by Ben? ... I'm spitting distance from his office.

* * *

Nancy was opening the office when I arrived.

"Roberta, what a surprise. Ben never told me you were coming by this morning."

I didn't know it was possible to surprise a psychic. Either I was becoming adept at running brain wave interference, or she was actually honoring her promise to exempt me from her up close and personal version of the Patriot Act. "It's more of a spur of the moment thing."

"Is that why you're wearing the same outfit you had on last night?" Ben's voice came from behind me. "Not that I don't like it, I just prefer it ironed."

I cast my eyes down upon my wrinkled, unkempt clothes and tried to surreptitiously catch a whiff of my breath. *Pooh!* Discreetly, I placed my hand over my garbage mouth.

Though I knew Ben was only teasing, my faux pas made me acutely aware of how my appearance contrasted with Nancy's quintessential California surfer girl perfection.

"I had another Remote Viewing encounter."

"This must be your Woodstock look," Ben joked. "Why are you talking through your hand?"

We walked into his private office.

"Can I get you anything, Roberta? Coffee? Facecloth?

"Okay, enough with the yuks. I'm yucky enough for both of us. I fell asleep in my car."

"Was Jack driving?"

"No. I was alone. In the UCLA Medical Center parking lot. Richard Baxter's wife was taken there last night after being rescued from a fire at their home. He may have set it to get her out of the way. I was hoping to bump into him at the hospital. He stole LaVonne's file from my office."

"It's fortunate you didn't find him. He may have harmed you." Ben sounded genuinely worried about my well-being. "What did the police have to say?"

"As you can see, I'm fine." Other than the crushing embarrassment my appearance was causing me, I never felt better deep down inside. There was something anomalously invigorating about this work. "I reported the file missing, but left it at that."

"Roberta, you're not a detective," Ben admonished. "This situation is getting dangerous." He picked up the receiver from the phone on top of his desk. "I'm calling Officer Sanchez."

"What are you going to tell him?"

"Uh ..." He stared blankly into space.

I knew that would stump him. "Let me rephrase the question. What are you going to tell him that he'll <u>believe</u>?" I folded my arms and tapped my foot, waiting for his response.

"Give me a second," he said with obvious aggravation. He put the receiver back in its cradle. "You win. I give up."

"Now that you understand my dilemma, can we move on to my latest Remote Viewing escapade?"

After reviewing all the details leading up to my Erica Baxter vision, Ben concurred with my assessment. "Your fatigue, combined with your unrelenting search for the truth, has created the optimal conditions for initiating unprompted Remote Viewing episodes. I may have to conduct a study on you."

I wouldn't object to an in-depth probe.

"Let's assume what you saw today did take place. And Karen Hall is not Richard Baxter's daughter."

"Assume? You're not sure?" His doubts unsettled me.

"Not one hundred percent. You could be filtering through information while sleeping—processing, sorting, and cataloguing whatever you can't make complete sense of while awake."

"But I recognized Erica Baxter, a woman I've never seen before."

"That you can <u>recall</u>. You may have seen her picture in a newspaper, a magazine, or on television. I've seen her before."

"You have? Where?"

"On the society pages."

Clearly, there's much left to discover about my fiery beau. "You read the society pages?" *Are they even called that anymore?*

"My mother has press clippings from various awards banquets and charity functions she's attended. Erica Baxter was at some of them. She's a trust fund baby."

"There's another thing I didn't know until my alleged dream took place." I felt vindicated by his revelation. "While on the phone, she bribed Richard with her daddy's millions."

"You may have read it alongside a picture."

"I only read the entertainment section," I blurted, proudly wearing my inexcusable ignorance like a badge of honor.

"And her husband headed a huge entertainment company bankrolled by her fortune."

"Why are you playing devil's advocate all of a sudden?"

"Part of my clinical training. If the rest of the world is ever going to take parapsychology seriously, stringent trial methods must be employed. Empirically speaking, ninety-nine percent of me believes you have been Remote Viewing. In spite of this, I can't simply ignore the remaining one percent of the equation. It should be easy enough to test though."

Huh?

Ben typed furiously on his computer keyboard; his keen intellect astonished me.

*He's probably devising an intricate mathematical formula and test-
ing procedure to verify our findings ... dressed to the nines ... we'll
humbly accept the Nobel Prize together.* "What are you doing?"

"I'm googling Richard Baxter.

Catch ya later, Nobel Prize. "How will that help?"

"It's amazing what you can find out about people nowadays. For
instance, say someone called me up and left an anonymous threat on
my voice mail."

*Something like this?... listen up, mister ... you have twenty-four
hours to get that celibate ass of yours in gear ... or I'll be forced to come
over there and jump start it for you.*

"Using the caller ID feature on my phone, I could get a hold of
their number. Then google it. And next thing you know—I have
their name, address, and a map with directions to their location."

*Good ... that'll give me time to chill some wine ... and slip into a
revealing ... yet flattering ...*

"Watch, I'll google your number."

A multi-colored street grid with a highlighted red star, pinpoint-
ing my house, appeared on Ben's monitor.

*Wonderful ... now I can go to bed at night ... and worry about be-
ing stalked by techno perverts and cyber voyeurs.* "I suppose that's how
Richard Baxter tracked me down."

"You said he got your address and phone number from Jack,"
Ben corrected.

"You're right. Guess he's an old-fashioned killer at heart."

"I've been meaning to ask you something. If Chicago Karen Hall isn't his daughter, doesn't that rule him out as your murderer? She did say it was her father who stabbed her."

"Well, Richard thought he was her father until Erica dropped the bombshell on him yesterday. She must have had the same misinformation," I said, defending my hypothesis.

Ben shook his head. "Doesn't fly. It's not kosher. Chicago Karen Hall discovered her fiancé was her father from the results of a premarital blood test—conclusive evidence. It was also a blood test that proved Richard wasn't the father of Lori Taylor's baby—more conclusive evidence. Leaving us stuck in a quandary with two contradictory conclusions, casting serious doubt on the guilt of Richard Baxter."

Damn that makes sense … I've got to start writing this stuff down. "Do you have a pen and paper?" Ben handed me a legal pad and ballpoint. "Run your premise by me again."

"Think about it. Either we're talking about two different men or something's faulty about your information."

"Meaning I dreamt Erica Baxter's meeting with the nun, your one percent factor?" The idea was disheartening but survivable.

"That's one explanation," he said, tentatively.

My other alternative was a lot less favorable. "LaVonne's suffering from an overactive imagination?"

"Or both, or neither."

"Aren't you glad I left the police out of the loop?" *Maybe I should slip that loop over my head and hang myself.* "Otherwise, I'd feel like a bigger fool right now."

"For what it's worth, I still think you're on to something here," Ben consoled.

"Yeah, but what?" I glumly asked. "I'm not a detective, remember?"

"You'll work it out." He glanced at his wristwatch. "Wish I could help you further, but I'm late for a conference call."

"That's all right, I have to get home and wash up before my first client. Can I keep the notepad?"

"Sure. I'll have Nancy look deeper into Richard Baxter's past."

" 'Look'—as in crystal ball?"

Ben raised an eyebrow. " 'Look'—as in source out some of this Google info."

"Don't stare at me that way," I said defensively. "It was an honest mistake."

CHAPTER THIRTEEN

MUCH TO MY AMAZEMENT, I made it through the rest of the day without difficulty. A humdrum nap at lunchtime was restorative, but lacked the vibrant luster of my Remote Viewing escapades. I wrapped up with my last client at four o'clock.

It was Friday, a week to the day since LaVonne Jefferson and Ben Cohen had walked into my life. They transformed my black-and-white, mono existence into a pulsating, digitally enhanced, Technicolor extravaganza. There were drawbacks though; nothing made sense in this topsy-turvy world. No easy answers, no reliable compasses. I had to chart my own course and trust it would lead me in the right direction.

Under the heading—"WHAT I KNOW"—I jotted notes on the yellow legal pad:

1) Chicago Karen Hall—Lori Taylor's dead daughter— was murdered by her fiancé/father on the fourteenth of February, nineteen ninety-three.

2) Richard Baxter—Lori Taylor's former manager and lover—is not Karen Hall's father.

3) LA Karen Hall—Lori Taylor's hospitalized daughter—is an imposter.

4) Paul Graham—Lori Taylor's old singing partner—is the husband of her imposter daughter.

5) All roads lead to Lori Taylor. She's the key to solving this mystery.

FOOTNOTE – Lori Taylor is suffering from Alzheimer's.

Dead end … examine other options … LA Karen Hall must know something … she's trying to pass herself off as a dead woman … she may soon be a dead woman herself … does Paul Graham know what she's up to? … he did engineer the entire mother-daughter reunion … what about Erica Baxter? … she definitely knows LA Karen's faking it … is that why she ended up in critical care? … but, who put her there? … probably the person responsible for running over LA Karen … what if both accidents are nothing more than, accidents? … the only people left to talk to about any of this are Paul Graham and Richard Baxter … I've left a message for one … and don't know where to find the other.

There it was all laid out before me on paper and I was still no further ahead.

Stick to what you know, Roberta … hypnosis … I need to put La-Vonne back into trance … and get a name from her … except Reverend Jefferson won't let me anywhere near his daughter … if I was more adept at this Remote Viewing business … I could transport myself back to the scene of the crime … and take a look at the perpetrator.

I placed a call to Sharon Jefferson.

"Hello, Sharon. It's Roberta. How's LaVonne doing?"

"She slept soundly last night," Sharon replied with relief.

"What about Reverend Jefferson?"

"I'm sure he's dog-tired. He spent the night praying over her."

"Can't he see how much she's improved since we started doing our work together?"

"He's claiming last night's slumber triumph for the Lord."

"Then another session is still out of the question?" I asked dejectedly.

"The man makes Jerry Falwell look like a liberal. I've agreed to let LaVonne spend the next week with him. If she doesn't show continued improvement, he's promised to allow me to proceed as I see fit. I told you he'd come around."

My hands were tied. There was nothing left to do, but wait. If I were correct about Richard Baxter's culpability for the break-in at my office, along with the recent rash of accidents and the murder in Chicago, LaVonne would be safer with her father. Reverend Jackson's address and phone number weren't listed in her stolen file. I hesitated bringing up the topic with Sharon. My conjecture didn't need to be the cause for unwarranted panic.

"Roberta, thank you for freeing my little girl. I know the nightmares have stopped due to your efforts."

"Don't thank me, yet. They may still return," I cautioned her.

"Not if Karen keeps her promise. During trance she said LaVonne's torment would stop when her murderer was discovered. Yesterday you did just that and my daughter slept like a baby for the first time in weeks."

"I sincerely hope you're right. According to my recollection, Karen said she would stop the day her murderer was <u>caught</u>. If it's who I think it is, as far as I can tell, he's still at large. One more session with LaVonne would confirm or deny my suspicion. Maybe then we'd have something solid to present to the police. I consulted with my brother on this case; he thinks I have the wrong guy."

"Your brother?"

"Yes, Dr. Daniel Law. He's a psychiatrist and somewhat of an authority in the field of past life research."

"I've heard the name before. Didn't he write a book?"

"Several."

"I wish there was something more I could do to help. That poor woman's bloody, battered face still haunts me after all these years."

Sharon's words hit me like a triple espresso. "There is something you can do. Let me hypnotize you."

"I don't understand. What good would that do?" she asked, stunned by my extraordinary request.

"You were there."

"I told you I didn't see anything."

"You saw someone run out of the alley. We can work with that image. Have you ever heard of Remote Viewing?"

We set up an appointment for Saturday afternoon.

It was after six. I had promised to pick up Danny and Louie at seven for dinner. We'd made plans to eat in Toluca Lake, so I needed to get a move on.

* * *

Bumper-to-bumper traffic greeted us as we turned off Riverside Drive and into the parking lot at Mo's restaurant. I'd forgotten Friday was classic car night at the Bob's Big Boy across the street.

"Isn't that Jack and his Thunderbird over there by the bevy of carhops?" Louie asked as the valet handed me a parking chit.

I squinted past the scores of muscle cars, hot rods and dune buggies. My bass-playing gasman was working the adoring crowd, handing out pictures and signing autographs.

"You know, I didn't notice the other night when I met him," Danny casually remarked, "that guy looks a lot like the bass player from Sound Squadron."

"He is!" Louie and I confirmed in astonishment.

"You remember him, but you forget Paul Graham?" Louie added.

"What can I say? I was a Sound Squadron fan. The longer I'm off my meds, the clearer my memory."

Louie gave Danny a slight kick.

"Are you crazy?" I cried. *Poor choice of words.*

"According to some," Danny said dryly.

"Come on. Let's say, hi." Louie pulled Danny away from me, in an effort to shield him from the torrent of my foreseeable wrath. "Jack, how's it going?" he shouted out.

They weren't going to get off the hook that easily. I followed them across the street.

"I hear you met Roberta's brother, Danny, last night," Louie said.

"More like early this morning," I chimed in.

"He's a big fan of yours," Louie continued.

"You've got great taste in music, bro." Jack gave me a lustful once-over. "And sisters. Glad I bumped into you, Red. I'm doin' some promotion for my Hell's Papas gig in Reseda tomorrow night. See ya' at midnight." He handed me an autographed picture. "Details are on back."

"We wouldn't miss it for the world," Louie answered for me. "I need a good rock and roll band on my roster."

I looked askance at Louie. "You represent actors."

"Lots of musicians crossover to acting—J.Lo, Britney Spears, Ice Cube, Will Smith," Louie listed.

"Elvis, Mick, Bowie," Jack continued.

Apparently ... my brother isn't the only mentally unbalanced member of our group.

"We're on our way to Mo's. Why don't you join us for dinner?" Louis asked. He knew I wouldn't get into an argument with Danny in front of a virtual stranger. "We'd love to hear more about the band."

"Scarf down a burger and a brew with my babe?" Jack wrapped a predatory paw around me. "Bodacious."

"Copacetic." I gritted my teeth and cast a dirty look Louie's way.

"Are you two seeing each other?" Danny asked ingenuously.

"On and off," Jack said playfully.

"What about Ben?" Danny asked.

Jack gave my rump a possessive slap. "He's on, when I'm off."

"Well, sis, I didn't know twin flames were allowed to burn the candle at both ends. If you're not careful, you'll run out of wax."

"No need to fret." Jack proudly patted his privates. "My wick's renown."

"Tell me about it!" I unwittingly babbled, recollecting our Woodstock get together.

"I read some groupies made a bronze cast of it," Louie zestfully contributed, relishing the marriage of his two favorite topics—penis and trivia.

"Can we talk about something else?" I begged.

Jack obliged my request. "So where ya think Lori Taylor is?"

"I'm sure she's quite distraught about her daughter's accident," I said protectively. "When she's emotionally able to handle it, she'll visit her in the hospital."

"She better hurry," Jack said. "Heard on the radio Karen almost died today."

The color drained from Louie's face. "I really need Richard to come through for me now."

"He will," Danny said confidently.

I was still odd man out on the Richard Baxter issue.

"The hospital said it was an oversight. One of her machines came unplugged." Jack paused. "I don't see how takin' off's gonna help things. Lori always was an unpredictable sorta chick."

"What do you mean by 'takin' off'?" I asked.

"Vamoose, amscray, frappez la route. She hit the road," Jack replied. "The media's all over it. Paul Graham's offerin' a reward for any information on her whereabouts. He says she may be behavin' erratically—like that's news."

"Poor Paul," I empathized. *No wonder he hasn't gotten back to me.* "He already had enough to handle with his wife being hospitalized." *Lori's Alzheimer's is way too much for him to deal with on his own.*

* * *

After dinner we parted ways with Jack. He wanted to finish promoting his Reseda gig and I was bushed. Louie and Danny graciously agreed to spend the night in my guest room. I still hadn't replaced the locks on my living room window, and I knew I'd have a more restful sleep with some company in the house. Louie turned in first, giving me the opportunity to get some more of Danny's input on LaVonne's case.

"How can you be so positive about Richard Baxter's innocence?" I asked.

"My years of experience have taught me a thing or two about human behavior and motivation. The man who committed this crime is a classic psychopath. I'm willing to wager we have some schizophrenic undertones operating here. If there are blackouts involved he may not even be aware of his actions, or may only remember them as part of a distant nightmare."

"From what Jack's told me, the guy's a supreme son of a bitch," I countered.

"In his youth, by his own admission, Richard Baxter was a greedy opportunist. The man had an authentic epiphany when he was in rehab a number of years ago; it transformed his life. Doesn't your Remote Viewing incident with his wife verify he isn't your culprit?"

"I suppose so."

"Are you planning on pursuing this further with the child? The key to solving this crime is still locked inside her."

"Her father won't allow any more sessions. He's opposed to hypnosis for religious reasons."

"It may be best to respect his wishes. The Wheel of Karma will eventually take care of this matter without any help from you."

"I don't think her mother's willing to wait that long."

"Would you like me to speak with her?" Danny asked, missing my sarcasm.

Though the proposal sounded well-intentioned, I had long grown out of needing big brother to rescue me from problematic situations in my life.

"I've got things under control." *Not bad ... I almost believe that myself.*

* * *

"Lex, stop barking." My brother's voice carried into my darkened bedroom. "Uncle Danny will give you a biscuit."

The clock on the bedside table said six a.m. Other than my afternoon appointment with Sharon Jefferson, my schedule was clear.

Go back to sleep ... Danny knows his way around your kitchen.

The reassuring clatter of pots and pans lulled me back into slumber.

* * *

The tempting aroma of fresh coffee and hot bacon reawakened my nose. Then my stomach. And, finally—me. It was more than I could resist.

Early as it is … I have to get up … nothing's stopping me from climbing right back into bed after breakfast … Danny and Louie won't mind … after a quick bite … they'll be on their way … anxious to enjoy their weekend together.

I put on a robe and went to join my visiting chefs.

"Look who's up," Louie said. "I was about to bring you breakfast in bed. Don't you have any clients today?"

"Not until two o'clock."

"Cutting it close." Louie held up two eggs. "Fried, scrambled, or poached."

"Poached. Why am I cutting it close?"

"It's one in the afternoon."

"No way," I objected. "I heard Danny poking around in here about an hour ago."

"Don't think so." Louie pointed at the clock in my microwave. "He left hours ago."

"I must have been really out of it," I said, pouring myself a coffee.

"You were. In addition to short order cook, I took it upon myself to act as your personal secretary." He handed me some message slips.

Ben and Nancy called. "Why do they both say they'll see me tonight? We haven't made any plans."

246

"I invited them to join us at the Double D Club in Reseda."

Jack's euphemism for the demise of his rock and roll career came to mind. "For an old-fashioned evening of drugs and disco?"

"Drugs, maybe. Disco, I doubt. Hell's Papas doesn't strike me as the name of the next KC and the Sunshine Band."

"Louie, you didn't? I was going to take a pass."

Clubbing in Reseda is about as appealing as a vacation trip to Barstow.

"Come on, Roberta. It'll be fun, like old times. Danny promised me he'd be there."

"Where is Danny?"

"He woke me up at five-thirty saying someone had called him. There was important business he had to attend to."

"What kind of call?" I asked warily. Danny had been known to receive calls from ethereal voices prompting him into dubious actions. "Did you hear a phone ring?"

"No, I was asleep."

Louie's stubborn naiveté concerning my brother's mental illness frustrated the hell out of me. "How long has he been off his meds?" I snapped.

"I don't know. The first I heard about it was yesterday morning."

I studied Louie's face looking for the faintest hint of deceit or collusion in his eyes. "You swear to Judy Garland?"

"Yes," he said without vacillating.

"I hope he's not slipping into another episode. He promised to meet us at the club tonight?" Danny had an obsession about keeping his word; even a mental haze wouldn't deter him from honoring it.

"He took down the address before he left."

Seemed I had no choice but to attend the festivities at the Double D Club.

Ben may be able to subtly assess Danny …and help me wrestle him into a straitjacket … if it looks like he's approaching the point of no return.

Two pieces of sourdough bread popped up from the toaster.

Louie reached for the butter dish. "You're out of jam."

"I know. Thanks for making me breakfast."

"Brunch," he corrected.

I sat at the dining room table. Louie set a plate down in front of me. Dropping the phone messages, I picked up a fork and dug into my meal. The back of one of the notes caught my eye. Louie had drawn a small heart and beside it he'd written, "Ford '93."

"What's this?" I passed him the paper.

"Nancy wanted you to know Richard Baxter checked himself into the Betty Ford Center on Valentine's Day, nineteen ninety-three."

How could he have been in two places at once? … two places nowhere near each other. "You and Danny were right about Richard Baxter. He's innocent. Chicago Karen Hall was murdered on Valentine's Day."

* * *

After wolfing down brunch, I jumped into the shower, dressed, and was in my office by two minutes to two. It was all up to Sharon Jefferson now. I intended to turn back the clock, regress her to the night of the murder, and then convert it into a Remote Viewing. If I had her arrive at the scene earlier, she'd be able to get a better look at the murderer as he exited the alley.

Having never done anything quite like this before, I was more than a little apprehensive. Experimenting on clients was not my standard M.O.

The doorbell rang; I went to the door.

"Hi, Roberta." Sharon entered my office and took a seat. "I just spoke with Frank. LaVonne's had another good night."

"I'm glad to hear that. However, since we haven't completed our work, there's no guarantee this will last." *Best to err on the side of caution.*

"Oh, I understand. Getting Frank to understand is the problem. Maybe your brother will be able to talk some sense into him."

"My brother?"

"Yes. You mentioned you had consulted with him. I was surprised to see him show up at my house though."

I never gave him Sharon's address ... he must've poked around in my office to find it. "When was he there?"

"Early this morning, I was just getting home from work."

"Please excuse my brother, Sharon. He's prone to overzealousness." *That's the understatement of the year.*

"He was a bit wild-eyed," she said reflectively. "Poor man was worried sick about LaVonne. Said he knew of a way to stop those nightmares permanently. I told him she was doing fine, but he said he needed to see for himself."

If I wasn't certain before, this confirmed it. Danny was in full tilt wig-out mode. "Sorry he disturbed you. My brother's getting together with me tonight, I'll make sure this never happens again."

"He asked for Frank's address. I gave him his phone number. Frank doesn't appreciate unannounced callers, which I always thought was pretty nervy for a person who doesn't think twice about going door-to-door spreading the Good News."

"Will you excuse me for a moment," I said, exiting my office in search of Louie.

He was in the living room watching *A Star Is Born*, the Streisand version. "Did you know Barbra originally wanted Elvis for the Kris Kristofferson role? Colonel Parker talked him out of it."

"I don't have time for trivia. You've got to find Danny. He's out of control."

"Relax, we'll see him tonight." He continued watching the movie.

I picked up the remote and turned off the TV.

"What you go and do that for?" he protested. "It's coming to my favorite part, when they spray paint 'Esther' backwards on the staircase wall."

"It can wait. This is more important."

Louie reached for the remote. "Now play nice or Santa won't bring you TiVo for Christmas."

"Danny unexpectedly showed up at the home of one of my clients this morning. He's acting strangely and I need to stop him before he runs my practice into the ground."

"What can I do about it? My driving license is still suspended."

I handed him the phone. "Call him on his cell."

"He lost it."

"If his phone's missing how'd he manage to receive a call on it this morning?" We looked at each other uneasily; the answer was glaringly apparent. "Try the Zen Center. If he's not up there, see if anyone knows where he is. I'll be back to help you after I finish with my session."

When I returned to my office, Sharon was fast asleep in the recliner.

"I'm back," I said, lightly tapping her on the shoulder.

She jumped back into awareness. "What happened?"

"You fell asleep."

"Was I able to identify the killer?"

"Don't know. I haven't put you into trance yet. Do you want to postpone?"

She shook her head. "It's those extra shifts at the hospital. I'm not as young as I once was, it takes me longer to get used to them. I have to report back to the hospital at eleven tonight. Could you throw in a few suggestions for vitality?"

"You got it. Shall we begin?"

"Will you tape it for me?"

"Thanks for reminding me." I got up and put a blank tape in the recorder. "This may be the only evidence we ever get."

Fearful she would drift back to sleep while in hypnosis, I put the renewed energy suggestions in prior to regressing her. I wanted her to be alert and observant when she returned to the alley.

"Sharon, visualize or imagine a large picture window. A gigantic calendar hangs near this window. With your consent, we're going to travel back to the year nineteen ninety-three."

She languidly lifted her head up from off her chest and let it drop back down, giving the okay.

"One by one, the calendar pages fall away. As they do, the world spins backward in space. Look through the window, watch the seasons whirl by. Feel yourself grow younger. Count off the fading years as they fly past. Ten—nine—eight—seven, each number bringing you closer to our final destination."

Her breathing was measured. I lifted one of her arms and let it drop lifelessly to her side. She had crossed over from alpha mind state deep into theta.

"Six—five—four—three, when I reach zero it will be nineteen ninety-three and you'll be living in Chicago. Two—one—zero— deep sleep!" I snapped my fingers. "Sharon, look out the window. It's winter. The month is February, Valentine's Day to be exact. In a moment, we'll revisit a place you were at long ago."

Appearing agitated, she twitched nervously in the recliner. Symptoms of anticipatory anxiety brought on by an awareness of what happened on this day.

"Before we venture outdoors, an invisible, protective shield will encase your entire body. No harm can come to you while you wear this shield. In fact, no one will be able to see you. Inside this, you are safe."

She relaxed back into the chair.

"All right, Sharon. The shield is forming. There's a full-length mirror behind you. Turn to look at yourself. No one is there; you're completely invisible to others. Outside the picture window, you see a deserted street near an alley. It's late at night. You pass through the window undetected, and stand near the alley. A crime is taking place. In a moment, a man will run from the alley. You will see him. Not only will you see him, you will also recognize him. Look directly at him, his face will be clear as day. When I ask you his name, you will identify him." Not knowing if there'd be another prospect of getting this information, I wanted to ensure a positive ID. "When you are ready, nod your head."

Her head made an almost imperceptible bob.

I crossed my fingers—hoping—needing this to work. "You hear footsteps, the man is darting from the alley. Do you see him?"

"Yes," Sharon mumbled.

"Take a good look at him. Sear his image on your brain."

Tears welled up in her eyes. "A woman's screaming. She needs my help."

"You are helping her. Describe the man to me." I wanted to elicit a description while it was still fresh in her mind. "Whom do you see?"

"I see me."

"You?" I wasn't expecting that. "How? You're invisible."

"Across the street, on my way to work."

Of course she sees herself . . . she was there that night.

A horrendous scream cut through the stillness of the room. Sharon's body erupted into violent convulsions.

"What's wrong?" I yelled over the tumult.

The brutal thrashing continued unabated.

Seeing herself set off a fierce chain reaction … if I don't bring her out fast … she could disassociate … and spiral into a full-blown personality break.

I plugged the handheld microphone into my tape deck and switched on the PA function.

"Sharon, you are no longer in Chicago." My voice exploded through the speakers. "You are in Los Angeles. Nineteen ninety-three is long past. It is the present. You have a ten-year-old daughter—LaVonne."

Hearing her daughter's name quelled the riot inside her. She lay there panting and sweating, but in trance nevertheless.

My heart raced, I knew it was time to bring her out. Yet, I found myself resisting, unable to leave without getting what I was after.

I put down the mic. "Can you hear me, Sharon?"

She stirred ever so slightly.

"Sharon, can you hear me?" I asked forcefully.

"Yes." The voice was frail and hollow.

"You are floating on a cloud of peace in a sea of love. All cares, concerns and worries are gone. They have been replaced by a profound calm."

Her brow unfurrowed.

"Allow the serenity to soak through you, enveloping every muscle, nerve, fiber and cell of your being. In this place, fear and pain do not exist. Events from your life may be viewed safely, without emotion or judgment."

Her breathing returned to a light theta range. She had reached homeostasis.

"Sharon, earlier you saw a man; without recalling the event, evoke his face. Can you see him?"

"Yes," she whispered.

"Tell me whom you see."

"Your brother."

She must have gotten her wires crossed. "Chicago—nineteen ninety-three—a man runs from an alley. Whom do you see?"

"Dr. Daniel Law." Her torso quivered.

I recalled the "Jane Doe Murder" clipping in Ben's blue folder. On back was the article about Danny's appearance on *Oprah*. He was in Chicago at the time of the murder. It was a month before he experienced his first psychotic breakdown.

"You are floating on a cloud of peace in a sea of love. I'm going to count up from one to five. When I reach five you will be fully aware, awake and refreshed." I shut off the tape recorder. "Except for an overall feeling of well-being, your conscious mind will have forgotten everything that took place here today. One, two, three, four, five. Eyes open, wide awake!"

Sharon squinted, readjusting to the light in my office. Yawning, she stretched her arms and legs. "I feel fantastic. What did you do?"

"Nothing special. Just what you requested, a few suggestions for vitality," I replied with a gnawing sense of guilt.

"I may have to schedule another appointment, if this is how I can expect to feel afterwards." She reached for her purse and took out a checkbook. "May I borrow your pen?"

"This one's on me."

"No, that wouldn't be right."

"I insist. It's my way of making amends for the tape. It started to unravel inside the machine, I had to stop recording."

"Too bad. I was going to listen to it on my break."

"Next time."

"Did it work? Were you able to find anything out?"

I sucked back what remained of my integrity. "No, regrettably. It was a long shot to begin with."

"Let's pray Frank's right and LaVonne's nightmares are over."

"Why don't you leave me his address and phone number? I'll feel better if I can check in on them." *And make sure they're still alive.*

CHAPTER FOURTEEN

R EVEREND FRANK JEFFERSON'S phone line was terminally busy. There's something plain wrong about a person who doesn't have call waiting. Wanting to reach him before my brother did, I placed my first call the instant Sharon Jefferson left my office. Ten calls later, I was starting to have second thoughts.

Would Danny hurt LaVonne? ... could Danny hurt LaVonne? ... my brother's not a violent person ... all this regression and Remote Viewing business could turn out to be a load of supernatural hogwash ... false memory syndrome must be at play here ... hypnosis isn't a foolproof tool for gathering facts ... the California judicial system declared testimony obtained in this manner inadmissible in court ... why should I accept it as gospel truth?

I replayed the tape I made during Sharon's session. Some of my questions could be considered leading, lacking in clinical objectivity. Others were somewhat dubious in their interpretation and capable of producing false assumptions, unfounded conclusions.

One suggestion in particular echoed back at me—"Sharon, earlier you saw a man; without recalling the event, evoke his face."

Danny was at her house in the morning; she may not have understood which event I was referring to. Or another plausible scenario—if unable to make out the face of the man who ran from the alley, it's likely she would fill in the blank with some other face lodged in her subconscious. One that was fresh and accessible. Hypnotic subjects are eager to please.

Having convinced myself of Danny's innocence, I began to contemplate his guilt. *Could he have had a child by Lori Taylor? ... the baby was born in Chicago ... he's never lived in Chicago ... Lori toured a lot ... conception could have taken place anywhere ... he was a teenager ... it was the sixties ... a sexual revolution was underway ... okay ... I'll give the possibility a yes ... no ... not possible ... Danny's gay ... yes ... possible ... Danny came out of the closet when I was a teenager ... back in the seventies ... he dated lots of women ... however ... Jane Doe was impregnated in the nineties ... he was involved with Louie then.*

Last evening's conversation with Danny resonated in my head—"The man who committed this crime is a classic psychopath; I'm willing to wager we have some schizophrenic undertones operating here. If there are blackouts involved, he may not even be aware of his actions or may only remember them as part of a distant nightmare."

Danny was diagnosed with schizophrenia after going to the doctor complaining about blackouts ... was he unknowingly trying to tell me something?

I called Reverend Jefferson one last time. *Still busy.*

I walked into the living room and checked back with Louie. "Is he at the Zen Center?"

"No. They said he's visiting his sister in LA."

"Will you come with me to Orange County? For my own peace of mind, I have to make sure he's not there."

"And if he is there?" Louie asked.

"Pray to God nothing's happened."

* * *

An hour later we were in Orange County pulling into the driveway of a green stucco bungalow. I'd tried calling a few more times before we arrived, but continued to be thwarted by a persistent busy signal. Not wanting to cause a greater commotion, I decided not to share the full extent of my qualms with Louie. The only thing that mattered to me was making sure LaVonne wasn't in any danger.

"Who's place did you say this was?" Louie asked as I rang the doorbell.

"I didn't say." It was getting rather challenging to maintain client anonymity. "I just need to make sure Danny isn't here."

No one came to the door. I rang twice more and knocked. Nothing.

"Looks like nobody's home." Louie turned to leave.

"Hold on." I reached for my cell. "Let me call again."

Louie waited on the walkway.

"Beep, beep, beep!" I said, my aggravation level going up a decibel or two. "Why do I keep getting a busy signal if no one's home?"

"Blame Moses," a female voice responded. An elderly African-American woman was watering a bed of flowers on one of the adjoining properties. "He's always knocking phones off the hook. Caught him doing it in my house one day. Had to chase him out with a broom."

Another religious fanatic … I must be a magnet for them.

"That cat has some serious attitude." She finished her watering and turned off the hose. "If you're looking for the Rev, he's not there. He and his daughter are spending the weekend at the Big Tent."

"Camping?" I asked.

She let out a laugh. "The Rev isn't much of a one for camping. That'd be too much fun. They're up at the Big Tent Revival in Claremont."

"When do you expect them back?" I asked.

She gave Louie and me the once-over. "Are you two Jehovah's Witnesses?"

"No," I said defensively.

"Too bad," she sighed. "I don't suppose you're Mormons?"

Is this poor woman lonely? … in search of human companionship … regardless of what strings may be attached?

We shook our heads.

"Didn't think so," she said dolefully. "I love to watch the competition get a rise out of that old bag of wind."

Evidently, I had misconstrued her true intentions.

"I'm a friend," I explained.

She frowned and looked at me dubiously. *As if to say—I may be old, but that doesn't mean I'm stupid, honey.*

"Of his ex-wife," I added.

My qualifier put a smile on her lips. "How's she doing? Lord, I miss that woman."

"She's fine."

"Will you tell her Betty Robinson was asking after her?"

"I will." With the social niceties out of the way, I returned to my main mission. "Is the Reverend returning soon?"

"Don't expect him back till late Sunday; his whole congregation's up there with him. Not much point coming back to preach in an empty church."

I could relax for a while; LaVonne was safely tucked away. Her father didn't have a cell phone. If you didn't know where he was, there'd be no way to reach him.

"The Rev's mighty popular today. You're the second person to come by looking for him."

Break's over ... back to being stressed. "Did you speak with this person?"

"After a fashion, told me he was a doctor. But when I asked him about my bursitis, he didn't know a thing about it. Said he wasn't that kind of doctor."

"Was he a psychiatrist?" Louie asked.

"I thought you were a mute," she responded.

That's a first.

261

"He looked like he should be <u>seeing</u> a psychiatrist. Not quite right in the noggin," she said, knocking on her head. "He'd fit in just fine at the Rev's church."

"Did you tell him about the Big Tent Revival?" I asked.

"Not on your life!" She seemed astounded by the sheer audacity of such a suggestion. "I'm not doing any recruiting for that group. The world's got enough troubles on its plate without shoveling on another mound of Holy Roller cornpone. I'll be eighty next month. Those people've been carrying on about the last days long before I came into this world, and they'll still be shouting about it long after I'm gone."

I hadn't just touched a sore spot; I'd ignited her entire central nervous system.

"If our days on this good Earth are dwindling, all the more reason to party till you drop. When the train of life pulls out of the station, you'll find me in the bar car."

It wasn't difficult to imagine her with a cocktail in one hand, a cigarette holder in the other, surrounded by a host of adoring studs. This old woman was more Auntie Mame than Grandma Walton.

"You wouldn't happen to know where in Claremont the event is being held, would you?" I had to reach them first; Danny was resourceful and would figure out where they were before long.

She carefully sized me up.

"I'm not planning on joining," I offered, attempting to assuage her fears.

"What about you?" she curtly asked a shrinking Louie.

"Me? I doubt they'd want me. I'm gay."

A wide grin graced her dour face. "I wish I could go along with the both of you, but tonight's my tango lesson. Give me a moment, I'll look for the leaflet the Rev left me." She moved toward her front door. "I'm pretty sure I know where I put it."

Betty returned holding a badly soiled sheet of paper by the corner. "Sorry for the muck, I used it to wrap up some catfish heads. It does my heart good when I can turn useless garbage into trash with a purpose."

* * *

"Why the rendezvous with Elmer Gantry?" Louie asked me on the drive to Claremont. "Betty said she didn't tell Danny where they were, and even if she did, he wouldn't know who to look for."

Perhaps I was being overcautious. Reverend Jefferson thought I was in cahoots with the Antichrist. My showing up at his religious celebration wasn't going to earn me any holy medals. But, if he had to choose between that and being killed by my brother, I felt certain he would excuse the intrusion.

"Have you ever seen Danny lose his temper or fly off the handle?"

"Plenty of times," Louie responded.

"I mean violently. Did you ever see him hurt anybody physically?"

"Danny? He wouldn't let me use a flyswatter in the house." Louie shot me a wary glance. "Is that why we're on this wild goose chase? You think Danny's going to harm someone?"

"I don't know. He may be sicker than we realize."

"It's not in his nature, mental illness or no mental illness."

In my heart of hearts I knew Louie was right, but a niggling feeling persisted nonetheless. A woman with an apparent link to LaVonne was brutally murdered in the past, and two women with a connection to the victim were in the hospital clinging to life. A clear and present danger charged the atmosphere; when and where it would strike again was anyone's guess.

Forty minutes later we pulled into the city of Claremont. Using directions on the flier Betty gave us, we navigated our way to the site of the Big Tent Revival. Wending along the broad tree-lined streets of the Disneyesque community, it was inconceivable this slice of small-town Americana could be situated so close to the urban sprawl that is Los Angeles.

"Don't Wally and the Beaver live somewhere around here?" Louie joked.

We turned a corner and came upon a large park area packed with tents and booths and people. Brightly colored balloons and banners, proclaiming—"JESUS IS LORD!" and "HAVE YOU BEEN SAVED?" and "THIS WAY TO THE RAPTURE"—wafted on a warm inland breeze, accompanied by the raucous strains of a gospel choir. My Beetle chugged itself into an open spot between two mini-vans.

"Aren't you coming?" I asked Louie as I stepped out of the car.

"Maybe I should wait here. I didn't notice any rainbow streamers on display out there."

"It's too hot to stay in the car. I could also use your help searching for LaVonne and her father. This is quite a sizable crowd."

"I know; that's why I'm staying put. I don't want to see them turn into an angry mob. Ozzie and Harriet aren't the type to socialize with Will and Grace."

"How will they know you're gay? We'll institute a policy of 'Don't Ask, Don't Tell.'"

Louie seemed unconvinced.

"The sooner I find them, the sooner we leave."

Begrudgingly, he opened the door. "I'm only doing this for Danny's sake. He doesn't need to make another religious conversion. Zen Buddhism suits him."

"Do you think he's here?" I asked with apprehension.

"If you're right and he's going off his rocker again, this would be one of the first places I'd look for him. It wouldn't shock me to pick up a program and see him listed as keynote speaker."

"That's a great idea." I towed Louie over to an information kiosk. "The Reverend may be scheduled to speak."

"Whoopee," Louie said with mock delight. "I can hardly wait."

"The Lord does work in mysterious ways," I said, scanning the packed agenda. "He's speaking right now in the main tent."

It took us ten minutes to make it over to the massive red, white and blue canvass pavilion nicknamed Camp Christ. We pressed our way in among the sweating, swaying, shouting multitude.

"I never knew Jesus was American," Louie said, surveying the patriotic paraphernalia, intermingled with crosses, decorating the interior of the tent.

"And a Republican to boot," I said, pointing up at the stage. Reverend Jefferson was framed by a big screen image of the Savior on one side and President Dubya on the other.

"Praise the Lord and pass the ammunition!" Louie hollered, much to my chagrin.

The remark was greeted by some random "Hallelujah, brothers" and "Amens" as we melted into the inflamed multitude.

"We need to get closer to the front," I said. "Or he may disappear on us once he's finished speaking."

Louie motioned toward the aisle that ran up the center of the tent. "Looks like there's only one way to get there."

People flowed from the back, front and sides, magnetically progressing toward the awaiting Reverend Jefferson. One by one, he placed his hands upon each new arrival's head and their bodies instantly crumpled at his feet. This was the greatest display of mass hypnosis I'd ever witnessed.

"I've see him somewhere before," Louie said, moving into the aisle. "Does he do this on TV?"

"Maybe."

"I'm going up for a better look. Are you coming?"

I felt my body being pushed toward Louie.

"Go with your husband, sister," an unknown voice urged. "Be slain as a couple in the Spirit before burying yourselves in the waters of baptism."

Can't say I like the sound of that.

It was too late to turn back. My body, caught up in the tide of mounting religious fervor, moved along without my assistance.

What am I going to do once I reach the Reverend? … what will he do? … his eyes are closed … maybe I can sneak by without causing too much of a scene … I'll wait for him behind the stage.

"I'm sure I know this guy," Louie said, fast approaching the moment of truth. He stood three souls away from redemption.

"Let's get out of line while we still have a chance." I grabbed ahold of Louie. "I came here to save LaVonne, not to be saved myself."

"He looks a bit like one of the old Motown R&B artists. This could be a potentially rare autograph find. I need to get closer."

Two linebacker-sized ushers cleared away the fallen body of a rather rotund woman in a shocking pink tank top and leopard print capris. She was crying and shouting, "Jesus saves," over and over again.

Louie stepped into her vacated spot. "Wal-Mart saves you more."

I froze, hoping no one heard his flip remark.

Reverend Jefferson roared, "Did you say something, brother?" He opened his eyes and looked straight at Louie.

Half expecting Louie to be smited right then and there, I tensed up and backed away from the sacrificial lamb. No one needed to know he had come there with me.

Holding his ground, Louie gave the Reverend a questioning look and responded with one simple word, "Frankie?"

"Lou?" Reverend Jefferson replied in stupefaction, and fell to the ground at Louie's feet.

The audience went wild. En masse they pushed toward the stage. I couldn't tell whether they were planning to crucify or deify Louie. The linebackers snapped into action and whisked the Reverend out of sight.

Exposed and alone onstage, Louie picked up a mic. "The Reverend is all right. Please return to your seats."

Ignoring his plea, the crush continued.

"Reverend Jefferson was overcome by a vision," Louie shouted forcefully.

The pushing and shoving subsided.

That got their attention.

"What did he see?" a man called out.

"What did he see?" Louie repeated.

Thinking now would be a good time to get out of Dodge, I tried to catch Louie's eye.

"He saw through this veil of tears and into the Promised Land!" Louie exhorted.

Heaven help us … he's in high gear performance mode.

Assorted "Praise the Lords" rippled through the audience.

Judging by Louie's peacock-like strut, this only added fuel to the fire. "A promised land where brother embraces brother and love flows freely!" he continued.

"Oh, happy day!" a woman cried.

"That's right, sister! It'll be the gayest day you've ever seen. Will you all join me now in song?" Louie reached down and pulled me up onstage with him.

"Can we get the hell out of here already?" I whispered in his ear.

"That's what I'm trying to do," he answered, before turning back to face his fans. "All right, all together now."

Louie put his arm around my waist. Before I realized what was happening, we were kicklining our way offstage singing "Get Happy."

The congregation rose to their feet singing, shouting and cheering.

"People always love a kickline," Louie said as we exited backstage.

A procession had formed, snaking its way through the tent and outside into the sunset. Saint Judy Garland had saved the day.

In a dark corner underneath the stage, huddled in a fetal position, we found the Reverend Frank Jefferson.

"What happened back there?" I asked Louie.

"I guess he never expected to run into me again," Louie said. "We haven't seen each other since we fell in love at Boy Scout camp."

"Frank Jefferson was your first teenage summer romance?"

Louie nodded wistfully. "First and last of my scouting years. We were both kicked out after his mother discovered our assignation."

All the pieces from the Reverend's unplanned hypnotic regression fell into place.

"Seeing you must have plummeted him into a prenatal state." I went over to comfort this broken shell of a man. "Where are those bodyguards? They have no business leaving him unattended in a state like this."

"I sent them away," the Reverend said with a tremor. He lifted his head, laughing uncontrollably. "I didn't want them to see me like this."

"He's in a state of hysteria," I said.

"I'm fine." Reverend Jefferson picked himself up off the ground and dusted the dirt from his navy blue, three-piece suit. This was not the Frank Jefferson I knew. "Lou, you haven't changed one bit. I always felt good about myself when you were around. How have you been? I see you still have your theatrical flair."

"You were doing pretty good up there yourself," Louie complimented him.

"Aw, that was nothing. After our enforced split-up, I spent the rest of my summers in Bible Camp. Preaching was the closest I could get to performing."

"Your mother must be proud. How is the old battle-ax?" Louie asked.

"The good Lord took her home five years ago." Reverend Jefferson cast his eyes down. "He had no choice; Lucifer wouldn't take her."

This triggered another laughing jag, punctuated by the trading of a series of guffaws and hoots with Louie. When Reverend Jefferson finally regained his composure, he turned his focus on me. All residue humor drained from his face, the stern and sour man I met in my office reemerged.

"I never expected to cross paths with you again," he said in an austere tone. "But since you're here, I'd like to have a word with you."

Here it comes … an inexhaustible litany of fiery accusations … and litigious threats.

"Can I give you a hug?" he said with arms outstretched.

Is this a setup? … is he planning to crush me to death? … and blame it on overly enthusiastic fellowship? I cautiously consented to his impending assault.

"Thank you," he said, clinching me tenderly. "Whatever you did to me that day in your office has given me my life back. Now I truly know what it means to be born again. I feel like a colossal burden has lifted from my heart. Seeing Lou, the boy I left behind, reminded me of another boy who was taken from me that day. It's high time I reclaim him and begin to live the life the good Lord meant for me to live."

To say this confession stunned me would be an underestimation of biblical proportions—pun intended. "Are you going to remain a minister?" I asked.

"Absolutely," he said without hesitation. "I may have to switch denominations though. Any suggestions, Lou?"

"You're asking the wrong guy about that, Frankie. I'll have to introduce you to my friend, Danny. He's something of an expert on the subject of switching religions."

Danny! I'd entirely lost sight of the reason we were there. "Where's LaVonne, Reverend Jefferson?"

"Please, call me Frank. She's over in the Kids For Christ tent with the rest of the children."

"Do they spell Christ with a 'C' or a 'K'?" Louie inquired.

"With a 'C.' Believe it or not, even the Pentecostals aren't that kitschy," Frank replied in earnest. "Although, I have heard some of the brethren refer to it as Camp KFC."

"Has anyone come up to you looking for LaVonne?" I qualified, "Anyone you don't know."

"No. Why would someone do that? She's a child," he said, looking puzzled.

"Can we check in on her just to make sure everything's okay?" I asked.

"She's stopped having those dreams, you know?"

"I know. Sharon told me."

"Then why wouldn't she be all right?" he pressed.

I had to tell Frank exactly what was going on; at this point I had no other choice. "Because I think someone may be after her, a man who murdered her in a past life. He was never arrested for the crime and LaVonne may be able to identify him. Well, not LaVonne per se, but the young woman she once was."

He shook his head and looked at Louie. "And I was just starting to like her."

"I know it sounds crazy, but it's the only thing that makes any sense. She stopped having the nightmares because she revealed who her killer was to me. If I don't bring him to justice, the nightmares will resume."

Absorbed in thought, Frank looked into my eyes before turning to Louie. "How long have you known this woman?"

"Long enough to know she's not imagining any of this or making it up," Louie answered.

"Who's the killer? Why not go after him?" Frank asked, not sounding fully convinced.

"I'm not sure who he is," I replied.

"Are you doing those designer drugs? Less than a minute ago you told me LaVonne revealed the killer to you."

"She did. It was the murder victim's father, but I didn't have a chance to get a name from her?"

"Why not?" Frank asked, probing further.

"Because you came back into the room and yanked her out of my office!" I burst out in exasperation. "Sorry, I didn't mean to yell."

"It's okay. I've been known to have that effect on women," he said with a surprising degree of understanding.

"All I can tell you is I have some ideas, but I'd prefer not to point any fingers. I've been mistaken before."

Frank appraised me one last time. "Fair enough, I'm no stranger to the sin of bearing false witness. Let's go check on my sweet baby."

Making our way over to the Kids For Christ tent was easier said than done. We kept bumping into people who either wanted to hear more about Reverend Jefferson's vision of the Promised Land, or to find out where Louie would be preaching next.

"You might want to consider becoming a man of the cloth, Lou. That was a tough bunch you played to back there."

"No thanks, Frankie. The only cloth that interests me is a loin-cloth, preferably hanging off my own personal Tarzan."

"Here we are," Frank said, stopping at a large, yellow and white polka-dotted tent bursting with children. "It may take some time to locate her."

"Aren't there any wranglers that can help us?" I asked, making a quick search through the sea of unfamiliar faces.

"Wranglers?" Frank snickered. "Last time I looked she was a child not a horse."

"She means kiddie wranglers," Louie explained. "They use them on film sets for rounding up and sorting through a lot of kids. It helps keep things organized and running smoothly."

"The Hollywood way of doing things doesn't sit too well around here," Frank said with a slight air of superiority. "The class is almost over. Let's wait in the back with the rest of the parents. She'll find us faster than we'll find her."

"Don't forget little ones," a saccharine-sounding matron chided from the podium, "it's a blessing to be living in these last days."

Her diminutive charges shifted restlessly in their seats.

"Sure there will be fires and floods, hurricanes and earthquakes, on top of famine and pestilence," she continued.

A smattering of tots wailed for their mothers.

"Crying for your mamas isn't going to help you now." She smiled serenely. "It's much too late for that. Only your Heavenly Father can save you. The righteous among you will rise up triumphant and in the twinkling of an eye be caught up unto heaven. What a glorious day—the rapture will have begun! You'll disappear just like that." She snapped her fingers. "Poof!"

If the intended effect of her declaration was one of comfort, this subtle nuance was lost on the ever-growing number of distraught children.

"All right, my little angels. You may spread your wings and fly to your awaiting parents."

The ensuing pandemonium was sobering. Even I wanted to run and find my mother.

"Where'd you pick her up?" a shell-shocked Louie asked. "Divine Dominatrix Boot Camp?"

"It's funny, this is the first I noticed how harsh she sounds," Frank revealed. "Let's find LaVonne and hightail it out of here. No wonder she's been having nightmares. I can't believe I hired the woman to teach Sunday School at my church."

"She really knows how to clear out a room," I said, observing the rapidly thinning assembly. Despite this fact, there was no sign of LaVonne.

"Do you see her anywhere?" Frank asked me.

I shook my head, hoping she had just stepped away to use the bathroom.

"Delores, have you seen LaVonne?" a concerned Frank asked the woman who had verbally terrorized us with her apocalyptic visions. "I can't seem to find her."

She clasped her Bible to her chest and exclaimed, "Praise be to Jesus! The Rapture has begun!"

A nearby woman, picking up discarded programs and candy wrappers from the floor, rolled her eyes. "She left with the doctor about half an hour ago."

"What doctor?" Frank asked with alarm.

"The one who treated you after your collapse," she replied casually. "He said you wouldn't stop asking for her."

"Isn't this exciting?" Delores beamed. "You were overcome by the power of the Holy Spirit, the same day your daughter was caught up by the Lord. I'm sure you'll be next to go Reverend."

"Will you shut-up, Delores? My daughter disappeared, all right. With a strange man, right under your oblivious noses! No doctor treated me," he fumed.

"Maybe this one should take a look at you," the woman tidying up mumbled.

Frank reeled around to face her, "What'd you say?"

Unintimidated by the Reverend, she went on. "He said he's a psychiatrist, Doctor Daniel Law. Told me LaVonne's a client of his sister. LaVonne said it was true and gave me her mother's telephone number to verify. Your wife said it was okay to let her go with him."

CHAPTER FIFTEEN

"I'M CALLING THE POLICE." Frank Jefferson stormed out of the tent.

"No, wait!" I chased after him with Louie hot on my heels.

"Wait? Wait for what? My child has been kidnapped!" he bellowed. "Now I see why you don't want to identify the killer. He's your brother."

"Danny's not a killer," Louie protested vehemently. "He's just a little crazy."

"Then what am I worrying about?" Frank said facetiously. "My daughter's only been abducted by an everyday, run-of-the-mill maniac, not a homicidal one."

"Let me call the police." I pulled out my cell and punched in a number. "Frank's right. I've been trying to protect everyone and, in the process, I've succeeded in protecting no one."

"LAPD, Van Nuys Division," a voice answered on the other end of the line.

"It's Roberta Law calling for Officer Sanchez. I have some additional information for him concerning the recent burglary at my office."

* * *

Explaining the entire confusing mess to Officer Sanchez wasn't as bad as I had anticipated. Turned out he had a degree in criminal psychology and knew of my brother and his work. An Amber Alert was put out on Danny and his car. Now came the difficult part, informing Sharon Jefferson. I had betrayed her trust and unnecessarily put her daughter at risk. Her forgiveness was something I neither deserved nor expected.

"Sharon, it's Roberta. I'm with Frank. There's something I have to tell you and I don't know where to begin." Pausing, I took in a deep breath. "It's about LaVonne. She's missing."

There was a momentary deafening silence before she spoke. "No, she's with your brother. I spoke with him not long ago. How's Frank? I heard he collapsed."

"Frank's fine. It's my brother who's not well. He's prone to delusions. I believe he's developed a fixation on LaVonne."

"Why would he go and do something like that?" she said in utter disbelief.

There was no avoiding the unpleasant facts any longer. "Because he's the man you identified as Jane Doe's killer today."

"No, I didn't ..." she halted in mid-sentence, "oh, I see."

The sound of disappointment in her voice was unbearable to me. "I was going to tell you, Sharon, as soon as I checked it out. It just seemed too ..."

"Unbelievable?"

"Yes," I said, humbled by her lack of vitriol. "The police have been notified. If they don't find him, I will. He's supposed to meet me …"

"Daddy! Daddy!" A very frightened looking LaVonne pushed toward us.

"Oh, my God, Sharon! It's LaVonne. We've found her," I shouted with joy and relief.

"Is she all right? Put her on the phone," Sharon demanded.

LaVonne was firmly ensconced in her father's protective arms.

"Sharon wants to speak with her." I passed my cell to Frank.

He held the phone near the trembling child. "It's your mama, baby. Can you talk to her for a minute?"

Wiping her eyes, she nodded timidly. "I ran away from the man, Mommy. The lady told me to. She said he wanted to hurt me."

"What lady?" Frank asked.

"The lady who lives inside me," Lavonne replied.

"Thank you," Frank said, casting his grateful eyes skyward and clutching his daughter tightly to his chest.

* * *

After notifying Detective Sanchez of LaVonne's safe return, it was decided it would be best to place her under protective custody at her godmother's house until Danny was apprehended. The godmother, who lived in nearby Covina, picked LaVonne up and returned home accompanied by two plain-clothed detectives. Sanchez also arranged for a stakeout at the club later that evening.

Not quite knowing where to go or what to do next, I stared vacantly at Louie and Frank. "Well, we still have a few hours before we're supposed to meet up at the club. I suggest we pay a visit to the Mount Baldy Zen Center. It's not far from here. Danny may have stopped in for a change of clothes."

"I'm coming with you," Frank said forcefully.

"We drove here in an old VW Bug," I said, looking down at his elongated limbs.

"You two can ride with me in the church van." Frank took out his keys and headed toward the parking area. "All I need are the directions."

"Oh, I think you know how to get there," Louie said with a mischievous smile.

* * *

"Hey, Lou! Isn't this the road to our Boy Scout camp?" Frank remarked as we made the ascent up Mt. Baldy.

"It sure is, Frankie," Louie responded. "Except the place doesn't belong to the Boy Scouts anymore. I think your mama's wrath scared them away. It belongs to Mr. Buddha now."

"I believe his given name is Siddhartha Gautama," I said.

"Whew, what a handle!" Frank hooted. "No wonder he changed it to Buddha."

"Buddha isn't his name. It's a title like Christ," I corrected.

Frank challenged me. "Are you telling me Jesus' last name isn't Christ?"

"Yes," I stated flatly. "And his middle initial isn't 'H,' either."

"Now that I knew," Frank said with pride.

"I thought the 'H' came from his Father," Louie added.

"Joseph?" Frank and I questioned.

"No, Harold," Louie came back.

"Harold?" Frank and I looked at each other.

"Yeah. Our Father who art in heaven, Harold be thy name," Louie chuckled. "Don't get to use that one very often."

* * *

Getting out of the van at the Zen Center, my heart skipped a beat upon sighting a purple Gremlin parked in the far corner. "He's here," I shouted triumphantly.

"No, he's not," a voice said from behind me.

"Ben! What are you doing here?" I said, wheeling round to face him.

"You brother called me. He said it was urgent, wanted my opinion on a patient he's treating."

"A patient?" I said with consternation. "He hasn't practiced psychiatry in years. I doubt he even has a license anymore."

"He said it was a favor for a friend. Since he's not here," Ben shrugged, "I guess the rest of it's irrelevant."

"Did he say anything else?" I asked.

"Something about his patient being in grave danger and needing to know whether or not I thought she was 'hallucinating the threat.' He said he finds it difficult to sort reality from fantasy with any degree of certainty these days."

Frank lunged at me upon hearing this news. "If your brother dares go near her again, I'll ..."

Ben intercepted him with a headlock. "You'll what?"

"Let go of me!" Frank yelled, struggling in Ben's grasp.

"It's okay, Ben. Let him go," I said. "This is the Reverend Frank Jefferson."

"What happened to turn the other cheek?" Ben released his hold. "Aren't you supposed to be working for the Prince of Peace?"

"He's LaVonne's father," I explained. "Danny attempted to abduct his daughter today."

"The police have an APB out on Danny," Louie added.

After being filled in, Ben extended his apologies and placed a call to Nancy. "Do you object to enlisting the aid of a psychic, Reverend?" he asked, eyeing the massive red cross and lettering on the side of the white van: "THE ONE AND ONLY UNIVERSAL CHURCH OF JESUS CHRIST TRIUMPHANT – REV. FRANK JEFFERSON, SHEPHERD."

"Frank readily acquiesced. "The Lord works in mysterious ways; be my guest."

"Nancy, it's Ben." He paused. "Oh, that's right. You already knew."

I gave Frank a reassuring nod. "Psychic."

"No," Ben whispered. "Caller ID."

* * *

We arranged to meet Nancy at my place. She had requested a piece of clothing or some object that had been worn by or belonged to my brother. It would help her track him down. I suggested the copy of his book Danny had sent me.

When we arrived, Nancy was sitting out front in her Miata waiting for us.

I got out of Ben's car and approached Nancy. "Have you been here long?"

"Ten minutes, maybe," she replied, getting out of her vehicle.

Louie and Frank screeched up in the Jesusmobile.

Ben joined us. "Thanks for stopping by on your day off, Nancy."

Louie jumped out of the van. "What'd we miss?"

"Nothing," I said. "We only just got here ourselves."

"Someone was prowling around when I arrived," Nancy said. "Seeing me must have scared him off."

"It may have been Danny," I said.

"I only saw him from behind. He disappeared into your neighbor's backyard." Nancy pointed to the blue ranch house on my right. "Is your brother bald?"

"He wasn't this morning. Of course, that doesn't mean anything," I replied, reflecting on my brother's mercurial ways. "Richard Baxter's bald, though."

"Wish I had a positive ID for you," Nancy apologized.

"You're clairvoyant?" Frank scoffed.

"No, I'm Nancy Perkins," she said, shaking his hand. "Reverend Frank Jefferson, right?"

"My name's painted on the van." He looked at Ben and me, duly unimpressed.

"You used to go by Frankie," Nancy parried. "In your Eagle Scout days."

Frank let go of her hand. "I stopped using that name after my mama yanked me out of scouting. So where's her brother?"

"After I touch the book he sent to Roberta, I'll let you know what I see."

"Psychometry," Ben said. "Nancy does some of her best work through the handling and touching of personal objects."

"Me, too," Louie added.

"Thanks for sharing," I replied.

"Exactly what I say to them." Louie was on a roll.

"Okay, enough with the hackneyed Catskills routine already." I led my guests up the front walkway. "Let's make sure I haven't been broken into again."

Inside, we discovered my living room window jimmied open. "Why do I even bother locking this place up?" I said in frustration.

"Officer Sanchez did advise you to have it repaired," Ben reminded me.

"Someone's coming on Monday," I said. "What do you suggest I do until then? Hire a security guard?"

"I'll stay with you," Ben said.

You could have knocked me over with a hologram of a feather. *Did I hear what I think I heard? ... Ben Cohen's going to spend the rest of the weekend at my place? ... if anybody or anything is out there listening ... thank you!*

"You're welcome," Ben and Nancy both replied.

"Roberta, why are you blushing?" Louie asked.

"It's the weather." I gave Ben and Nancy a warning look. "Prickly heat."

"Could be the change," Frank contributed his unsolicited two cents worth. "Where's that nasty watchdog of yours?"

Yeah, where is Lex? ... how come he didn't greet us at the door? "I'd hardly call him nasty. Beagles are highly intelligent animals. Lex! Lex!"

I heard the door to my office open and close.

"He is smart," Frank said in respectful amazement. "I never met a dog who could work a door like that."

"That's not the dog," I said in a terse whisper. "Somebody's in this house."

"Yes, and they are trying to work." Danny walked through the kitchen and into the living room. "So could you please keep it down to a dull roar until we're finished?"

"Danny! Where the hell have you been?" I demanded.

"I'm working with a patient." Danny looked over at Ben. "Good, you made it."

"You asked me to meet you at the Zen Center," Ben replied.

"Unforeseen change of venue," Danny answered. "No need to worry. I was confident an able colleague like yourself would figure it out." He motioned for Ben to accompany him back to my office. "Shall we?"

"Shouldn't we be trying to restrain this guy?" Frank made a start for Danny. "I don't much appreciate people kidnapping my child." He placed a stranglehold on Danny. "Call the police, Lou. I can't hold this guy forever."

Louie didn't move. "I could hold him forever."

"What's the matter with you people?" Annoyed, Frank tightened his hold on Danny.

"Do what he says," Danny rasped. "He's undoubtedly delusional, and possibly homicidal."

The front door opened, in walked Richard Baxter carrying Lex in his arms. Seeing the jam my brother was in, he dropped his hairy burden and rushed to Danny's aid. "Let go of him." Richard put a counter-clench on Frank.

Okay, now I'm totally baffled. "Can we have a time out here?" I tried to sound reasonable. "This doesn't look like it's leading us anywhere productive."

"It's not," a woman's tenuous voice came from the kitchen. "If you'll allow me to finish my session with Dr. Law, we may be able to sift through this chaos and come up with some semblance of a rationalization." A feeble looking Lori Taylor joined us in the living room.

Lex sniffed Frank's pant leg. "Call this cur off and I'll let go."

"He's not a cur, he's a purebred beagle," I carped. "He has papers from the American Kennel Club,"

"I wasn't talking about the dog," Frank growled. "It's the one behind me I'm vexed about."

Richard released Frank and, as promised, Frank let go of Danny.

"Okay, so where do we start?" I asked for lack of a better ice-breaker.

"At the beginning, I guess," Lori said, sitting on the sofa.

Following her example, the rest of us made ourselves comfortable.

"As I'm sure many of you know, I gave birth to an illegitimate daughter back in the sixties. Despite all my later success, wealth and fame never filled the void left inside me by that singular event." Lori made brief eye contact with Richard. "The man I believed to be the father of my child was married and not about to leave his wife. Due to the times and the circumstances, it was decided giving the child up for adoption was the only feasible option."

"You said <u>believed</u> to be the father," I interjected.

Richard continued the story. "Lori and I had been having an affair for about a year when she got pregnant. For obvious reasons, we assumed I was the father. An abortion was discussed, but they were illegal and much too risky in those days."

Frank Jefferson seemed visibly disturbed by the subject matter, but held his tongue in check.

"My divorcing Erica was put under consideration. When she caught wind of the situation, her immediate reaction was not what we expected. She came up with the idea of assuming custody of the baby and raising it collectively, in an open marriage type of arrangement." Richard looked simultaneously pained and relieved as he shared his story.

"Lori and I were ecstatic, but Erica insisted on having a paternity test done first. She was the one who gave me the results of the test over the phone. Her attitude had changed; she was bitter and angry. An ultimatum was handed down. She wanted me to choose either Lori and the child, or her and my career.

"Will you excuse me for a moment." Frank looked over-whelmed. "I need to use the restroom."

"I could use a break myself," Lori said forlornly. "Do you have any chai iced tea?"

"Lipton's Instant?" I ruefully offered, doubting I'd make a sale.

"A glass of water's fine," she replied.

"It's from the tap," I admitted with reluctance.

"Filtered?" she asked, hopefully.

I shook my gauche head in disgrace.

Frank reentered the room and shifted course toward the front door. "There's a case of water in the back of the church van." Eyes red and bloodshot, it was obvious he'd been crying.

Frank promptly returned with bottles for all, even his archene-my—Lex.

Louie took a swig. "I've never tasted holy water before," he said, attempting to lighten the gloomy mood.

"It sunk in that you were talking about my little girl," Frank said softly. "I always had a feeling she was an old soul. But there wasn't any room for such feelings in my former life. There wasn't any room for lots of things. So they've been sitting inside, all bottled up and hidden away until today." Sniffling, he removed a tissue from his pocket.

Lori gently touched Frank. "Your daughter must be the little girl Dr. Law told me about."

"Our daughter," he replied, caressing her hand.

"Yes," she said, delicately pulling away. "Our daughter and Paul Graham's daughter, too. The daughter he killed once and wants to kill again."

Why did I ignore my gut instinct about him?

"We had a one-night stand after a gig in Boston. It was a mistake. I was stoned and hurting; Richard wanted to cool things down a bit. Paul had always had a thing for me. So I figured, why not? As the song goes, 'Love the One You're With.' "

"He was my primary suspect until I was finagled by his confiding in me about your …" I didn't go any further, not sure whether or not it was appropriate to proceed.

Danny intuited my dilemma. "She doesn't have Alzheimer's, Roberta. He was trying to drive her mad by playing on her numerous fears and phobias, hoping to push her over the edge into suicide."

"It almost worked," Lori said. "Until I came across Vanessa's Florida driver's license, the day before I met you at the restaurant."

"Vanessa?" I repeated.

"Vanessa Griffin," Lori confirmed. "The woman who's been posing as my daughter.

It all came flooding back to me. "He called her Vanessa the afternoon I bumped into you at Inn Of The Seventh Ray."

"When he realized his slip, we beat it out of there. You can imagine his alarm at finding you on our doorstep later the same day."

"I ran an identity check on her. She's a grifter," Richard added. "The only thing legit about her is the fact that she is Paul's wife."

"Was she involved with the murder in Chicago?" I asked.

"I doubt it," Richard answered. "Lori doesn't think she has the stomach for murder."

"She helped me escape on the night of the car accident," Lori said, picking up the story again. "I was the one Paul was after and she paid the price for her compassion. Richard found me hiding in his shack."

"Why'd you take off on us that night?" I asked Richard.

"Much to my mortification, I am loath to admit my motives were entirely selfish. When I heard the police sirens, I panicked. Jack had Ecstasy on him and I've already spent time in rehab for drug violations. If we were busted, I was afraid I would be barred from taking my final vows."

"Why did you follow Louie and me to Inn Of The Seventh Ray earlier that evening?"

"I wasn't following you. Karen … I mean … Vanessa asked me to meet her there. I was hoping for a long overdue father-daughter reunion, but she never showed. Figuring she'd developed cold feet, I decided to hitch my way back to Mt. Baldy when Jack came along and picked me up."

"Paul and Vanessa had a big blowout after you two left." Lori looked at Louie and me. "Vanessa was tired of Paul's stalling. She thought it was the perfect time to have me committed. He said it was too risky; they needed to revise the plan, get me out of the way permanently by staging a suicide. Vanessa said she didn't sign on for murder and picked up the phone; Paul struck her in the face. She fought back, but he eventually knocked her unconscious. During all the confusion, Vanessa slipped me the bedroom door key before Paul locked me back inside. From my window, I watched him carry her body down to your SUV and drive away. That's when I made my final escape. I was hiding in the shack, paralyzed with fear, when Richard found me."

"Why didn't you take off in the Rolls?" Louie asked.

"Because she has a fear of driving," Danny told us. "Not to mention her fear of the dark and her fear of rats. It's a miracle she made it to the shack without having a mental breakdown. We were working on her phobic reactions when you showed up."

"And I was out hunting for your beagle," Richard said. "There was a noise at the side of the house. When I went to investigate, the dog took off."

"Did the sound come from the vicinity of this window?" I asked.

"Yes. It looked like someone was trying to break in. I think it was Paul Graham. He took off into your neighbor's backyard before I was able to get a good look at him. I chased him for a few blocks, but he got away."

I jumped up from the loveseat. "This is LA—he had to get here by car! I bet it's still parked on the street."

"I don't think so," Frank said with regret. "There was a guy skulking around outside when I went to get the water. Soon as he saw me come out of the house, he scrambled into a black BMW. I got a peculiar feeling, like he was sitting in there watching my every move. He drove off after I slid the van door shut."

Frank's physical description of the man matched Paul Graham.

"I don't understand. What's driving him to do this? What's his motivation?" The actor in me still needing to wrap my head around what makes a character tick.

"I have my theories," Danny said. "Of course, they're meaningless without any direct input from the subject himself. We're working with the flotsam and jetsam of information here. By piecing together what Lori knows—with what Richard knows—with what you know—my initial hypothesis is that we're dealing with a fragmented personality. Its incongruity has grown more acute with each passing year. A long festering resentment over the break-up of Graham & Taylor—compounded by his subsequent failure and Lori's enormous success—laid dormant, waiting for a triggering event to unleash his simmering rage. Assuming he had no idea his fiancée, the real Karen Hall, was also his daughter—that discovery, along with the fact she was carrying his child, was all it took. He's been in a tailspin ever since."

"Up until that point, Erica was the only one of us who knew Lori's child was not my daughter," Richard disclosed. "She had no way of knowing the true identity of the biological father, but that didn't stop Paul from setting fire to our house."

Though I suspected arson all along, I was woefully off the mark in deducing the true culprit; Angela Lansbury, I was not.

"Erica was none too thrilled when I told her I was going to let Karen and Paul use the Topanga Canyon house. When she found out Lori was staying with them, she exploded and told me the truth about my daughter—I didn't have one. She went over to kick them out, and later the same day a fire broke out at our Brentwood home. When I found Paul hovering around her bed at UCLA Medical, I knew she must have divulged the information about my not having a daughter. Paul and I got into a loud quarrel about it and were kicked out of the hospital. Without delay, I arranged to have Erica moved to the Grossman Burn Center in Sherman Oaks."

"We've got to notify the police," I said.

"I was about to do that very thing when our intruder showed up," Richard said. "They can stop looking for Lori and start looking for Paul."

"Better tell them to stop looking for Danny while you're at it," Louie added. "Roberta had them put out an APB on him."

"Whatever for?" Danny asked, scandalized.

"Ludicrous as it may seem now," I said with a self-protective reflex, "it seemed like the appropriate response after your disappearing act this morning."

"I told Louie I received a call and had to leave on business," Danny said, justifying his actions. "Hardly a reason to alert the police."

"You lost your cell phone," I pointed out.

"The call came in on your line. It was Richard; he was at the Zen Center looking for me." Danny explained. "They told him I was down in LA visiting my sister. He had Lori with him and wanted me to take a look at her before getting in touch with the police. I went up there to meet with them. Since I'm a bit rusty, I contacted Ben for a second opinion."

"Why didn't you wait at the Center for Ben to arrive?" I quizzed him further.

Danny heaved a sigh of frustration. "Well … if you must know … I forgot. Electroshock therapy does have its downside."

"Danny told me he had spoken with you on the phone, Roberta—about getting a second opinion—and that we should bring Lori to your office," Richard added.

"That was indisputably one of my non-telephone assisted calls," Danny confessed.

"Why did you pay a visit to Sharon Jefferson this morning?"

"I didn't." Danny looked completely flummoxed. "Did I?"

"I need to go out for a drink," I said, relieved it was all over.

Louie raised his hand. " 'I Second That Emotion.' "

"It would be nice to do something normal again," Lori spoke up.

"Yes, it would," Richard agreed.

"Can I interest you two in accompanying the rest of us to the Double D Club?" Nancy asked. "We have plans to catch Hell's Papas last set."

"Jack Hensler's new band?" Richard asked.

"The one and only," I said with affection.

"Count me in," Richard said. "If he hadn't come along and picked me up the other night, we might not have any cause for celebration."

"Is that old hound dog still around?" Lori marveled. "Jagger and Morrison were in awe of him. And I don't mean musically. I'm on board."

"I suggest we pay a visit to the local police station first," Ben said. "Get them to stop looking for Danny and Lori, and start looking for Paul Graham."

* * *

Officer Sanchez was going off duty when our motley crew piled into the Van Nuys Division and filed our report. At last, LaVonne was safe and Paul Graham was a wanted man.

Our caravan arrived in Reseda at the stroke of midnight. Though known as the bewitching hour in folklore, no detectable enchantment had been cast over the grubby environs of the Double D Club. While this detail, under more conventional circumstances, would preclude my opening the door and stepping inside—by this point it didn't deter me one iota. After all I'd been through in the past week, I looked forward to the opportunity to get down and dirty on the dance floor with Jack, with Ben, with anybody for that matter.

Assembled on a small poorly lit stage, the band was tuning up for their last set. Though smoking in clubs had long been banned, this revolutionary news had failed to breach the foggy nicotine shield of the Double D.

Crossing the throwback dance floor with cracked mirror ball dangling above it, we found an empty table near the long, hooker-congested bar. Scrutinizing the gargantuan attributes of the working clientele, I came to a tacit understanding of how the club had derived its name.

Thinking Jack had been too engrossed to notice our arrival, I ordered a Long Island Iced Tea and settled in for forty-five minutes of anonymous, mindless amusement. My false confidence was short-lived.

"Welcome back, folks," Jack's voice crackled over the worn-out speakers. "Some special guests have dropped in to join us for the closer. One of them is a lady who holds a very special place in my heart."

How embarrassing ... I hope he doesn't ask me to stand up or anything.

"And I'm sure she holds a special place in all of yours," he continued.

He must be stoned

"I'm glad to see she's safe and sound. Let's give it up for Ms. Lori Taylor!" Jack led the unbridled applause.

Lori appeared uptight at first, but relaxed when Danny nodded his head and took her hand. "Stand up and get your due," he said. "Let's see if any of the work we did made a difference."

Looking doubtful, Lori warily rose from her seat. The response was overwhelming and her self-assurance seemed to grow in direct proportion to the audience's reaction.

"Nice work," I said leaning into Danny. "Welcome back."

"She'll need some expert follow-up," he said. "Do you take referrals?"

I couldn't remember the last time things had worked out in such movie-like perfection.

"Excuse me," I got up from the table, "I should visit the ladies room before they start. Did anyone happen to notice where it is?"

Nancy pointed to a decrepit sign on the far wall. "It's on the other side of the room."

Expecting to slip by unnoticed, I traipsed back across the empty dance floor.

Jack spoke into the mic, "I'd like to dedicate this first number to the high-stakes filly trottin' past … 'Mustang Sally.' "

I made a hasty exit into the dark passageway that carried me to my toileted sanctuary. The lyrics ricocheted off the bathroom tiles. Rejecting my impractical brainstorm of spending the rest of the night inside the can, I reasoned everyone had forgotten about me after two more songs elapsed.

On my way out the door, my cell phone beeped; low battery. I had switched it to vibrate mode at the Big Tent. Moving back inside the relative quietude of the restroom, I instinctively checked my voice mail before returning to the fray.

Sharon Jefferson had left a message. "Roberta, I spotted your brother at the hospital when I started my shift at eleven. He was walking into Karen Hall's room. When he saw me coming, he took off. He disappeared before I could catch up to him. I called the police and they said not to worry, he was no longer wanted; they're looking for Paul Graham. Did you know this?" Conking out, my cell automatically powered itself down.

Danny wasn't at UCLA Medical Center at that time … he was with me … oh, God! … Paul Graham's been passing himself off as my brother.

I had to call Sharon, make sure she was safe and fill her in on the latest developments. Having noticed a pay phone in the hallway, I stepped back outside digging around in my handbag for some loose change. Dropping a couple of quarters into the slot, I plugged in some numbers on the keypad. A hand reached out from behind me and disconnected the call.

"Cut it out, Louie. Now's not the time for kidding around."

The hand stayed put and a body pressed into me. My quarters clinked down into the coin return, the sound of their fall scarcely audible over the ear-splitting wall of music from the club.

"Didn't you hear me?" I hollered.

Another hand covered my mouth. "Yeah I did, bitch!" Paul Graham's voice invaded me and swamped my senses. "The only thing I want to hear from you is where you're hiding that kid."

I struggled to break free of his hold; he twisted my right arm behind my back.

The band stopped playing and Jack spoke, "If I can get her to agree to it, I have a special treat in store for you next."

Yes … I'll agree to anything you have in mind … make somebody go find me.

Tugging me by the hair, Paul hauled me toward a back exit.

"Lori, would you grace us with a song?" Jack asked.

Applause spontaneously erupted from inside the club.

Paul pushed open the door; a desolate alley awaited us on the other side. Kicking my legs into the air, I refused to go peacefully to my death.

Lori's melodic voice rose up, underscoring the cataclysmic closing scene of my life. "Ill conceived, you never were a part of our plans. Ill conceived, I'm drawn by the sweet siren call of fans."

Paul's tenacious hold on me loosened.

"Traded my soul for a ticket to the top," the song continued. "Now I pray the ride will stop."

Lori's voice, the lyrics, or a combination of both had a mesmerizing effect on Paul. Zombie-like, he moved away from me and toward the source of the music. Keeping a safe distance, I followed. Paul stopped, unobserved and transfixed, in the dim center of the dance floor.

All eyes in the room were on Lori. "It's too late to take it back. Devil's at the door, handing me my wrap," she sang.

"You deserve to rot in hell," Paul bawled out.

The other spectators registered their irritation with demands of—"Shut-up, buddy"—"Be quiet"—"Keep it down."

Their taunts only fanned the flames of Paul's rising fury. "What the fuck do any of you goddamned leeches know?" he cried, turning on the crowd.

"Paul, is that you?" Jack asked, shielding his eyes from the glare of the stage lights. "For Christ's sake. If I'd known you were gonna freak out on me, I'd never've invited you to the gig. Put a plug in it and let us finish the set. Go on, Lori."

Visibly shaken, Lori's hands trembled on the mic. "You invited him?"

"I thought you'd patched things up," Jack replied innocently. "What with him findin' your daughter and all."

The audience murmured among themselves, fascinated by the spectacle playing out before them.

"You killed our daughter," Lori spat out venomously.

"It would never have happened if you hadn't thrown her away," Paul retorted. "I loved her."

"Yeah, you loved her all right," Lori said. "You loved her right into pregnancy."

Paul pulled out a knife. With a maniacal yelp, he dove for the defenseless woman standing onstage.

The house lights went up and half a dozen cops surrounded him. In the center of the fracas, I spotted Officer Sanchez slapping a pair of cuffs on a prostrate Paul.

I pushed through the crush of photo-snapping gawkers to let everyone at my table know I was okay.

Richard went over to comfort Lori while the police took a statement from her and the band.

"What took you so long?" Louie complained. "You just missed the gossip event of the century."

"I'm sure there'll be a blow-by-blow recount from the media for weeks to come," I said, referring to the sudden increase of cell phone activity in the room.

"Minus the messy paranormal elements, no doubt," Ben added.

Officer Sanchez approached us, while the other uniforms escorted Paul Graham out the door and into a squad car. "I thought you might want to know I contacted the Chicago PD," he said. "They have some preserved DNA samples from the Jane Doe slaying. If the results come back positive, we can add murder to the existing attempted murder and abduction charges."

"What made you decide to show up here tonight?" I asked out of curiosity. "You were going off duty when we turned up at the station earlier."

"I dunno. Hunch I should stick around?

"Premonition?" Nancy proposed.

"Could have been," he conceded. "A call came into the West LA division from Sharon Jefferson. She reported seeing your brother, but it didn't matter because we no longer had a warrant out on him."

"By the way, what exactly was the warrant for?" Danny asked. "No one bothered to tell me that part of the story."

"Attempted kidnapping," Sanchez said. "We hadn't gathered enough solid evidence to tag on the murder and attempted murder charges."

"Charming," Danny wryly remarked. "As if being crazy isn't enough."

"If Sharon's call made no difference, why'd you bother to mention it?" Frank Jefferson astutely observed.

"Because a short while later she put in another call. Something made her check the visitor log. Only one person had signed in to visit Karen Hall this evening—Paul Graham. A buddy of mine at West LA took the call and tipped me off. I was listening to an oldies radio station—a fan called in with a scoop about a Lori Taylor sighting. She said Lori was no longer missing, and was in fact singing at the Double D Club in Reseda."

Maybe I need to soften my stance on the ritual of media bloodsucking.

"Before we stopped looking for Dr. Law and switched our focus to Paul Graham, a stakeout had been planned for this location. It was a simple matter of reactivating Plan A," Sanchez said self-effacingly. "Anyway, I've got to get back to the station. I'll be in touch."

His exit marked the end of a very long week and my work with LaVonne. It was time to go home and crawl into bed.

"Doesn't look like you'll be in need of any protection tonight," Ben whispered softly in my ear.

"Hey, babe. This looks like a wrap." Jack approached me with a rapacious look in his eyes. "Whadda ya say? My place or yours?"

Roberta to Ben … Roberta to Ben … mayday … mayday … Ben are you there?